8 PALMS

PUBLISHING

THE GIFT CERTIFICATE

The Story of a Love Relationship that Transcends Time

TONY DE ANGELO

8 PALMS PUBLISHING CALIFORNIA

8 PALMS
PUBLISHING

Cover Artwork: Katherine DeAngelo

Cover Design: Guy Hopshtein

Library of Congress Control Number 2017917360

Published by 8 Palms Publishing California, Coto de Caza, CA 92679
www.thegiftcertificatebook.com

The 8 Palms Publishing name and logo are trademarks of
8 Palms Publishing California.

ISBN 978-0-9996185-0-9

First Edition

Printed in the United States of America

For Amy, my compass of life, boussole de la vie

*"I believe in intuitions and inspirations.
I sometimes FEEL that I am right.
I do not KNOW that I am."*

— Albert Einstein

CONTENTS

Preface
Acknowledgments

PREFACE

The Gift Certificate was written for all those looking to have a positive mindset and live a meaningful life.

The inspiration for this book was to create a fictional story describing a natural pathway toward this ideal for everyday living, to live a naturally positive life, to be internally comfortable with all decisions made, and to find a path toward the most fulfilling aspects of why a person is put on this earth.

For me, this process began with the understanding of how to find and truly follow my own inner voice on a consistent basis. This is a process of naturally blending the mind, emotions and spiritual development into one strong and unified method of living.

The Gift Certificate is a story of a love relationship that transcends time.

The story is set in the context of a fictional love relationship, but it is often love and romance that drives humans to investigate their deeper meanings of life and create an introspective pathway to follow their heart. The story creates a fictional set of characters, relationships, dialogue and settings to show how to inter-relate these concepts, uses the pathways of hope and faith to follow your heart, and ultimately shows how to trust and follow your own inner voice. It has become my daily roadmap for all that is meant for me to experience during my life and relationships on this earth and thereafter.

This concept is something of a bridge between the secular and spiritual worlds. It is also a bridge between those that have a cerebral approach to life, but need to find a way to incorporate the emotional aspects and especially the spiritual development that is a deep craving for many. Everyone has this capability, but many do not fully utilize it. They either don't believe it is possible, don't believe in the idea of it, or they talk themselves out of it. Doubt makes it difficult to follow your own inner voice.

While I have always had a deep desire to help the human condition, the road has taken many forms and turns over the years. Somehow, my personal mindset always returns to this basic desire. We are all a work in progress, but sometimes that work reveals plateaus of success that are worth sharing. I am not speaking about a monetary or social level of success, but an internal level of success – an internal comfort that your life is on the right path, and the larger picture of life and spiritual development is finally on the right course for life. As you move through life, you realize that it is no longer about yourself, but how to help others. However, this road must begin with a deep level of self-awareness, before it can be reconciled and released into beautiful blend of selflessness to your children, family and friends.

The key is how to listen to your inner voice, understand when it is part of your true pathway, trust it, and then not be talked out of it. This is a process of life, combining awareness with positivity, intuition and spiritual development. When you both trust and obey these deeper realizations, the rewards are endless. The story also shows how hope is the starting point, but faith is the finale. There can be symbols along the way to show you that you are on the right path.

A logical creature by nature, I have had to work at how to follow my own emotional underpinnings, and develop a spiritual foundation to my life to trust and follow this path on an hourly and daily basis.

After much conscious effort, I no longer need to think about how to do it, but simply follow the natural flow that it lays out for me. After many years, I have finally settled into this deeper connection and satisfying avenue for my life. I hope in some small way that this fictional story will help you to do the same.

Tony DeAngelo

October 24, 2017
Coto de Caza, California USA

ACKNOWLEDGMENTS

To Amy, my compass for life, a stylist and educator, an
exceptional mom, friend, and the love of my life,
To Nicholas, Katherine, Michael and Matthew, for the humor,
talent, strength, intelligence, creativity, adaptability, and allowing
me the honor to be your father,
To my father Jim, who endured through great personal physical
loss to allow me a pathway to creativity,
To my mother, Mary, who defeated age and simply endured,
always calm during the storms of life
To my in-laws, Jim and Jean, who have always been genuinely
supportive,
To the mountains of Coto de Caza, who speak to me every
morning and guide my outlook on life,
To the ocean at Santa Monica beach, my sunset for life,
To the California mind set, may it always have wisdom,
To my European descent, may it always be liberated,
To Italia, for my Italian-American ancestral heritage,
To my grandparents, who endured the trek to Ellis Island,
To British Airways, for my first trip to Europe as a youngster,
To New York City, where I 'grew up' in the world of art,
architecture, literature and culture,
To the Empire State Building, who took me to greater heights than
its finial,
To my Uncle Ralph, who first introduced me to the idea that a
person could be an architect,
To Chakrapani in Los Angeles, for helping me to better understand
myself and encourage me to be a writer,

To Jim Mumford in Madison County, who understood the legal side of my brain,

To Nick, for his love of reading, music, work ethic and insight into health, diets, fitness and DNA,

To Kat, for her fashion sensibility, composure, and helping me to understand a teenage daughter,

To Miguel, for his humor, creativity, physical endurance, genuine kindness, and deep ocean of love,

To Matty, for his focus, commitment, leadership, confidence, and a certain *je ne sais quoi,*

To Orange County, the inspiration for the Vintage Rags setting,

To Rancho Santa Margarita, the inspiration for The Pond setting,

To Michael Petted, for his creativity, love and support,

To the Waggoner's, for simply being great friends,

To Sharon Moalem, and his book "Inheritance", for my greater understanding of epigenetics,

To Paris, for its creative flair and incomparable setting,

To the *Parisienne*, for their greater understanding of the love of love,

To the fashion industry, may they continue to impress,

To Saint-Émilion, may every small town keep its heritage over the centuries,

To America, the land that I love,

To the Angels of the Lord, who have given me my surname, and who protect and guide me every day,

And most of all, to my Lord, who loves me, and who has given me all my skills, ideas, hopes and desires, and guides me in all my skills, ideas, hopes and desires.

THE GIFT CERTIFICATE

CHAPTER 1

The Mannequin

It was another beautiful day in Southern California. John pushed through doors of the coffee shop with his freshly made extra hot latte in hand. Winter was hardly noticeable, and it was type of day that encouraged you to slow down and take notice of the local sounds and surroundings. The air was warm, crisp and clean, and the plants and flowers were soaking up the sun and light breeze in a familiar way as they had done on many days before.

Just to the east of the coffee shop, an outdoor mannequin was stylishly dressed and placed outside of the adjoining store. John had noticed this figure on several prior visits to the coffee shop. This figure was always wearing something different, and its clothing, accessories and jewelry had always seemed to match in a very artful way.

John took a moment to consider that there was a distinctly artistic and talented person who was dressing this figurine every morning. The figure was strangely real. John had never seen the person that dressed the model figure each day, but suddenly became intrigued by the store that had placed it on the sidewalk.

His wife and daughter had both shopped inside this small boutique on many prior occasions. For some reason, he had barely noticed the actual store before today. Many beautiful clothes and accessories were arranged along the display window, which drew him toward the glazed reflections.

In the middle of the stylish fabric displays, the sign behind the glass read *"Gift Certificates Available"*. John had seen those signs before in many storefront windows, but something was different this time. Something was different in this place.

"May I help you with something today?" came a voice from his left.

John was slightly surprised at the question sent in his direction. After all, he was still on the outside of the store and simply peering through the store window from the sidewalk.

"I don't believe so," replied John, who was very analytical and somewhat wondering why this sales associate was asking him questions on the sidewalk. This was not the best way for a sales associate to begin a conversation, he thought, since asking an open-ended question such as this gave him the perfect opportunity to push away and continue along the sidewalk. Yet he didn't leave the storefront.

"I am very impressed by your display window, and you seem to have some nice items in the store," continued John, somewhat surprised by his own response since he typically was not a fan of pushy sales associates. The sales associate maintained a genuinely kind and steady smile, as if she already knew that John would soon be evading her question and continuing along the sidewalk. John was somewhat fascinated by this reverse psychology that was pulling him in.

"I noticed you were looking at the blouse," she replied. John's eyes were frozen on the white spring looking linen shirt that had reminded him so much of his wife. She had worn this type of garment on many occasions prior to her sudden disappearance just two years prior. Until the sales associate mentioned it, he had not realized that he was staring at it so intently.

"Yes, it is quite beautiful, and I noticed you have gift certificates available," said John. And just that fast, the sale was done. John immediately knew that he would be making his way to the sales counter to purchase a gift certificate. As he crossed the door threshold, he pondered the realization that this sales associate was quite magnificent at her job.

"Yes, we do," she replied, as she led him toward the check-out counter.

John noticed that there was nobody else in the store, and it was probably a bit early in the day for most people to be shopping for clothes. Then he realized that the store had just opened a few moments prior at 9:00am, and he must have been the first to arrive. The sales associate must have just unlocked the door, turned on the lights, and placed the mannequin outside. She wasn't being pushy at all, but had simply been at the front door to open the store when she greeted him on the sidewalk. There was a small white name tag that was pinned to her shirt with the name '*Amelie*' printed on it, in small and understated black letters.

"Yes. We. Do," she repeated, each word stated distinctly and individually elongated. "I love the idea of giving gift certificates," she continued.

"Amelie," John stated, seeing the name tag and thinking aloud about the possible meaning of her name. "Is that French?" he continued.

"Yes," stated Amelie, "my mother was French and she loved the name Amelia, but she wanted me to have the original French spelling since it reminded her of a close childhood friend that she had many years ago."

John's mind began racing in several directions. Something was eerily familiar, yet at the same time strangely distant. The name Amelie had a very historic meaning to John and brought about images of Saints and Princesses, but also was a very trendy and popular name when spelled Amelia in the United States.

Amelie continued, "some people call me 'Amy', and some friends call me 'Mia'.

John went silent. He nervously scanned the store with his eyes as she began ringing up the cash register transaction. John finally responded in agreement, "My wife's name was Mia….. Is Mia". A rush of emotion came over John as he pondered his long-lost Mia.

"Yes, gift certificates are great," continued John, as if the whole name conversation had never happened. He was too stunned to continue discussing the immediate similarities that he was noticing between Amelie and his wife Mia. They both had an innate striving for excellence that immediately shined through from their personalities when you first met them. They both had a streak of calm confidence, competence, and independence that came through upon first meeting. They both had an artistic sensibility for clothing and a demeanor as a creative stylist that was eerily familiar. John took a drink from his extra hot latte, which by now had mostly cooled off.

"I've always believed that there is a much deeper meaning to gift certificates," said Amelie.

John knew immediately what she meant. This is also something that Mia would have said. Mia loved giving gifts, and never had an excuse for not giving a gift. Even when she did not have an idea for a gift, she would think about the person's favorite category of gifts and purchase a gift certificate on their behalf from the appropriate type of store.

Right on cue, Amelie continued, "I think that it is important to let others choose their own gifts, but within a particular set of parameters."

For Mia, this idea went well beyond a store gift certificate. It was a way of life for her, helping others as an educator to determine how to make their own decisions and live with the results. The decisions chosen were always within a general set of guidelines, such as what might be a person's unique set of skills, passions, interests, or natural tendencies. After that, Mia guided her students to trust their decisions and never look back, choosing which of their individual gifts to pursue, within a predefined set of individual talents.

"Are you OK?" asked Amelie.

John realized that someone was speaking to him. "Are you OK?" repeated Amelie.

"Yes, thank you," replied John. "I'm fine".

John was clearly not fine. Amelie gave John his gift certificate and receipt. She had noticed that his description of Mia was both in the past tense and in the present tense, but did not raise the question.

John was always known by his friends to be the coolest of customers in tense situations. At this moment, however, there was much for John to consider as both his mind and emotions had been rattled to the core, thinking about a wide range of emotions that had resurfaced about Mia in a mere fifteen minutes.

He said goodbye to Amelie and departed the clothing store.

As he departed, he noticed her genuinely kind and steady smile, the same one that he had received from her before entering the store, as if she already knew what John would be thinking about as he continued down the road.

CHAPTER 2

The Veranda

John gazed at the soft blue sky from the rear deck of his home. He had stretched out on his long chaise lounge chair, which had been strategically placed to point him toward the magnificent view across the pool area and to the distant mountain tops of Coto de Caza. The chair was soft and comfortable. The place had become his personal escape from the usual hectic pace of the day. He had let his mind drift across the green terrain on this sunny afternoon, and was faintly aware of how the tree tops merged seamlessly with the distant mountains.

The soft blue mix of cumulous clouds and sky melted away the afternoon, and left him in a miniature trance as he listened to the flowing water from the pool area. John had always delighted in the flowing sounds of the waterfall. It helped to heighten his awareness of the senses, more than any other experience that he could think of.

Although a logical creature by nature, John had a very romantic way of viewing the world. The pool sights and sounds helped carry him into his safe place, where he could relax his mind and process his random thoughts. He had always carried phrases and thoughts in his mind that sometimes made him chuckle, never quite understanding where some of the strange and foreign thoughts had originated. The pool area helped him reach a second level of relaxation and mind clearing, so that he could freely drift into this comfortable but unusual state of mind. He had always enjoyed a private humor of stringing words together in his mind that few people would ever say during a normal conversation. The phrases, messages and identifiers were consistently unusual, and had a bit of a marketing flair: Attic salt romance, carbon fiber rhapsody, protectors of the Mandalay, Zyrian myths and iterations, and abaya blue science were just a few of the odd composites that would roll poetically through his thoughts. This internal phrasing and variety of random rhymes revealed an inner flair of creativity, but which had mostly been locked up in an internal private vault. He was a very private person as it related to his deepest inner thoughts, and rarely shared this side of his personality even to his closest of friends.

Water was of course a key to life itself, but to John this thought was rather basic and incomplete. This interesting wet element was much more than contemplating the usual sequence of evaporation, condensation, and precipitation. For John, water signified something with a much higher mystical quality, beginning in an unknown place and flowing off somewhere into an equally mysterious ending point. Infiltration, vents and volcanoes, seepage and streams, fog and dew, were all part of a literal and mystical approach to both life and its various states of daily emotional living. John rarely let others see this internal emotional river, but it certainly was a part of his DNA like plants needing sunshine.

The dichotomy was striking. The sites and sound of the beautiful day and the flowing water were supremely gorgeous. At the very same moment, John was a total wreck. The questions kept coming, as they do for a person that is suddenly out of control with their own thoughts and purpose of life. What was John to do with this information that was suddenly eating at him? Where was his wife, who had suddenly disappeared just two years earlier? Was she alive? Was she dead as they had speculated? Had she been kidnapped, or had she intended to leave? The upper right part of his stomach set off a warning flair, and then took a nose dive into a crater of pain in his lower middle stomach area.

John's mind, searching for the balance and comfort of the flowing water and breathtaking view, was concurrently racing with considerable angst. His thoughts had become erratic and disjointed, and were beginning to make his legs and lower back ache with pain. Why had this small shop even grabbed his attention this morning? Why was he suddenly having a massive level of uncertainty about his future?

The clothing store was very understated, part of a small strip of shops within a larger neighborhood corner retail center near Laguna Beach. It was unassuming, peaceful, and non-descript. This was a small inline group of stores where you could choose between flowers, donuts or postage. The clothing store was not a grand space nor was it a well-known name brand clothier. But there was something that this small unassuming shop had done: it had shaken his world deep into its core, past his aching stomach, and into the deep and small crevices within his back. Most of all, it had brought back an avalanche of both good and bad memories from the past.

Thinking back a couple of hours earlier, the ride home from the clothing store incident was supremely terrifying to John. He had been visibly shaken, had taken the wrong rode home, and had ended up at a dead-end cul-de-sac in a neighborhood about three miles from his home. He had no idea how he arrived at that location, what speed he may have been driving, or how many pedestrians or children he had raced past along the way. As he finally pulled into his driveway, his neighbor Hugo noticed something very distant and unsettling about John's demeanor. The conversation was very abbreviated, as John squeezed out a brief hello and pulled into his garage without delay. Hugo asked, "Is everything alright?" but John had already pulled past him and closed the door behind him in haste.

Sitting on his open veranda, John drifted in and out between the inspiring beauty of the day, and the sudden turbulence in his life. He could visualize his wife's face like it was yesterday, and wondered if she looked the same now, thought the same, or even had the same mannerisms and interests that he had come to know and love. Maybe she had been kidnapped. Maybe she had intended to leave. Maybe he didn't know her as well as he thought.

The county sheriff's report had placed her on the "Missing Persons List," with a photograph and date of her disappearance. A missing person flyer had given some basic details about her height, weight, and hair color, and simply stated that "her whereabouts were unknown." The case number was still active, and had two digits, followed by a hyphen and four more digits. Publicly, they continued with their active Missing Person posting, in case someone came forward with additional information about Mia's disappearance. Privately, however, the sheriff's office had told John that they believed that she may no longer be alive.

Contrary to the Sheriff's private statements, John had always believed that she was still alive – living somewhere, in some way, and under either the same or an assumed name. The possibilities were endless, but his deepest instincts told him that she was still alive and not anywhere to be found in the local area that she had lived for many years. He began to speculate that she was probably not in California. He began to wonder if she had somehow departed from the Unites States. How could this have ever happened?

None of the numbers in the case number were John's favorite numbers.

Two more hours passed, as if it were ten minutes. John continued to examine the unlimited possible outcomes that may have taken place. How would he ever know the truth? How might he ever know the true reality, the end of the story? The calm blue sky above his home was not revealing any secrets. The flowing water was tempting and taunting as it passed through John's universe.

John began to sense that the neighborhood was strangely alive. It was probably like this every day, but for some reason he seemed to be noticing it more than usual. John did spend a lot of time at work during most weeks of the year. Today was possibly the longest single stretch of time that he had ever sat on this beautiful chaise lounge chair in his rear yard.

A small green lizard darted across the planter area as if he was heading for home. Where exactly was that little lizard man going? Was it a 'he' or a 'she'?

The clouds continued to move across the sky in a slow but poetic motion. John realized that the lounge chair had become more of a symbol of comfort than a place for his comfort during the past two years. He really should sit in the chair more often, instead of just looking at it from inside of his house.

The dogs were barking in the distance. The dogs had done that on many occasions, but John was noticing today what seemed to be an interesting conversation between two or three of the neighboring breeds. Do they have problems that they discuss with each other every day? John accepted the realization of how little he really knew about nature, and about life outside of his office. How might a lizard choose a good home? Maybe lizards each have several homes. Maybe that cute little lizard has a family. Whether male or female, it certainly seems to be content with what life had placed upon its table. John had a desire to be more content with his life.

The lizard crossed back into the planted areas, and John drifted back into a time several months before. The first year after his wife's disappearances had exhausted him enough to last two or three life times. It had haunted his very existence, and the newly revived questions in his mind began to once again press into his skull. The ultimate question had always been like a flying marsupial looking for a landing spot inside of his aching brain: Where. Was. She.

John knew that he needed to cross into new territory. Nothing made sense, and he was concerned that the potential answers to his grief could no longer be based on logic. This was completely terrifying for John, who was one of the most logical creatures that his friends had ever known. He was a lawyer by trade, which perfectly suited his personality. He could solve nearly any problem or dilemma that was sent his way, and could follow the facts and lead his clients to a pragmatic decision based on the most relevant factual data. He had done this successfully for many years as a lawyer, and could solve any number of complex conflicts, while others were often whirling within their emotional hurricane and high stress emotional outbursts. Emotional outbursts to John were always viewed as a curious waste of time, and they seemed to always get in the way of a reasonable and swift resolution.

This day was different. The insight that can be found from a different spectrum than he had known was the only way that he would be able to answer his most burning question. Nothing else had worked. Logic had certainly not worked. Something deeper needed to be attempted. Something unfamiliar needed to be learned. For maybe the first time in his life, he began to contemplate that the land of emotions, spirituality and internal messaging might be the only path to answer his most burning question. Where would he begin? Who could help him understand this brave new world? It hit him like a thunderbolt: He must find out how to enter and comprehend the world of things that are unseen.

John's mind jumped across the centuries of history, trying to scan the names that had entered a brave new world in one way or another. Magellan was the only name that came to mind. He was an explorer, after all. How did he know where to explore? Maybe he just started sailing and let the ship lead him to a distant land. That would be completely uncomfortable for John. John always had a map and charted a course. What about the Mayans? They were mystical and spiritual.

This was a topic that was difficult for him to know where to begin. It was uncharted territory that was not within his core of knowledge. Maybe he did need to be more like Magellan. How might Magellan go about looking for his lost wife? It was always a cold reality for John when he came across a topic that he didn't much understand – but his persistence had always served him well, and this topic would require a deep reserve of both determination and luck. He must somehow learn to understand the unknown, the spiritual signals, the emotional indicators in life, and what many people had always referred to as a gut feeling.

How could you ever depend upon a gut feeling to give you a viable answer? It was not rational or quantifiable. It was not logical or easily definable. They didn't teach him this in law school.

John ventured deeper into trying to relax the pain around his lower back. He chuckled at the irony of the deep pain that started in his stomach area, and then had moved in a circular fashion to the lower regions of his back. This was the same type of migraine pain that had been residing in his head over the past twenty-four hours.

"Oh, my goodness," thought John, "I have never been so incredibly happy and intensely sad at the very same moment."

CHAPTER 3

A New Dawn

John's leg lifted with a short spasm as the sunrise caught his right eye. There was an unusual sound in the distance, as if someone was pulling a rope that moved a mechanical pulley system of some sort. "What is that? Wait, where am I?" thought John, without attempting to answer either question.

John was still sitting in his lounge chair on the rear deck of his home. A new day had emerged, with the morning sunshine piercing into his face. John looked around to locate where the incessantly productive woodpecker was laboring heartily in the distance.

The thought came like an electric flash. "It's time to figure this out."

John could not get Mia or Amelie out of his mind, and was newly determined to figure it all out.

Reaching for his mobile telephone, he finally found it trapped between the lounge cushions and the side arm of the chair. John quickly called the office before all power had been drained from his usually dependable device. "Janey, can you tell Jordy and Raney that I'll be taking the day off today?" a combination of both asking a question and making a statement.

"John? Are you OK?" asked Janey.

"Yes, I'm fine, can you tell them please?" continued John in a determined voice.

Janey had never heard John call in and say that he was not coming into work. Like oil with vinegar, or salt with pepper, it was unusual for the two to be separated. She had worked there for nearly two years, and immediately sensed that something was wrong.

There was a long silence from Janey.

"Are you there?" asked John, concerned that his phone was out of energy.

"Sure, John, should I have one of them call you?" said Janey, trying to absorb if she should inquire any deeper.

"No, I'll check in later, thanks," said John, and just like that he was gone.

John was generally known as a no-nonsense type of character, but was extremely social and normally not this brief and confusing as to the reason that he was conveying information. To Janey, their loyal office manager and communications coordinator, this seemed well out of character to receive an early morning call such as this from John. She also knew that both Jordy and Raney, John's law firm partners, would find this call to be highly unusual.

John ended the call and strangely squinted at the fence area beyond the pool.

"What is that?" he ruffled under his breath, as this new day continued to test his resolve.

"When did you arrive?" he asked the feathered creature.

"That's not a woodpecker," he thought to himself, as the woodpecker continued to tap on the tree branch in the distance.

"What exactly was this unusual bird sitting about twenty feet in front of me on the fence?" he thought, "and what is the deal with birds, anyway, on this particular morning?"

One bird was auditioning as the noisiest inhabitant in the neighborhood, and the other was sitting on the fence with a quiet resolve like it was the king of a thousand lands.

John repeated his private murmur, "What kind of bird are you, anyway?"

He had seen this type of feathery creature before in books and photographs, but could not remember if he had ever seen one in person. John certainly knew that one had never been directly in front of him sitting on a fence. This bird was strangely calm. How could a bird be so calm? He had never seen any bird be so calm and content, entirely unconcerned or skittish about what might be flying in his or her direction.

John sat up in his chair and rubbed his forehead. "I need a shower," he thought.

As he stood up and turned toward the house, the bird calmly remained on the fence. There was something very mysterious and magical about that bird.

John was beginning to sense that his life had already entered a whole new phase.

CHAPTER 4

The Wedding Shower

John did some of his best thinking in the shower. As a youngster, his family was not blessed with much wealth or many possessions, and he was always grateful for the simpler pleasures in life such as a good meal, a shower, and a warm bed to sleep in at night. The water running on his head had always helped to calm his nerves, and it was the place in which many of his most important decisions in life had been contemplated, such as the day he decided to ask Mia to marry him.

Most of his shower decisions were calm and deliberate, and made over time.

On this day, the shower brought John a sudden urge. He jumped out of the shower completely wet, grabbed a towel, and wiped off the wet phone as he began punching the front screen in a state of mild panic.

"Charley!" shouted John. "I'm glad you picked up, I need to talk."

Charley was as patient and loyal as a person could ever ask for. "Sure, John, what's up?"

"I don't know, I just need to talk." John was adamant about something that he had no idea how to describe, and Charley was always right there for him with the best answer possible.

"OK, sure, what is the general topic?" said Charley with full support.

"It's about Mia," said John.

The phone went silent, as Charley waited for John to catch up with his thoughts and emotions. John's voice had become choked off as he ventured further into his conversation and began to mention the name of his wife.

Charley new that John was not an emotional person, and was not great with handling emotional matters. The good news was that emotional cross roads had rarely occurred. The bad news was that it was occurring today.

"OK, John, how about if we get together for coffee and see where it leads?" said Charley patiently.

Perfect. Done. John's best friend and most trusted confident had aced the exam again.

"How about in 30 minutes at *BP's,*" continued Charley. *The Bean Plantation* was the local java house where Charley and John had spent many hours together over the past three years.

"Yes," said John, "I need to make a quick stop first and will meet you there at about 10:00."

Except for Mia, and his daughter Jordan, Charley was the one person that he could call and talk about the unique and strange things that can happen in life, and what the deeper meaning might be for uncommon occurrences.

Charley was also his most trusted source during the days and months following the disappearance of Mia, and was someone who John could trust without judgment or condemnation. Charley was a good listener, but more than that, Charley was good at explaining the unknown, the more emotional and spiritual side of life.

John set down his wet phone, and noticed the picture of his wife on the master bedroom wall near the entrance of the bathroom. She was standing with him and their daughter Jordan along the beach front, in a photo that he had always cherished. Both Mia and Jordan had a beautiful smile. They were both calm and serene, with matching features at the corners of their mouth, shape of their nose, and composition of their cheek bones. The genetic match was remarkable in so many ways. DNA and genetics was always a fascinating topic to John, but one that he had never investigated in much detail.

John sent a blank stare into the distance, contemplating the days during which the photo had been taken, and trying to gather himself from the clothing store discussion on the prior morning. Amelie had such a strange resemblance to Mia, both in her mannerisms and her features.

"How could they be so similar?" thought John, as he began to focus on any genetic knowledge that might be buried within himself.

John always had a deep need to know what he was thinking about things in life. Both Mia and Jordan had a great ability to go with the flow, to easily adapt to unusual situations, and to maintain their calm, serene smile during the most intense occurrences. He had always envied how they were able to do it, and wished that he could do it as well. At the same time, John was humble enough to realize that is was not his best quality.

The events of the prior day, the evening on the rear deck, the morning call, and the photo of his dearest two ladies, had all sent him into an internal dilemma that was becoming difficult to manage.

John wandered throughout the bathroom area, still dripping water across the floor area, and began to question which type of a person he really was. Externally he was always known as a logical and pragmatic thinker, who was calm under pressure and could solve most any problem that he confronted. Internally, he knew that he had some additional emotional and spiritual traits that he had rarely revealed to friends or associates. If he really did have several emotionally creative qualities, why had they been locked inside his own body like a stone vault without a door?

This sudden awareness was both frustrating and liberating.

John began to dress, and ran through the confusing thoughts in his mind. Maybe there was something to his private thoughts that he could and should be using in his everyday life. Not just rolling phrases through his mind, but digging deeper and following the origins of his thoughts and patterns of thinking. There was something deeply spiritual about the way in which thoughts, emotions and spirituality balanced and interchanged with each other, and John longed to have this higher degree of balance in his life.

John began to think about some of his associates, friends and others that he deeply respected.

His mind ran through them like he was describing a variety of ice cream flavors:

- Maria, she was emotional and spiritual – very conversational.
- Mason – logical and emotional – how did he balance them?
- Jeff – logical and spiritual – this was very interesting. John considered how this person might be most like him.

John looked down and saw his suit and tie. He had been so focused on the personality types and had dressed himself in full work attire.

"Oh, crap," said John, as he swiftly unthreaded the tie and grabbed a hanger for the suit pants.

Remembering that he was not heading into work this morning, he quickly changed into a casual shirt and pants. This was a very uncomfortable feeling for John to be so far outside of his typical routine and emotional comfort zone.

CHAPTER 5

No Returns

John raced down Oso Parkway in Orange County on his way to meet Charley at *BP's*. The rhythm and bass of the guitars vibrated across his dashboard as the music blared along the landscaped boulevard, "all this feels strange and untrue, and I won't waste a minute without you."

The words cut through in an unusual way as he thought about Mia, his life, and his sudden change of perspective about what was important in life. "My bones ache my skin feels cold, and I'm getting so tired and so old", the lyrics pounded forward, "I want so much to open your eyes, 'cause I need you to look into mine."

Did John need to open his eyes? It was as if someone was suddenly telling him to open his eyes.

"Tell me that you'll open your eyes, tell me that you'll open your eyes, tell me that you'll open your eyes," as the chorus echoed in his mind from the Snow Patrol song.

John was enjoying the song, but also mumbling at the broader symbolic meaning. "Is this song talking to me?" he thought. "Why are so many strange things happening lately?"

John had always tried to escape from lies and false truths, it was part of his profession. Uncovering the truth had become a mission in life. In a sense, it was like trying to find the light, and he could relate to the verse "and you'll walk from this dark room for the last time."

The song continued, "Tell me that you'll open your eyes, tell me that you'll open your eyes." John needed his eyes to open and understand what had happened the past twenty-four hours.

"All this feels strange and untrue, and I won't waste a minute without you." The song ended with a direct message for this strange timeframe that he had entered. John wanted very much to be reconnected to Mia. He wanted to never waste another minute without her.

The pain in his head returned, and was becoming oppressive. It weaved throughout his body like a racer in Le Mans. The hurt took a sudden leap into his lower back area, made a crazy left turn into his middle back, and then headed north up the turnpike to some upper back muscles that he didn't realize had existed. It then left the roadway, and landed directly in the pond next near his middle stomach area.

John locked up in sharp pain, as his right shoulder blade began to send distress signals all along the highway.

He pulled up toward the front of the clothing store at 9:45am, just as he had done the day before an hour earlier. The difference on this day was that he needed to pull his right shoulder pain out of his left lower neck area.

As he pulled into the parking lot, he noticed the large letters above the clothing store with the name *"Vintage Rags"* above it. Wait, the name of the store was *VINTAGE RAGS*! He had been in that parking lot on dozens of occasions, maybe even over a hundred times, and had never noticed the name of the clothing store.

John always thought of himself as an observant person, collecting all the fine details of a piece of art, a person's mannerisms, or the unique flow of a conversation. How had he missed the name?

The morning dew was burning off the pavement, and the morning sun filtered through the lightly peppered sky above. A light breeze began to make it easier to breath. This was a welcome relief, because breathing had not been so easy for John the past twenty-four hours. John could see the window directly in front of him that had strangely captivated him on the prior morning.

The store had not yet opened, and the mannequin was not yet out on the sidewalk.

"Wait, what? Where is the mannequin?" John thought. "And why is the store not open. What day is this?"

John checked the small black on white sticker on the inside of the door window that showed the days and hours of operation.

This was Tuesday, and the store was set to open at 10:00am. In fact, the sign says that the store opens at 10:00am every weekday, including Monday.

"Wait, what?" John repeated to himself, as if his mind had played a second trick. Yesterday was Monday. He widened his eyes and read the sign again. "The store opens at 10:00am EVERY day?"

John wondered why the store did not open until 10:00am. It had opened at 9:00am yesterday. Yesterday was Monday. Monday was yesterday. Was Monday yesterday?

John took a walk down the covered retail corridor, pacing off his nervous energy and killing some time until the store was to be open.

He began to check into what else he had missed along this covered retail area. Postage, donuts, flowers. Just as he had remembered. "Alright, something still makes sense," he grumbled, but John could still feel some panic pressing into the upper part of his throat.

The next ten minutes seemed like an eternity. John nervously checked his phone to see if anything else in his life had begun to spin out of control.

As the 10:00 hour approached, John waited near the corner of the storefront glass, peering into the display area with a much different outlook than the day prior.

The lock clicked open, and in slow motion the sign on the door was turned to say *Open*. He could see a nicely dressed lady on the other side of the glass.

John was in a much different mindset than the day before, when he was trying to avoid the pesky sales clerk at the same sidewalk area of the store. Barely allowing the lady to return toward the sales desk, John pushed through the glass entry door.

"Is Amelie working today," bellowed John, before saying hello, good morning, or any other type of small talk introduction.

The lady in the store was dressed much in the same style that was displayed throughout the shop. She had a gracious and patient demeanor, with a calm looking facial expression, but her features turned into a slightly confused look at the question that had been posed by John.

"Who?" answered the softly spoken sales lady.

"Is Amelie working today?" John repeated, thinking that maybe she did not hear him clearly on the first try.

"I'm sorry, but we don't have any girls named Amelie that work at our store," responded the nice lady.

The blank stare that John had recently developed about his life had returned to his face, and settled in again for a nice long stay. His eyes widened, and his mouth was suddenly unable to produce any coherent sounds.

John tilted his head slightly to the right, and nervously scratched his hairline directly above his right ear.

He finally pushed forth a response out of his throat area. "Not working here?" he asked. "She has never worked here?"

"No, I'm sorry," responded the nice lady again, "maybe you are thinking of a different clothing store?"

This was a very nice way of telling John that she thought he was lost or crazy, but was not the type of person that wanted to directly hurt his feelings.

John continued with his blank stare, in silence.

"I am the owner of this store, and we have never employed any girls here with that name," she continued. "Are you certain that her name was Amelie?" trying to unveil the silence. "We have several different girls that have worked in our store over the years."

"No, thank you," responded John, expressing it more as a question than as an answer.

After a prolonged delay, John turned and slowly left the store. He had never noticed her name, or made mention of anything other than the person that he had come to see. She must have thought that he was a very odd person, showing up just after the door had been unlocked, and departing in a daze just moments later.

"Thank you," came out again as he reluctantly reached the glass entry door. He looked back toward some of the very familiar display areas in the clothing shop, and slowly pushed on the horizontal stainless door entry bar.

John's eyebrows remained in the raised position, as he halfheartedly exited the familiar clothing store.

CHAPTER 6

The Illusion

John had always loved his gatherings with Charley. The two of them normally had so much fun catching up on life, sharing jabs, dissecting experiences, and solving the problems of the world.

It had been several months since they had been able to get together. Meeting for coffee was one of the most enjoyable social items in his life at present. John was not dating anyone, had not gone to any dinner parties for a long time, and rarely attended his office holiday parties. Other than getting together with his daughter Jordan, which he truly cherished, this was one of the few social events that he would alter his schedule to attend.

However, today was different from one of their usual gatherings for coffee – today John *needed* to meet with Charley. Today John had serious business to discuss about life, perceptions, and if maybe he was beginning to lose his mind.

"Charley, you won't believe what just happened," John blurted out as he scraped the chair against the tile floor.

"Good morning," responded Charley, ignoring John's introduction and smiling at the fact that John had completely lost his manners.

"You won't believe it, there was no Amelie there today, she has never worked there," and then with a slight pause, "I can't believe that she has never worked there!"

"I'm sorry to hear that," responded Charley. "Who is Amelie?"

John began to fill in Charley about the strange occurrences at the store next door over the past twenty-four hours. There was no Amelie, and the store does not open until 10:00am!

John recounted the entire conversation with Amelie just the day before at the clothing store. Charley knew that John had been very content with his life at present, had a very successful career, was doing very well financially, and had a wonderful daughter that he truly loved. The only part of his life that had been put on hold had to do with his missing wife Mia, who he truly loved. John had figured out a way to manage things without her, out of a purely survival type of necessity.

Charley knew that John would someday need to make a final resolution of the matter regarding Mia. He had always tried to be positive in discussing the topic with John, given that it was such a delicate matter and an unresolved part of his life. Charley certainly knew that the current event with the girl at the clothing store had created a newly revived set of emotions and thoughts about Mia, and now that it was raised again may take a great deal of time to be adequately resolved.

"Did I imagine this?" hastened John. "Did I actually meet with Amelie?"

"Yes, it sounds like it really happened," inserted Charley, knowing that John had drifted off into this new internal world of questions and concern about what he had seen or not seen in the clothing store the morning prior.

John shook his head up and down in agreement, knowing deep inside that the event had really happened.

"The store wasn't even open at 9:00am," muttered John.

Charley was a good listener.

"Was it a dream, an illusion, or some other bending of the mind?" quizzed John. "Remember those 1970's movies, where you never really knew what happened?" he continued. "That's what I feel like, a 70's movie where you never find out what actually happened."

Charley smiled and continued listening as he tasted his coffee.

Charley always knew when to speak, and when to be quiet. This was a fine art that many people had not yet learned. Charley scanned his eyes across the variety of people in the coffee shop, who was meeting with whom, and the different individuals and groups that were waiting to receive their special orders.

"I know it was not a dream," John continued. "I know that I actually walked into the store and had that conversation with the girl who called herself Amelia." Thinking further, "but the owner today says that there is no girl by that name who has ever worked in the store." He was half asking a question toward Charley, and half trying to remember what she had said.

John was breathing heavily and stressing about the various options that may have occurred. Had Charley not known him so well, he might have become concerned about where this all was leading. John continued his stream of consciousness, and Charley allowed it to play out as he listened to the random thoughts coming from John.

John and Charley had often discussed topics of this type over coffee or dinner. They would jointly examine all sides of a problem, joy, or crisis, and make Aristotle proud of their sound and logical conclusions. But it was always much easier to determine what someone else should be doing with their life, thought John, what someone else should be changing about their life.

Yes, on this day, it was different. On this day, it was about John himself, on a topic that was not easy for him to understand. Life in the spiritual world was a complicated matter. The spiritual world worked from a set of principles that were quite different from the physical world. The spiritual world was not necessarily rational, or logical, or sequential. The spiritual world was based on faith, hope, inner peace, and tapping into a greater plan for your life that could not possibly not be described in physical terms.

"Was it an illusion?" continued John, venturing into the next possible answer for what had happened.

"Well," thought Charley, "an illusion is generally a thing that might be wrongly perceived or interpreted by the senses, so basically a form of deception."

"Then it would be some sort of deceptive appearance or impression that I had about the discussion?" asked John.

"Yes, something of a false idea or belief," said Charley.

This reminded John of the old 'trick of the light' trompe l'oeil paintings, which he had remembered from studying French art. They had used this technique to deceive the eye of the art observer, using realistic imagery to create an optical illusion which made objects appear to be three-dimensional.

"Yes," said Charley, "something like that. A deceptive or falseness to what you were trying to believe to be true."

John knew that an illusion was a distortion of the senses, but the questions about it kept coming. Was it really an illusion if he was so certain that it had happened?

John continued with his stream of perceptions. "If an illusion is a something that is or is likely to be wrongly perceived or interpreted by the senses, maybe a deceptive appearance or impression, then wouldn't that mean that my meeting with Amelie was really a false idea or belief?"

John paused and then continued, "but I know that I actually spoke with Amelie, or at least I think I know it."

"Exactly," repeated Charley. "You think that you know it."

The words began to roam through John's mind like they had done during many other private settings, words to describe his current dilemma. "Who knows what it was, a delusion, misconception, mirage, apparition, or figment of the imagination?"

Charley listened as John worked through the possibilities. "Yes, an illusion may be wrongly interpreted by the senses, but is not necessarily deceptive," said Charley. This is merely a description of the physical world, but does not fully incorporate the spiritual world. When you add the spiritual world, you come out with a different meaning."

"How did the mind normally organize and interpret sensory stimulation?" persisted John.

Charley knew that John had been doing some heavy thinking about this event and the meaning of his life over the past day, and the topic was continuing to gain momentum.

John was unrelenting in his questions about the strange occurrence. "Illusions by nature distort reality," and then with a slight pause, "but are they shared by most people?"

"Yes, I think so," bantered Charley, thinking that it might be time to break John's stream of consciousness. "Illusions could occur, I suppose, with any of the senses, but visual illusions are probably the best known and understood."

"Optical illusions," stated John, processing the answer. "Why don't we hear about the others?"

"Yes," replied Charley. "I think probably there is an emphasis on optical illusions, because vision often dominates the other senses."

Charley was a very smart man. He had a way of explaining concepts and making them sound so simple. "Some illusions might be based on assumptions that your mind makes during perception," he continued, trying to calm John that there may be an explanation to what had occurred.

Good grief. "Perception," repeated John.

"Yes, perception," continued Charley. "I think it is a matter of how your brain is perceiving something based on assumptions, and based on various perceptions, all of which lead to a specific sensory distortion."

Charley was on a roll.

"Unlike a hallucination, which is a distortion in the absence of stimulus, an illusion describes a misinterpretation of a true sensation," Charley continued. "For example, hearing voices regardless of the environment, would be a hallucination."

"So, you think I was hallucinating?" John surmised.

"No, because you were hearing her voice in a specific environment, in a specific store." Charley was examining all the possibilities that John had presented, as he often had done in analyzing highly spiritual matters.

Charley took a short bathroom break, as John thought about his descriptions. It was great for John to hear all the possibilities, so that he could sort back through each of them and get to the best available answer.

Charley returned from the bathroom, and continued in rare form. "It sounds to me like it was an illusion created by an angel," he summarized.

"By an angel?" The words left John's mouth in an abnormally high pitch, which had come from some unknown origin.

"Yes, I believe that you may have had a highly spiritual event, John. It may have been a spiritual experience, which created a temporary illusion to convey the message to you in a way that you could understand it," said Charley.

Now Charley had crossed over into new turf, which he had stated without apology and in a very factual manner.

John wondered if that was possible. "How does an angel manifest itself? Do we know if we've ever seen an angel?" asked John.

"Sometimes it is represented by a dove," said Charley.

"A dove?" asked John.

"Yes, an angel can take several forms I suppose, but is generally thought of as a spiritual being believed to act as an agent or messenger of God. It is often represented in human form with wings and a long robe, but can also be represented by a dove, or a white feather," said Charley.

"You think that Amelie may have been some sort of a saint, sent here as a messenger to speak with me?" asked John.

"Well," said Charley, "God sent an angel to talk to Gideon. He is certainly capable of sending someone to speak with you. Most of them serve either as intermediaries between Heaven and Earth, or as guardian spirits. In Christian Science, the word 'angel' is used to refer to an inspiration from God."

John wondered how Charley knew this.

"I think there is a message in this for you," continued Charley.

"Message?" John had asked more questions today than ever before in many previous gatherings.

"Yes, someone is trying to communicate with you through this clothing store experience," Charley said, "Maybe even Mia."

"Mia!" repeated John. This was a new one, and possibly Charley's most hopeful thought of the day.

"Yes, it is possible that Mia is sending you a message." Charley had finished his startling reflection in a most calm and measured way.

The coffee shop whirled with noise, bad acoustics, and chairs scraping noisily across the tile floor. Silence ruled for a short time at the table of Charley and John, as John continued to think and stare into the distance. Charley had outlined a startling set of possibilities for what may have happened. It was as if the fog was trying to be lifted from the shoreline, as John tried to focus on the best option. In a matter of minutes, Charley had passed through, analyzed, and summarized the idea of illusions, hallucinations and angels, all of which combined into the thought that John had seen an angel and was being given a message from the spiritual world.

John could not help but think how far his life had changed in a very short time. One day he was enjoying his life, or at least had effectively put it on hold, with a great job, good friends, and a wonderful daughter. Now he had entered a world of complete misery, wondering if Mia was out there somewhere, maybe lost, maybe in pain, maybe trying to find her way back, or maybe even trying to avoid coming back. Who knows what really happened to her, and how would he ever find out.

John peered into the small hole at the top of his latte cup, and with a slight shake became resigned to the fact that it was empty. He searched around for where he might focus his eyes next, and his large round pupils finally tried to focus on a distant light pole in the parking lot.

"An angel?" repeated John.

Charley let him absorb the thought.

"Spiritual experience?" said John, as he continued to gaze into the distance.

"Mental?" followed another long pause.

"Both?" said John, following an even longer processing delay.

"Yes," cheered Charley, "all the above," with an ease that would make a school girl laugh, as if he had known the answer all along.

"Have you considered speaking with a Doctor?" said Charley. The words came slow and soft from Charley's mouth, as he continued to bring John along slowly and carefully.

"About me?" John nearly winced at the thought.

"No, I think you are fine," Charley continued. "About Mia."

John stared at Charley, still trying to absorb all the topics covered the last hour. Now Charley was talking about seeing a Doctor. John took a breath and considered what had just happened. What a difference twenty minutes can make. John knew he was a mess, but appreciated Charley's insight and perspective.

"About what could have caused her disappearance due to a medical condition," Charley continued, proceeding slowly and cautiously. He was not certain if John was still listening.

My goodness, thought John, this certainly was a new avenue to consider. John had given such great thought to the causes for Mia's disappearance, but just realized that they were all from the police perspective - was she injured, was she kidnapped, was she dead. Not once had he ever considered that she may have disappeared due to a medical condition.

"No, I haven't, but I will," agreed John.

It was time to go. Charley had pressed John's brain beyond his current limit for coping with reality, and it was time for him to go collect his thoughts. There were many new possibilities to consider. The scraping chairs and bad acoustics in the coffee shop had all gone silent. It was time to exit to the sidewalk.

"Just remember," Charley calmly stated as they maneuvered through the parking lot, "follow your gut feelings, and be sure to follow your internal messaging, as they are from your spirit and they know the answers that you are currently seeking."

"Ya?" eked out John.

"Yes," Charley replied firmly, "they know the answers long before you will hear them."

After a slight pause, Charley continued, "you will hear it in your spirit before it will come to pass."

The sage had spoken.

CHAPTER 7

Find Your Horizon

John turned off the motor and slumped in his car at his favorite place near the ocean in Santa Monica. It was the location that he often visited when he needed to think through a difficult situation or idea. He watched the sun begin to set as it developed a broad yellow band in the distance, with a sea of blue extending from left to right across the broad horizon.

The power of nature was simply breathtaking, as the ocean, sky and mountains interlocked into a scene that was normally reserved for paintings and photographs. The trees in the foreground framed the view like a master artisan. The car music remained on low in the background, just soft enough to complete the mood of the moment as the sun continued to change and evolve in color across the horizon.

John always loved finding his horizon, and the blue mass of the water always helped him to set his internal horizon. He looked out for the leveling effect of the water in the distant ocean, and often used it as a reminder to focus his life in a broadly balanced manner. John was constantly attempting to balance his mind with his emotions and deepest spiritual desires, although his wife and daughter were the only ones that really knew this fact about him. He had a deep internal need to always be operating with this balance, and knowing that both his physical and spiritual aspects were balanced in all aspects of life was a supremely important factor to be considered.

The yellow and orange mix of the distant sun continued to expand as the minutes ticked away. The broad band reached a magnificent point, as if it was passing forth a beautiful wedding band to the world beyond.

As the sun began to set, the tall palm tree down the street and over his left shoulder caught his eye as it reached desperately for the sky. The tree was on the opposite side of the street, and it leaned over the curb and reached toward the ocean.

The slender palm tree was shooting into the sky with reckless abandon, almost as if it were a small boy laughing ear to ear and running wildly away from his mother. It didn't know exactly where it was going, but it knew it had to sprint toward the latest opening and express itself with incredible reach. This is possibly how a young boy running from his mother had felt, as he watched his legs running so fast down the sidewalk instead of watching where he was going. It might be some time later before both the boy and the palm tree would figure out just how far they had reached.

John began to feel this same way as he sprinted into his future, without any clear idea of where he was going or where he might end up. He just knew he had to do it, and at some future point he would be able to look back and see just how far he had gone.

This idea of sprinting into the future was very liberating for John, but it was a sensation that he had not felt in many years. It was a form of hope, running wildly toward something that could possibly be caught, and John began thinking that maybe there could be nothing more hopeful than that. Effort had to be involved, along with maybe some sound planning or ideas about where to go, but certainly some wild abandon had to also be involved. Maybe the three combined would somehow help guide him to find Mia.

As the orange became more yellow and linear across the distant horizon, John considered how far he had come in a short period of time. The world had begun to open to him, but the greater truth was that the world had mostly forced itself open. The question now was how would he handle it.

The discussion with Charley at *BP's* was quite a revelation. It helped John to begin to see the world more clearly, and especially to see the unknown world more clearly. This was tricky business, this unseen world, and more difficult than law school could ever have been.

The connection to all of this, as he gazed across the distant sunset, had to begin with hope. It had to lead to hope. Hope had to be in the same generation as the eventual answer. Without hope, why try. Without hope, why live. In a small way, he had not realized until this very moment that finding Mia had been buried inside of him all along in a miniature ball of hope. Without consciously realizing it, it was hope that had kept him going, believing all along that Mia might still alive, and someday might return home. Hope was the vehicle that had helped him through the past two years, and he was mildly embarrassed that he had just realized this fact.

The man of facts had missed a huge one. Things came so clearly when he visited his horizon, his favorite place to think and dream. For John, the first step in this new process would be to fully understand and embrace the idea of hope, as difficult as it might be to sustain.

He began to run the ideas through his mind, analyze it, and commit it to his eternal memory.

Hope meant possible joy. Joy was the happy anticipation of something good about to happen.

Possible joy could be found through hope. Hope was not the end, but hope was the possibility of finding the end. Why not enjoy it while you searched for the end of the rainbow? Somehow this all made sense to John.

At the same time, this was not an easy process for him. After all, he had a natural tendency toward hopelessness, rather than hope, given the tragic situation that he had faced. He wanted to be hopeful, but he could never really do it, or so he consciously thought. The inability to find Mia in the past had left a cast of doubt on much of his life. Outside of his work, this pain of disappointment has stopped him from expecting anything good. But down deep, internally, he had secretly maintained a high degree of hope, buried within the stone vault. Now was the time to permanently turn this around, and fully remove the oppressive feelings of hopelessness. Maybe today was the day to chart a new course.

"If I can stay in hope," he thought, "maybe I can bring about the miracle resolution that is needed to find Mia." It was worse than a finding a needle in a haystack, but at least John knew that somewhere in the stack of obstacles was an actual needle to be found.

Some internal voice was beginning to communicate with him. Except for the time that he spent with his daughter Jordan, his friend Charley, and a few other selected individuals, work had totally consumed John since the disappearance of Mia.

John pulled up his internet connection and began to read about the topic. "When you are full of hope, you are happy. Joy is energy. Your attitude is yours, good or bad. No one can make you have a good one if you don't want one. We get what we believe for."

These words were good, but somewhat hollow. What did they really mean? How could they be fully realized in his life, and not just repeated from a book?

"Be aggressive in hoping," it continued on, "don't wait to see what happens. Faith causes you to believe that good things are going to happen. It is what you decide to believe, and what you decide to say."

John had always heard that you could literally talk yourself into a better mood, but he was not the best at doing it. His personal life had disappointed him with the disappearance of Mia, and he became a vehicle of denial that this area of his life could be reversed and improved. On the surface, hope had become the enemy, something that mocked him and that could not be easily solved. It's a simple recipe, yet he had rarely wanted to cook that dinner. The problem was that it never stuck. He would start to be hopeful, and then dropped the idea like bare feet on hot pavement. It might be barely tolerable for a couple of steps, but it was wiser to get off the pavement.

But on the inside, a voice of some sort was trying to tell him today that maybe his spiritual sensibilities were trying to resist that external idea. Maybe he was fortunate that his internal clock had not fully listened to his external reasoning. "Sometimes you think too much!" was a phrase that Mia had often repeated to him in the past.

If hope was the happy anticipation of something good, he needed to begin consciously anticipating it.

The text on his research device continued, "Something good is going to happen to me today, and something good is going to happen through me today. Hope is a positive attitude and mindset. Remain hopeful in thought, attitude and conversation, all the way through to victory."

"Oh, my," thought John, "it sounds great, but I have so far to go." Ten days prior he would have considered this pious nonsense, but he was beginning to make the connection that the ideas you put and consistently maintain in your mind will become a reality if you truly believe them and speak them into reality.

John did believe it. Not the lofty words or descriptions, which were a bit on the promotional side of things, but the feeling he was beginning to receive deep in his soul of what was right and good with the world, and what the universe in its entirety was somehow trying to tell him.

John also agreed with the main point of this text: Anyone can *decide* to be hopeful. He had not done it in the past, but he always could have done it if he had chosen that path. If you can decide today to be full of hope, and if you can make yourself happy, why had he not done it? Why would anyone not choose to do it?

John could use some additional input from both Charley and Jordan. Gut feelings were still not his most highly developed quality. He was also exhausted. In all his late nights at work, he had never felt this exhausted. His heart ached for Mia, and he knew she was alive. He *knew* it. How did he know it? This one thought carried him through the evening, and continued to roll over and over through his brain: "How did he *know* it?"

The link on the web page emerged, and John wondered where it came from. He had not specifically clicked on this link, which read "Fight for yourself. Fight for your family. Break the habit of expecting bad things. Remove the evil forebodings." It was from *Proverbs 15:15*.

Something told him that he was supposed to see that link. Something told him that he was supposed to be at this location today. Something told him that he was supposed to have that interaction with Amelie in the clothing store.

"Who is telling me these things?" thought John. They were ringing in his mind as clear as the sunset in the distance, but there was no audible voice telling him these words. They were coming from somewhere within himself, and they were the types of messages that he had always tried to talk himself out of.

Mia always knew how to trust her inner voice, and had always trusted John's gut feelings and reactions to various situations that they were involved with. She knew that they were locked inside his vault, but she always trusted it nonetheless, and tried her best for John to understand where it came from. John and Mia were two peas in a pod, but this was the only topic that John had difficulty agreeing with Mia. He had relied so much on his rational thought processes in his daily work and had never given the topic much credence, until today.

This was complicated stuff, thought John. He had gone to law school, passed the bar exam, and helped clients for years get out of a variety of messes and predicaments that many others would not know where to begin. But this spiritual component was complicated, or maybe too simple. Either way, it was a topic that he had always struggled with understanding, how to balance the real world with the spiritual world, whatever that may be.

John remembered how much Mia trusted his inner voice, and had always had told him to follow it no matter what. She trusted it, so he should trust it.

Somewhere deep inside his spirit he felt that she was giving him this message right here, right now. The reality of following his gut feelings was beginning to become real.

Mia always had asked him, "If not for yourself, please try it for me."

John remembered the one thing that Charley had told him at *BP's* as he was leaving the parking lot earlier in the day: "You will hear it in your spirit before it will come to pass."

These thoughts from both Mia and Charley were beginning to take root.

CHAPTER 8

The Bird

As the thin yellow horizon turned to darkness, John's exhaustion took him toward a light trance. The extensive activity in his mind over the past thirty-six hours had finally turned off, and John's head involuntarily leaned back against the driver's side head rest.

The bird from his fence suddenly reappeared in front of him like it has been there all along.

John could see something flying in the distance, but the bird was entirely unaffected by this activity behind it. John noticed that the bird also had something on its shoulders, some sort of wings that appeared to be much larger than might be needed for a regular bird, but which the bird was not using.

An airplane appeared behind the bird that was getting ready to take off, and beyond that were some passengers standing with their baggage. One of the passengers was holding a shopping bag with French writing on it, and had many friends and travelers with her.

Most of the travelers had sturdy travel trunks with them, such as you would have seen in the mid-1880's or so, with several travel stickers on them. John could see a familiar interlocking logo on one of the main traveler handbags, but could not make out the print.

One of the other passengers walked over toward John and handed him an envelope. John was surprised at the traveler coming in his direction. John took the envelope from the man and opened the envelope, but could not see any message written on the inside. The traveler asked him to look again. John looked again, and noticed that there was some printing on a small card in very light italic print, barely decipherable, but he still could not make out the text.

John looked back toward the traveler for assistance, but the traveler had disappeared.

One of the stickers on the suitcase was a block type sticker with the words 'Fight On'. This was a well-known college phrase for anyone living in Southern California, but what was it doing on an 1880's luggage bag in the middle of France?

John felt his phone buzzing on his lap, as if it were trying to send a distress signal from the European coast line.

John grabbed his phone, turned it upright, and answered the call.

"Daddy, where have you been?" His beautiful daughter Jordan's voice pierced unmistakably through his telephone. "I've been trying to reach you all day!" she said.

John realized that his caller identification had more than twenty calls that he had missed, ranging from office calls, to close friends, and several from his daughter Jordan.

"Sorry, hun," John replied apologetically, "it has been a crazy couple of days and I must have fallen asleep at the flats."

Jordan knew exactly where that was located, and felt relieved at his answer. They had spent many hours together at the place that they had coined "the flats", which was the elevated linear palisades park area high above the ocean front. She knew it was one of her dad's favorite places to sit in his car, walk, think, and watch the sunset.

"I've been worried about you all day, because Janey said that you did not come into work today. We were planning to have lunch at *De' Palma*!" shouted Jordan.

John felt completely terrible that he had lost touch with reality and missed lunch with his daughter.

"I'm so sorry, Jordan, I am not thinking right at this moment, we should get together and talk," muttered John, with his eyes still half open. "What time is it?"

"It's 10:15 at night, do you need me to come over there and pick you up?" Jordan was always ready to help her father upon a moment of notice.

"No, I'm ok, I'm going to go home now. Can we talk tomorrow?" responded John.

"Yes, of course," answered Jordan. "Daddy, what's going on? I need to work in the morning, but call me tomorrow and we can talk. I have been getting this feeling inside of me that you need my help, what do you need me to help with?"

"I will, hon, I will, no worries, we will talk tomorrow," said John. "It's about your mother, I think, I know it sounds crazy but I keep getting the feeling that she may still be alive."

"Me too, daddy, me too, I think that it may be true. I have this feeling she is trying in some way to communicate with you," responded Jordan without delay, as if she had been waiting for John to say those exact words. "Call me tomorrow and don't forget! Call me tomorrow."

"OK, I will, no worries, we will talk tomorrow," and John ended the call.

That was exactly what I have been talking about, thought John, how did she know that we needed to talk? "That is just the sort of thing that Mia would have said," he murmured aloud. "The two of them are so much alike."

John thought about the bird on the fence, wondering why it had reappeared again while he was sleeping.

"What kind of a bird is that, anyway?", thought John, as he pulled himself together and headed for home. He continued thinking about the message from the French train passenger, who was hanging out at the airport.

CHAPTER 9

Doctor Doctor

John arrived early to meet with the Doctor that Charley had recommended. John sat in the waiting room, listening to the music and waiting for Dr. Gregor to arrive.

The Doctor was a good friend of Charley's, which John had previously met at a couple of business gatherings. Dr. Gregor had a very fun wife that had hit it off well with Mia, and both Mia and Jackie always had the best time getting together, usually laughing and talking in the kitchen area at most of the parties.

John had known Doctor David Gregor from this type of social setting, but had never discussed any medical details with him prior to this day. In fact, John was not entirely sure what type of Doctor he was, but knew that everyone had always called him "Dr. G". Since Mia's disappearance, John had lost touch with both David and Jackie, but was happy to be catching up with the Doctor on this morning.

Dr. G was a humble and unassuming figure, very bright and always very conversational and friendly. He never seemed to take himself too seriously, even though his education, background and talents were quite exceptional.

The music in the waiting room moved from one song to another. Hearing it lightly in the background, the words on the current song hit him again as they had done the day before, "Tell me that you'll open your eyes, tell me that you'll open your eyes. " John needed his eyes to open further and understand what had been happening over the past couple of days.

John began to think about all that had transpired since the song came on the car radio yesterday, as he heard the strong voice ringing into the waiting area, "Hello John, I haven't seen you for a long time, please come in."

And just like that, John was sitting opposite Dr. G in his private office and catching up on the past.

John moved quickly from the social niceties to the point at hand, "Charley tells me that you can give me some insight on how genetics might impact a person. I still have a feeling that Mia may be alive and living somewhere, and we were wondering if their might be any medical explanations for what might have occurred to her in the past that may have caused her to disappear."

Dr. G always had a big smile and was ready to help. He would not meddle in the lives of others, but once they asked for help he was always quick to assist.

"Yes, I spoke with Charley and he gave me some general background information about your conversation," Dr. G offered. "It is conceivable that there may at least be a possible explanation for what could have happened to Mia, although a variety of things would have needed to occur and we don't have any genetic background information specifically for Mia."

"I see," stated John, ready to be in full listening mode. "Can you please give me any info that you can share about how all of this generally works, and how it might apply to Mia?"

"Well, yes, in simplified terms," quipped Dr. G, "Epigenetics is the study of biological mechanisms that will switch genes on and off."

"On and off?" repeated John. "What does that mean?"

"Yes, well, as you may remember from biology class, cells are the fundamental working unit of every person," explained the Doctor. "All the instructions required to direct their activities are contained in a person's DNA. DNA is made up of billions of bases, but the important thing is that the sequence, or the order, of the bases is what determines our life functions. Genes are the specific sequences of bases that provide directions of how to make important proteins."

"So, in short," continued the Doctor, "with this basic understanding of genetics in mind, it is epigenetics that controls the genes. You see, our latest findings show that certain circumstances in life can cause genes to be silenced or expressed over time. The genes can become dormant or active."

"Silenced or expressed?" repeated John, trying to absorb the scientific basis of it all. "Dormant or active," John continued, not realizing that he was becoming a parrot of the doctor's words.

"Yes," continued Dr. G., "in other words, the actual genes can be turned on or turned off."

"Really," stated John, in a long, low soft voice, raising his eyebrows slightly as he stared blankly at the horizon. "Turned on or turned off." John was becoming well accustomed to his blank stare.

"Yes, turned on or off," continued Dr. G, being patient with allowing John to absorb this new information. So many doctors were impatient with their patients, realizing that they were not trained in the same field, but nevertheless needing to not spend too much time repeating the same concept. Dr. G was different, he knew that he did not know the law as John knew it, and that John would not naturally know medicine as he knew it. He was a real person.

"Epigenetics is everywhere," continued Dr. G, trying to continue the teaching moment without sounding condescending to John. "What you eat, where you live, who you interact with, when you sleep, how you exercise, even aging!"

Dr. G paused, then continued, "all of this can eventually cause chemical modifications around the genes that will turn those genes on or off over time. Plus, in certain diseases, such as cancer or Alzheimer's, various genes will be switched into the positive state, away from the normal and healthy state."

"What you are saying then, is that a person's environment can cause a change in their genes, and cause them to function or appear differently in some way, depending on the entire set of circumstances?" relayed John, summarizing what he had been hearing.

"Yes, that is correct," answered Dr. Gregor.

"And did you say that their genes can be reversed back into a normal state based on their *environment*?" continued John, with his thoughts focused on the word environment. John loved to drill deeper once he grasped the basic concept, and his legal training often sent his mind and words down a fact-finding tour of questions.

"Well, potentially, yes," answered the Doctor. "Depending on the type of genetic condition, physical location and maybe some other factors. Normally it can be a difficult process to reverse the genetic condition, but there are environmental, diet, and other factors that can certainly help reverse it in certain circumstances."

John pressed forward with more clarification, "So it can *potentially* be reversible?"

"Yes, epigenetics can potentially be reversible, depending on the entire set of circumstances. Some epigenetic changes can be inherited, but different combinations of genes can be turned on or turned off. There are over 20,000 genes, so potentially the results can vary as different combinations of genes are turned on or turned off."

There was a sudden ray of hope in the life of John, as it related to Mia.

"In theory," continued the Doctor, fully pleased that John was grasped the potential ramifications of these relatively new scientific findings, "if we could map every single cause and effect of the different combinations, and if we could reverse the gene's state to keep the good genes while eliminating the bad ones," the Doctor cautiously paused, "then we could theoretically cure cancer, slow aging, stop obesity, and so much more."

"That is incredible," nodded John with eyebrows raised, "the possible permutations would be enormous."

Dr. G further clarified, as many often do with a level of caution for a topic so sensitive as this, "There are of course already wild 'self-help' claims in the marketplace by some that are beginning to exploit this idea, and offer 'panaceas' that really don't exist, but the basic fact remains that the future scientific possibilities are endless."

John felt a sigh of relief, like he had just been given the answers to a test, and discovered a whole new reason to be hopeful. This was not necessarily a direct answer for the conditions surrounding Mia, but for the first time in two years, he felt a sliver of confidence that he might one day find Mia, and the information just gained might be a critical aid to understanding how it might apply to her life.

Dr. Gregor stood up and walked toward the exterior glass wall. He placed his face close to the glass, as he stared for a moment into the distant sky.

John contemplated the good news, but was curious about the thoughts that might still be filtering through the brain of Dr. G.

"What," stated John, knowing that familiar look when a new thought had come across someone's mind.

"I was just thinking," continued the Doctor, "Have you considered PTSD?"

John stared at the Doctor and listened.

"Post-traumatic stress disorder," continued the Dr. "It can happen to someone who has been kidnapped, stressed, escaped, or could even cause memory loss from the anxiety of the situation."

The Doctor continued staring out of the office window. The outside breeze fluttered the pine branches in the foreground, just beyond the glass window. A parking lot in the distance had some red and white streamers that hung in intervals across a long wire, and were snapping in the breeze. The mountains beyond in the far distance created a perfect backdrop to the local terrain, and shared a light haze of cloud cover pressing up against its strong and majestic profile.

The Dr.'s mind was both in and out of the conversation, as if he was both thinking through the possible explanations and then summarizing the concept at the same time.

Dr. David continued, "People with PTSD often have lower levels of the stress hormone cortisol in their systems, and you often see it with combat veterans. After much research on the topic, it is safe to assume that our genes do not forget our experiences, even long after they have occurred. Some people may not be able to be around certain sounds which will make them ill, or in some circumstance they may block out the past. Sometimes even trauma Doctors can suffer from post-traumatic stress."

The Doctor watched how the hazy blue sky that had first been seen in the distant mountains tried to connect to the land forms and the buildings in the foreground. He was not being rude with his back turned to John, but was simply trying to think through some of the possibilities.

"All these things combined, it is also possible that there could be an epigenetic traumatic inheritance, possibly passed down from many prior generations," continued the Doctor.

John listened intently. He had been around a lot of great minds over the years, and learned to listen all the way through the thought process when someone had entered their stream of consciousness. The prospects of this topic were fascinating to John. It was like watching a great movie, he thought, where you sensed the end but really had no idea where the story might lead before you reached that final climax.

"Yes," summarized the Doctor, liking where these thoughts had been leading him. He finally turned back toward John, "Let me do some additional research on these possible connections and I will give you a call in a couple of days. I am also getting the distinct feeling somewhere within that your wife may indeed be alive, John. She may simply not have the ability or awareness to be able to reach you at present, but I would need to think through some of the conditions that could have led to this outcome."

John let the thought sink in.

"Thank you," replied John, as the Doctor shook hands with his patient. He had met with John as a part of his friendship with Charley, but was still the consummate medical expert trying to give his best advice.

"Please send my best regards to Jackie," offered John, with a smile.

"I will call you in a few days," confirmed the Doctor, "have a great week and we will talk again soon."

CHAPTER 10

The Pond

John pulled past the *No Parking* sign and stopped at the curb, while electronically rolling down the passenger side window, "Hi sweet heart!"

"Hi daddy!" shouted back his beautiful daughter Jordan, as she opened the car door and bounced into the seat.

A kiss on the cheek, and off they raced down the boulevard in sunny Southern California.

"Where should we go?" continued Jordan.

"I don't know, how about the park, and then we can grab some food at *O'Hanna's?*" responded John, two of his favorite places near home.

"Ya, sure," said Jordan, "and I can stop at *Zara* real quick on the way and pick up my blouse that I ordered last week for in-store pickup."

"OK," said John with a smile. Jordan was always multi-tasking, but she was also making a great effort to spend some time with her father.

"Hey, I wanted to ask you," continued John, "speaking of fashion items, what was that logo with the large 'V' on it that Mom used to love?"

Jordan thought on it a minute, "you mean the interlocking logo? Yes, that is Louis Vuitton, one of Mom's favorite designers."

Jordan always discussed her mother Mia in present terms, as if she were currently upstairs in the shower or down the street at the local marketplace. Jordan had always been so grown up, even at a very young age, and just like her mother she was beautiful both inside and out. John and Jordan had a very close relationship, with an extremely high degree of trust. Anything John said to his daughter could be trusted with 100% certainty. During all her years growing up, John had never said anything to Jordan that was not completely true and in her best interest. He always had done it respectfully, and with a cautious kindness, but he had always committed to telling her the full truth so that she could make the best decision for herself on how to handle the challenges of each day. In addition to that, John had always followed through on his promises to her, right down to the smallest of details. This, in return, gave Jordan the trust that she could say most anything that she wanted to her father, and be completely honest in return. He knew that she always meant it in the best way, without any ulterior motives to hurt him or undermine his trust in her, and was always open and honest in return about her thoughts and ideas.

"Louis Vuitton, the French designer?" responded John with curiosity. "Seriously? I think that might have been the interlocking logo that I saw in my dream. There was an 'V' in the middle, and I couldn't quite make out the other letter."

"Yes," said Jordan, "it is a very famous logo that they have used for many years. Those interlocking logos are known by all the fashion types. Mom loves Louis Vuitton and especially their LV handbags."

"LV handbags," said John, and with a brief pause, "He was born in France, right?"

"Yes," said Jordan, "he was born somewhere in France, and I think he might have moved to Paris at a young age. He started with designing some canvas type trunks, a long time ago."

"Canvas trunks?" asked John, somewhat surprised at that thought. "You mean the old leather looking trunks that were sort of rectangular?"

"Yes, that's them," stated Jordan in a factual manner. "Luggage for travelers, hat boxes, and other storage and travel items. Sometime back in the 19th Century, I think, he designed products for the elites in Paris."

"Paris, huh," pondered John. "Those must have been the trunks that I saw in my dream, but they had stickers all over them."

"Your dream?" asked Jordan.

"Yes, I'll tell you about it at the park," said John. "Do you want a Frappuccino on the way?"

"Ya, for sure, thanks daddy," said Jordan who loved her double chocolate chip Frappuccino's.

The two peas in a pod continued discussing the event of the day, the week and the month, as they moved down the boulevard and through the café drive thru window. It was part of their usual routine to drive, chat and drink a latte on the way to a simple but fun event, such as sitting in the park and watching the ducks paddle across the water.

Since they both were experts at multi-tasking, they could cover a variety of topics in a very short time period, using their time together in the most efficient way. They had an ability to get right to the point and find time for the deeper meanings, and this was the essence of the close and trusting relationship that they had shared for so many years. Jordan had her own apartment at college now, but still spent a great many nights sleeping at home whenever she desired. During her busy times, she would still find the time to check in with her dad and make her best efforts to catch up on all the new events in her life and discuss the things that they loved to share talking about at the park, the shopping mall, the movie theatre, and a variety of other locations.

They pulled into the parking lot near the park, and could see the rippling water in the distance. "I'll go grab my blouse and meet you at our bench," she said.

"OK," said John, as she bounced out of the car with the same enthusiasm that she had bounced into it.

John loved their time at the park, and especially the time at 'their bench'. This was a particularly favorite bench, that had been placed in the park as if it were especially located for them, oriented toward the views, landscaping, trees and water forms that they had most enjoyed. Jordan had coined it 'their bench' a few years prior, during a time when her father helped her talk through a very difficult boyfriend situation.

John was always happy when 'their bench' was free, unused, and not being loaned out to others.

He pulled out his smartphone and began some quick research from his thoughts in the car. John searched the internet for the Louis Vuitton name and logo, and came across an old French print ad that read, *Malles Et Sacs De Louis Vuitton*. It showed a variety of rectangular and other travel trunks that were sold at 1, Rue Scribe in Paris, France. The print font was in the old French style of the day, and appeared to be one of the original print advertisements that might have been printed in the local newspaper or on a poster board of some sort.

John continued reading about the famous designer in an adjoining article, "the Louis Vuitton Monogram is one of the most recognizable fashion brands out there, and the interlocking LV's are known by all."

"He was born in Anchay, France in 1821, and moved to Paris at the age of 15," continued the text description.

Jordan knew her fashion stuff.

The trunks were exactly like the photos in his dream, except for the stickers posted all over the outside of them. There were trucks for women in the ads with the heading *Malle pour chapeaux de Dames*, and trucks for men, noted as *Malle Pour Hommes*.

John sat back in his bench with a quiet amazement, trying to recall additional details from his dream.

"LOOK at this!" shouted Jordan, as she joyfully bounced back with her new white silk blouse in hand that had bell sleeves. She was holding it up in front of her for John to see the great style and fit.

"Outstanding," responded John. "You are quite the fashionista, my beautiful girl." John was of course impressed with her fashion style and taste, but was more impressed with her incredibly positive spirit and joy of sharing her life and thoughts with others.

Jordan could wear almost any type of clothes, with an ability to put combinations together in a stylish and perfect blend of materials, colors and patterns that others might never think of wearing together. They were normally a very simple mix, with just the right amount of jewelry or a special accent piece.

"You ARE your mother's daughter," said John mostly to himself, but loud enough for Jordan to hear it.

Not to be outdone, Jordan replied, "Well, I am ALSO my father's daughter," never wanting her dad to be left out of the conversation.

"Yes, you are, a blend of both," said John in agreement. "But you do have some distinctive qualities that are EXACTLY like your mother – your wit, your kindness, your intelligence, your sense of fashion, and that beautiful smile with the twinkle you get in your eyes when are laughing and that set off your cute little freckles on your upper cheeks."

"Oh, daddy, I'm not!" said Jordan.

"Ya, right," laughed John, appreciating the quick summary and extreme condensing of words when Jordan wanted to move on to a different topic. "I'm not" always really meant "stop embarrassing me and let's talk about a different topic."

John was not deterred, "and you also have that psychic sort of thing like your Mom, reading people, understanding dreams, knowing what might be coming next in life."

"No, I don't," repeated Jordan in a new way, ready to take the focus off herself. She knew her father loved her, and she secretly appreciated the compliments, but she had already heard these before and was ready to move onto new ideas and events of the day.

One thing did catch her attention, however, among his last set of compliments, and prompted her question, "So tell me about your dream."

The next group of ducks floated past them in front of their favorite bench, and this was always a sign that things were good and insightful in their lives. Every conversation of any significance at 'their bench' always has a group of ducks floating past them at some point or another.

They had often discussed and appreciated the ducks for a variety of reasons. Jordan watched them pass and remembered how her father used to say, "have you ever watched the ducks?" Jordan would always say yes, but then he would say, "no, have you ever really watched the ducks?" John always liked the way that the ducks were never deterred from their mission, and Jordan had come to appreciate this point. The ducks, when confronted with some obstacle in front of them, would simply swim around it and keep moving forward. John often followed this metaphor for life, when confronted with a problem he would just keep moving forward, not let anything stop him, and just go around the problem if it tried to get in his way. Jordan had also acquired this philosophy of life, and the meaning of letting the water roll off their back, just like the ducks. If you fed them, they would stop and eat, but if you tried to deter them from their mission, they would just continue forward and swim past the problem.

The two sat and enjoyed the view, the ducks, and the newly blooming vines and flowers in the area. This had often happened at 'their bench' many times prior, where they would start a conversation about a topic and then come back to it many minutes later.

"So, are you going to finish telling me about your dream?" continued Jordan.

"I already did tell you about it," responded John.

"No, I mean are you going to tell me what you are going to do about it?" insisted Jordan.

"That is a very different question," responded John. "I never know what I am supposed to do with my dreams. There is so much new information coming at me this week, my talk with Charley, my meeting with the Doctor, my dream at the ocean, my strange interactions at the back yard of our house, songs with particularly strange messages that have come on the radio, and all of this discussion around feelings, inner voices, illusions, and epigenetics, I don't even know where to begin."

"Wow, daddy, something big is trying to get your attention," responded Jordan, without even beginning to ask about all the details of the week. She already knew that she would hear about the details when the time is right, little by little if necessary, until they have a chance to catch up on everything. This was a common thread in their relationship.

Jordan continued, "Why don't you just go look for her?"

This was John's special daughter to be sure, cutting through all the possibilities to get right to the most important point.

John had considered this idea on more than a few occasions over the past week, and they were on the same wave length as he muttered out, "Where would I look?"

"I don't know, you just seem to be getting more clues than usual, and you should trust yourself. You'll never know if you don't look," said Jordan.

They watched the ducks to their left as they had moved well down the pond shoreline and circled into a small cove area.

Jordan continued, "How about France?"

John looked at her with a wispy smile. "France? Why France?"

"I think it might be obvious, daddy, your dream, the travel bags, the LV logo, it might be a place to start," stated Jordan in a simple but convincing way. "It is also where Mom was born, you know."

"France," repeated John. "It couldn't be the Napa Valley or something closer?"

He had not considered the fact that her place of birth might have an impact on these recent events, since it was so long ago and she had not actually grown up in France.

They watched the ducks turn back out of the cove and continue further down the edge of the pond.

After a long pause, John continued, "Do you believe in dreams?"

"Yes, you know that I do," said Jordan, "not in a literal sense sometimes, but they can be your own personal message, I think, coming from deep inside your subconscious. Carl Jung always talked about this, and if you follow your internal messaging system maybe you will be able to find Mom."

They both gazed across the pond, hearing the birds and other rustling noises in the background.

Jordan continued like a wise old soul, "Maybe she is alive, daddy, you know that we both think that is true, and maybe she wants to be found, but she doesn't remember that we exist."

"That is what came into my mind when the doctor was speaking today about epigenetics and other topics," agreed John, nodding as she spoke. "He was trying to give me some scientific background into some possibilities of what might have occurred."

"You should listen to this, daddy, the messages are all around," reinforced Jordan, always resolute when she felt strongly about a premonition or an opinion.

Jordan continued, "I'm not a doctor, but I get messages all the time about my life and other things."

71

"What sort of things?" asked John.

"All sorts of things," continued Jordan, "and I get messages about you sometimes, but I don't know how to tell you about it."

"You do?" inquired John. "Like what?"

"Just like basic stuff about you and that you should trust yourself more," continued Jordan. "I've been getting these message about you more lately than usual. You are so smart and so successful with your business, but you don't trust yourself with other things about your feelings and personal life. You never go out on a date, and you never talk about your feelings."

John partly agreed, "I don't know how to talk about my feelings".

"Yes, you do, but you just choose not to talk about them," said Jordan. "You have some very deep feelings about things, but you don't want to get hurt again. But I think if you trust yourself, and trust your feelings, and act on it, maybe you can feel better again. Maybe you can follow the clues and find Mom. We both think she might be alive somewhere. I think these new dreams and meetings with doctors and conversations with friends like Charley is trying to help you find her, but you are resistant to act on it."

There was a long silence. Jordan was right. John knew it was not personal, and that they were a team in solving the mystery.

The pond was serene, and so was Jordan in her new approach and demeanor. "I also had a dream about you, daddy, about two weeks ago, and you were somewhere in Europe."

"Why didn't you tell me?" asked John, looking at her cute little freckles.

"I didn't know what it meant until now," responded Jordan, as the pieces to the puzzle began to fit together in her mind. "You were talking with some old relatives or something, I'm not exactly sure where you were, but you had this special scarf that you were carrying around on your arm, and you kept looking at it but never wore it – I don't think it was your size, but you kept carrying it around with you and looking at it."

"Hum." John was absorbing the message.

"I have a lot of dreams with you in them, like I said, more lately than usual, also more recently about Mom," she said.

"What are the ones about Mom?" asked John.

"In one she was teaching some smaller school kids, like she used to do a long time ago," revealed Jordan. "I don't know why or where, but the kids were very happy and loved her. It was a pretty short dream, but the scene kept repeating itself, with the kids passing in front of me again and again, like it was a lot of different days."

"That is really interesting," whispered John.

He continued, "What do you think I should do?" John had cut to the chase, always trusting Jordan's input, but conveniently forgetting her prior advice. He was not ready to accept the fact that he should pick up and travel off to some other country without any idea of where to look. John needed more facts, or at least some rational convincing before he would commit to a decision like that.

Jordan knew her father very well. She knew that he needed all the information at hand, and maybe have it repeated to him a couple of times, before he would commit to anything out of the ordinary or generally unseen by the human eye.

She thought about the best way to tell him. She hoped that he would listen, understand, and maybe consider acting on it.

"I think you should follow your heart, and not worry about what anybody thinks. That is what you always told me, right?" she asked.

John agreed, "Right."

Jordan continued, "You have lots of money, and you never take a vacation from work. You are not dating anyone. You have a happy life, but you will never be able to find out about Mom unless you just go try to find her."

Silence came over the pond with a light summer breeze.

John stared into the distant trees, "Where would I start, you know, when I arrive in France?"

Jordan's freckles turned upward. She was beginning to make some real progress. "I don't know, maybe just try to trust your inner voice and follow the messages. Things that friends have said, things that you are thinking, ideas and images from your dreams. I always know when I am receiving a message because it is different from the other things I think. It is not the same as the other regular thoughts. I feel it deep down in my spirit, almost like it is talking to me but I don't hear a voice out loud. It took me a long time to trust it, because I would try to talk myself out of it, it didn't seem rational. But now when I follow through with it, I usually realize later that I was happy that I did – it usually leads me to a positive outcome or solving a problem of some sort. I've learned to trust it. I'm always curious what the outcome might be when I trust it."

"You are wise beyond your years," stated John, very proud of what his daughter has become.

"Oh, daddy, I'm not," she said.

John looked at the side of her cheek and chucked.

"Just go find Mom," continued Jordan, "and if you don't find her, at least you will have worked in a nice vacation!"

"And I should start in France," reiterated John.

"Ya, sure, you seem to have already found your rectangular luggage!" stated Jordan, always the comedian. "So, go find an LV handbag, and be sure to send me one!"

They both laughed, and headed back to their car for a trip to the restaurant. The ducks had come through for them once again, and it was time to leave their bench in good spirits until next time.

The stop at *O'Hanna's* was always enjoyable for them, and the specially prepared food was comforting. This gave them time to catch up on Jordan's school, friends, car problems, and gather funds for the hair salon. The day had been a wonderful time for both, and there was a quiet comfort as John dropped her at the curb in front of her college apartment.

"OK, doll face, France it is!" announced John, as Jordan bounced out of the passenger seat. "I'll go shopping for you in Paris, let me know what else you might need."

"Awesome, OK daddy, be careful, and let me know where you end up!" and off she went.

"I will, Jordan, I will," as the door closed behind her. He thought to himself, "maybe I'll send you something from Avenue Montaigne."

CHAPTER 11

Non, je ne parle pas Francais

Air France Flight #065 straddled the runway and took off with a heavy thunder, rising over the Pacific to the west of Los Angeles. Turning on course to the southwest, the south, and eventually the east, the large jumbo jet headed across the United States and toward Paris, France. John was in Row 15, Seat A, looking out of the window over Orange County, and wondering what would be up next when he finally stepped foot into Charles de Gaulle airport in Paris.

The captain and crew presented their usual routine of announcements and videos, and John's eyes closed as the plane ascended toward the east. In his imagination, he could begin to hear the sounds and see the sights of Paris, from the Eiffel Tower to the Louvre Museum. The Latin Quarter was a place that he had remembered fondly from the time when he traveled across Europe after graduating from college.

It had been many years, however, since he last stepped foot in the Latin Quarter. Beyond counting to ten and the usual greetings and niceties, he had never been terribly good at speaking French. He remembered that the French did not generally appreciate that, and were somewhat resistant to American tourists and their lack of French language skills. John had been through it before, and was prepared for the impending impatience that he was about to receive. At the same time, he knew that there would be a few kind souls that would treat him well, and over the years maybe some of the American resentment had at least partially waned.

The French stewardess came across the speaker system again with that familiar French accent and creative French delivery of language. They certainly were a very creative society, placing great emphasis over the centuries on their architecture, fashion, fine dining, and vineyards, along with the many famous artists, bridges, outdoor cafes, and other romantic followings.

It would be an eleven-hour flight, so there was plenty of time to think about the trip, where he might go, and what he might do. For John, this prospect was at the same time both frightening and exhilarating. Fortunately, Janey at his office had booked a hotel room for him for a few nights, so he had a place to initially settle once he arrived. After that, he would be completely on his own.

Once a person decides to follow their path, they are usually a difficult thing to stop. John's trip to France was to follow his path, as much as he had initially resisted the idea of it.

Jordan's advice and intuition was settling in, and he was finally following his heart. He had spent so much of his life focusing on following his mind, and was not sure where that part of the body ranked at the current moment. He had often assumed, incorrectly so, that following your heart meant that you should be required to set aside your mind. "Was there really room for both?" mused John. Of course, there was room for both. But, was there really *room* for both?

John was a balanced individual for the most part, but he was not accustomed to having balance in his life where both mind and emotions were sitting on the scales of justice. For too many years, it was his mind only that ruled this part of his universe. Now, he had uncomfortably switched over to his heart for a short period of time, trying to follow it to Paris, France of all places.

John watched the linear lights dim along luggage racks of the airliner, as he contemplated whether the pendulum of his life would be able to find a balance point between the two extremes. He was certainly much further along with this process than even one week prior. In fact, he thought, he had moved *much* further along in the process in a very short time. For the first time, this realization gave him great comfort that maybe he was learning how to follow the clues and trust that he was doing the right thing.

The sun was still bright, and the clouds were few, but heading east always brought a quick close to the day. John partly slid down the plastic window cover about half way. He was beginning to imagine the sound of the French music throughout the streets of the French Quarter, and street sandwiches that he loved where the French fries were jammed inside of the sandwich.

John began to envision wine, cheese, white table cloths, and French nouveau architecture. At the same time, the discussions from the past week all began to filter through his mind. The insightful words of Charley at the end of their gathering at the coffee shop kept ringing through his mind during the week when he said, "you will hear it in your spirit before it will come to pass." This phrase had stayed with him during both day and night, and was something that came to mind each time he received a new message, dream sequence, or piece of medical advice.

John further settled into his seat in 15A, which had finally begun forming to his body. He considered the way in which thoughts could become clearer as you got away from the day to day cycle of work, routines, and pre-scheduled events. As John closed his eyes for a moment, he ran though again some of the additional events of the week – the doctor, the dream, the ocean horizon, the pond outing with Jordan, and the coffee shop with Charley. The words of the week rang through his mind again and again, almost as if he had entered a new classroom on the topic. Illusions, epigenetics, post-traumatic stress, hope, faith and inner voices, all intertwined together in a way that he had never previously considered. That very moment was bringing him an inner feeling that these things had all merged together for a reason, and that he had made the right choice by getting on this plane to France. It was maybe the first time that he really understood what Jordan had been saying all, that voice from deep within that should be both listened to *and* acted upon. Charley had essentially said the same thing. Other than Mia, these two were his most trusted confidants on the planet. If he could not trust their advice, there was probably nobody who he could ever trust.

The police report for Mia was probably still the most troubling aspect of his recent revisit to the situation. It was not that the police were doing a bad job, but that it had never been resolved on many levels, and still had left a great many unanswered questions. The idea of a kidnapping or a post-traumatic stress related incident rolled over and over through John's mind, as the plane continued east across the Rocky Mountains. What if there was something in the report that had been overlooked, which would have given some indication about what had happened? If she was still alive, how had it played itself out? If she was still alive, where would she find money, a place to live, or proper identification if she was in a new location and had escaped or recovered from a traumatic event?

He looked out through the sliver of the partially open window cover. He could see the Rocky Mountains below, coming up on the left side of their flight path and extending well to the north. The beauty from above was breathtaking, as the snow sat on top and across the many ridges extending north across the horizon. Between the mountains, the desert and the ocean, the American west certainly had an expansive and unique beauty.

John drifted in and out of his thoughts about Mia and her disappearance.

As the time passed, he thought about Jordan's reminder at the pond about Mia being born in France, and he wondered if there was any connection between the two events. Although it was true that she had been born in France, she grew up as an American and never had any longstanding ties outside of this country. John did remember that she had returned to France during college for a short time, as part of a work study program of some sort, and had apparently made a few good friends in Paris during that period. However, this was a year before Mia and John had met, and his awareness of any details about that period was sketchy at best. He remembered that she had written and received a few letters from abroad, but those were the days before smartphones, social media sites, and the internet, and it was not easy for Mia to maintain an ongoing relationship so far away.

The mountain tops drew closer as they moved toward the east, seemingly right below the path of the aircraft. There was still a great deal of snow across the higher elevations and peaks, which gave great definition to these magnificent land forms. The sun pushed hard from the opposite side of the plane, wrapping around the back and creating large shadows on the massive land forms below.

The French girl named Amelie at the boutique began running through his mind again and again, her demeanor, her style, and her unspoken wisdom. There is no way that she could not have been a real person, thought John. The scene was just too vivid, and the location right next door to a place that he stopped at every week. It was not a dream, and the fact that the owner confirmed that nobody by that name had ever worked there was extremely puzzling. If it were in fact an illusion, or even an angel, then there had to be a God or a universally significant creator that was trying very hard to get his attention. He was on a plane to France, so maybe this angel figure had worked her magic as planned, but there were so many questions yet to be answered that the thought of it all working out was immensely bewildering.

As he closed and rested his eyes, his mind drifted to the dream at the palisades park along the ocean front, and the visualization of the strong bird image that had been so significant in that dream. How did the bird tie into the interaction at the *Vintage Rags*, or was there any connection between the two?

His mind returned once again to the mannequin, and the great secret that she was holding firm.

As he thought about the attire of the mannequin, he considered about how Mia would have dressed that figure. She had a keen interest in fashion design in those days, and he remembered that her undergraduate work-study program in fashion was the reason that had sent her to Paris. He had not really thought about this aspect of her undergraduate work until now, but this possible connection began to add new meaning to his renewed search for Mia.

John began to think of a way that he might remember any of the names of her friends during those college years. The old postal letters were surely long gone, but maybe he would be able to recall a name or two from the return address label and piece it together. It certainly was a very long shot that the two ideas were connected, but John was shooting in the dark and was ready to latch onto any possible ray of hope that might lead him toward Mia.

As the plane moved through the afternoon and evening, the darkness arrived and so did John's time to catch up on some sleep.

John hoped that maybe the mannequin might return to him during his sleep and tell him the great secret that she held firm.

CHAPTER 12

The Parisienne

Following the long flight and the time zone changes, John traveled in a taxi from the airport and checked into the *Grand Hôtel de lucarne*, Paris at about 2:00pm. He marveled at the design of this boutique hotel and the quaint location that Janey had found for him in the heart of Paris.

"Good evening, monsieur," greeted the hotel attendant, who was surprisingly fluent in English. She had noticed immediately that he was a foreigner from some western location, most likely American or Canadian.

"Bonjour," replied John. "You have a very beautiful hotel, C'est un bel hôtel."

The attendant efficiently checked him in, with a gentle smile and surprising kindness in her eyes. This level of hospitality was not exactly what John had been anticipating. She completed the paperwork, and then reached across the counter with the room key and room number.

"And monsieur," she continued, "please join us at 7:00pm in the *lumiere Room* for a special welcome dinner that has been arranged for you, our *bienvenue diner*."

"A welcome dinner?" asked John, a bit puzzled at this gesture of kindness and if she was speaking to the right guest about this event.

"Oui, monsieur," your reservation did include our *bienvenue diner*, it is something we offer to new guests and old friends who wish to join us with other local guests, did you not wish this option when you made your *hotel reservation*?"

"Oh, yes," replied John. "Merci, it is wonderful," realizing that Janey must have set this up as a surprise for him when she booked the room.

"Merci," continued John. "Merci."

The porter assisted John and with his bags, and they made their way to the hotel room on the third floor.

John was excited to be in Paris, and always had enjoyed and appreciated the European history and life style. However, the long flight, the time zone change, the delays in luggage pick up, and the trip from the airport, had accumulated into a bundle of tiredness for him. His head hit the pillow for what he had planned to be a short rest, and before he knew it was out cold amongst his new cotton sheets.

Three hours passed as if it were ten minutes. The lengthy nap had been a needed refresher for John. It was time to get dressed and restart his day into the evening hours. John's body felt as if it were still on Pacific coast time, so it felt to him much earlier in the day than what was showing on the wall clock.

After a quick shower, John sat by the window for a considerable amount of time. He read his fictional novel about three travelers in space, and intermittently watched the events taking place along the streetscape below him. The old French windows opened wide, and the scene at the street came into the hotel room like the next dinner table at a restaurant.

John watched a young girl below strolling down the street in her long black coat and sunglasses. The mix of attire reminded him of Mia and their life together back in California. John and Mia were opposite sides of the same coin. When they were apart, friends would often marvel in the way that Mia would describe a story or situation in the same way that John had described it. They thought alike, described thinks alike, and yearned for the same sensory experiences.

Eventually, 7:00pm arrived and John made his way down to the *lumiere Room.*

The *lumiere Room* had skylights stretched across the back of the room, along a long thin rear courtyard area that opened to the sky. The Euro doors were wide open in the middle sections, and the late afternoon daylight worked its way down to the elaborate fountain at the base of the opening. Stone benches surrounded the fountain area, and guests were sharing coffee and wine at the tables long the back wall of the adjoining building with vines wrapped along the masonry façade. Wall sconces lightly filtered along and between the vine areas, although daylight was still the primary light source as the late afternoon filtered toward evening.

It was evident to John that the hotel staff had been trained to greet all guests for the special dinner occasion, and the waiter with the name Enzo on his lapel greeted John immediately with a glass of champagne and an offer to join the guests in the courtyard area.

"Welcome, monsieur," stated Enzo with an enormous smile on his face. His broken English was clearly adequate for basic communication, and much more developed than John's broken French, although both tried to honor each other with their respective native language.

"Merci, Enzo," replied John. "J'aime la cour." John really did like the courtyard.

Enzo introduced John to some guests at the back tables, and gently let him know that the other dinner guests had not yet arrived.

The French were notoriously late for dinner parties, especially the women, so John took the cue and took up the conversation with some British guests standing by the fountain benches.

"Are you an American?" said Rowan, happy to see that John had joined their happy hour at the fountain.

"Yes," replied John, "as authentically American as you might ever find."

"Well then, mate, come join us for a pint," said Rowan.

John proceeded to amuse himself with observing the other guests, as he would while away the next forty minutes with his newly found British friends. They proceeded to hash about the current politics of the day, the state of the European economy, and the way that Rowan had been brassed off with his barmy neighbor next door. John fit right in with most any social situation, especially the bantering of life and politics, and made immediate fast friends with his new acquaintances from across the English Channel.

The dinner guests began to arrive, predictably late by French standards, but predictably on time as expected by the hotel staff. The staff brought out a special cart holding bottles of champagne, and the dinner guests began gathering around the dinner event that was about to unfold. There were plenty of smiles to go around, and a couple of the girls hugged and seemed to know each other from previous occasions.

"Hello, my name is John," as he directed his attention to a third girl that did not seem to know the other two girls already caught up in a deep conversation. John always did have exceptional manners, and often looked out for dinner guests that might feel uncomfortable because they did not know many people in the room. He was generally considered a great guest to have at parties, because he never waited around for others to entertain him.

"Salut, mon nom est Sophie," responded the soft-spoken girl with long straight bangs that were cut well beneath her eyebrows, and with long flowing and medium brown hair. Her smile was wide across her face, with classically French features. She was wearing fashionable black and white striped shoes, with her casual shirt sleeves rolled slightly up along her slender arms, "Vous êtes américain?"

"Oui, madame," responded John.

John took note of the special fashion sensibilities of all three girls that had gathered near the champagne cart. The girl taking center stage had entered with a long black coat and sunglasses, and had immediately reminded him of Mia. She had put together a unique ensemble of wears, with the same flair and fashion sensibilities that he had admired in Mia. She was adorned with some very simple jewelry, and had one main signature piece that set her off, a leather purse.

The second girl had a similar style, with a slender build like the first girl, but with a touch of lighter fabrics and color shades mixed into her primarily black dinner ensemble, and a plain white shirt. Her jewelry was even more understated than her friend, and she had a slightly lighter hair color at about the same overall length.

The two girls looked as if they could be half-sisters of some sort, especially in the way that they posed in their dress heals and carried forth their long slender frames, as they talked simultaneously and appeared to finish each other's sentences. The only difference was that the girl with the lighter hair appeared to have a British accent as she spoke in French, while the girl with the sunglasses was clearly a *Parisienne* original.

Sophie, by comparison to the other two, was slightly more petit, but had a similar stylistic flair and hair color to the girl with the sunglasses. She had typically slender French facial features, especially around the eyes and at the corners of her mouth. Sophie appeared very comfortable in her slightly more casual approach, as much as the other two girls were very comfortable with their more elegant but sophisticated and simple ensembles.

"Le diner est servi, s'il vous plait, dinner is served," shouted Enzo, in his perfectly pressed dark suit. Enzo stood tall and proud in his immaculately cut suit, although his actual stature was of a standard height and build for a French male. The smile was continuously stretched across his face, and not one of a jaded middle aged European male. Enzo clearly loved his job, and was a proud member of the hotel staff. He did not seem to care that someone might find him less than cool due because of his overtly positive and upbeat demeanor. Enzo was delivering a message to be happy at all cost, because that was his true calling in life.

"Permettez-moi de faire quelques présentations, car la plupart de nos invités sont maintenant arrivés. Let me make some introductions, as most of our guests have now arrived," stated Enzo in both French and English.

"With the ladies first," continued Enzo, "we would like to first introduce Madame Anne Avé, who is one of our most renowned fashion designers in Paris, and who has been invited tonight as the very special guest of our hotel owner Monsieur Quentin Lacroix."

Enzo pronounced Anne as if there was a long '*e*' sound at the end, and the full name of *Anne Avé* had a nice artistic ring to it.

The hotel staff gave a round of applause to the special guest Madame Avé, who was clearly a crowd favorite of the hotel staff.

"To the right side of Madame Avé, joining us from London, England, a regular guest to our great city and hotel, and a good friend of our special guest Manquer Avé, may I introduce the delightful and talented journalist and magazine editor, Madame Laura Edwards."

Madame Edwards also received some warm applause and a side hug from her sister-in-arms, and gave a slight wave and large smile to the adoring crowd.

Enzo was very skilled at his introductions and making his guest feel as special as they had felt in several months.

"Next to Madame Edwards, traveling to us today from the French countryside of Lyon, France, is our very talented graphic designer, the beautiful Madame Sophie Masson, and may we welcome her for the first visit to our grand hotel!"

Madame Masson had also become a crowd favorite in a very short time, as she had a warm but unassuming style, and took the praise in a thankful and welcoming manner. She was somewhat shy and introverted, but was trying hard to be engaging in this social situation.

"And for our deux monsieur, this evening may I first introduce our visiteur américain, Monsieur John Marcomb, a successful lawyer and partner with his law firm from California near Los Angeles."

Enzo led the applause, and the entire staff and crowd had already warmed to the presence of this interesting American visitor. Quite unlike many of the previous American visitors that had stayed at the hotel, John had already fit easily and seamlessly into the mood and style of the European social class, and presented a humble but humorous approach to his earlier discussions with the hotel staff and guests.

"And to his left, joining us tonight we welcome Monsieur Arne De Vries, a financial partner and banker from Amsterdam in the Netherlands."

Monsieur De Vries received the final applause from the group, and was a classically looking Dutch businessman. Standing tall and light haired, with his hair line thinning across the top, he was clearly an intelligent and fun loving person. It was also evident, however, that his life had been more focused to the traditional business world than many of the other hotel guests. The Dutch were always known for their great art and liberating social norms, but Arne had grown up in a wealthy family and gone into an industry focused on wealth and commerce, working for one of the large Dutch banks. He had a great interest in art and style, and certainly an immense appreciation for cuisine, culture and the arts, but was a bit uncomfortable with his individual rendition of going out on a limb on his attire and conversational prowess.

Enzo waited for everyone to finish cheering for the new hotel guests, a ritual that always took place with the entire hotel staff in the room.

"*Bienvenue* to all our wonderful guests, will you please be seated?" Enzo took a slight bow of respect, and exited quickly through the doors to the rear kitchen area.

The hotel seated each guest in alternating fashion, first the female, then male, around the circular table, beginning with Anne. Sophie was placed between John and Arne on the opposite side, with Laura to the left of John at the end of the circle. This put the two fast female friends together at the close of the circle. A large tulip bowl sat in the center of the table, and held beautiful springtime Parisian flowers consisting of a mix of white and purple tulips. Candles crossed the table in intermittent vertical placements.

It was spring time in Paris, and there was nothing quite so delightful as walking the streets of Paris in spring. The city on this spring day still had a touch of cool in the air, but was generally becoming warmer outside as the days progressed toward summer. The hotel had left the Euro doors open beneath the skylight area, and the fountain continued to be a wonderful backdrop as the daylight began to turn toward dark. The hotel always had some light music in the background, more faint than recognizable, but enough to set a nice soft mood for the guests to relax and enjoy their stay.

"Bienvenue à vous tous," greeted Anne, the special hotel guest, who had played this roll before and had a great personal relationship with the hotel owner. She always knew how to get a crowd rolling, and enjoyed her role to help her dear friend Quentin whenever time allowed.

The hotel had always enjoyed offering these welcome dinners. They were a bit uncommon among the Parisian hotel scene, but had become an enjoyable surprise for the many guests who attended them over the years. They were not highly profitable for the hotel, but this gesture of goodwill toward their guests had paid off over the years, and had created a very loyal following for those that returned to the hotel month after month and year after year and in the long run had become a great source for business. The hotel was into its third year now of offering the *Bienvenue diner* one time per week, and friends such as Anne were a key ingredient in making it a continuous success.

John thought to himself how many flights, hotels, and car rentals Janey had booked for him over the years, and marveled at how she had found this unique opportunity for him in a country far from his usual path of travel, and on a Tuesday night no less.

The sounds of the city continued to bounce through the rear courtyard, past the long narrow skylight, and into the *lumiere Room*. The skylights along the back wall had served their purpose for the day, but in the evening hours began to reflect the lights from both inside and out. This in return gave off a reflective glow from the movement of people, lights and water elements throughout the space.

The hotel staff had arranged a classic and sophisticated table setting, sparing no expense with its cutlery and accents. The hotel restaurant was a respected destination, with a menu that served the best of Parisian cuisine and received the highest of reviews. The *lumiere Room* was arranged as a private off shoot from the main kitchen, so that guests could be served in privacy and with special access by the best waiters on staff. For many great French restaurants, dining out in the evening could be a lengthy ritual, with diners easily spending between two and three hours at the table. John could see that the evening was setting up for a high number of meal courses, and settled in for conversation that would surely extend well into the evening hours.

Anne was a pro at Parisian dinner parties, and made everyone feel at ease from the first moment that she entered the *lumiere Room*. All the remaining guests waited for Anne to be seated before they took their seats, which were comfortably padded chairs that could be lounged in for several hours.

"We love our *Ville de Paris*," continued Anne, "and the spring brings such new and creative energy to the generations, but we also want to hear tonight about where you live and some of your favorite activities and travels, from the French countryside to England and to Holland and across to America."

This female from Paris, or *Parisienne*, as they were known, most certainly had a way with words, and was a very curious study for all of mankind. She was the classically Parisian French female in some ways, both creative and quite outspoken by nature, but with a beauty and style of her own.

A girl from Paris could be shamelessly snobbish, and perfectly comfortable letting everyone know it. Anne appeared to have moderated this element of her personality. She operated with such a kindness, a flair for the creative, and a supreme confidence in her time on earth, that nobody minded that this outlook might be a part of her composition. The *Parisienne* often carried a rebellious side, and there was always a side to them that appeared to be never satisfied with their situation in life.

John noticed that Anne fit this profile perfectly, as a person who could be brooding and enthusiastic at the same alternating moments. However, Anne had appeared to grow past some of these effects, certainly never satisfied he imagined, but comfortable within her skin and what she had worked hard to become in life, a fully defined version what was uniquely a person known as *"Anne Avé, the designer of fashion."*

John was very good at observing human nature, and immediately enjoyed the mannerisms and confidence of the special guest at the table. He had noticed that she was late for the dinner, but knew that this was a common thread running through many a *Parisienne* - always late, busy, and certainly in their mind had other more important things to do than be at this dinner party tonight. Nevertheless, she arrived, excited, and giving her full attention to the guests at this table.

"Retour à paris, my favorite city of lights, north of the equator of course," came rushing out in a rousing way from the left of John, bellowed out by the effervescent Laura from London. John's head turned to the left like a swivel on a pole. Like a blue spark of lighter fluid, the dinner party was immediately well lit, and the flames had already begun to spread across the table.

It was immediately clear that there were two very strong female personalities at the welcome dinner tonight, and John enjoyed the prospect of a very interest evening of fireworks.

"My pleasure to meet all of you," stated Arne, in his conservative and respectful style. There was a slight discomfort for social interaction that was clearly painful for Arne, but he was in his seat trying his best and ready to enjoy some fine French cuisine.

John was not far behind in his opening bid for a warm and enjoyable evening. This was a perfect setting for John to relax and enjoy his deeper sensibilities. This occasion had placed him far from his regular work routine, and there were no predefined rules or expectations about what he might think or how he might need to communicate what he was thinking. John had a very creative and fun loving side, full of humor and wit. His profession, however, didn't always allow this side of his personality to come forward, so this was a perfect opportunity to enjoy the lighter side that had been trapped inside after years of love loss and the daily routine of the legal profession. The other side of his brain could finally get some good exercise, and he was already immensely enjoying the evening that was evolving.

Besides Arne, the other quiet one in the room was clearly going to be Sophie, at least to begin, who continued her initial presentation at the dinner table with a sweet and calm demeanor. She was a person who had been emerged in life from the southern French countryside, ready to enjoy every moment of the classic dinner preparations, but did not appear to be feeling any immediate need to express any overt or controversial opinions. In France, there was the countryside, and then there was Paris – it was mostly one or the other. Sophie was classically French, but a blending and composite of a creative French female that dearly loved the French countryside. Paris was a fabulously fun place for her to visit, but she always loved returning home to her native Lyon.

The impressively classy waiter made his way to the table, and began his personal introduction. "My name is Gabriel, and I shall be your server tonight."

Everyone acknowledged the impressive gentleman that would be bringing them their dinner courses this evening. For some guests, especially foreign visitors, waiters in France had often become immediate adjunct members of the family, given the lengthy amount of time that it takes for the many meal courses to be served.

"We shall begin with some hors d'oeuvre," started Gabriel, "but before that we shall begin with an aperitif?"

"Oui, merci," confirmed Anne.

"Très bonne madame," and Gabriel was off for round one in a series of eventful glasses and plates.

In the best restaurants in Paris, the dinners were always expected to start with a pre-meal drink called an apéritif, which would be accompanied by little home-made snacks, which the French call des amuse-bouche. This was a way to whet your appetite before the multi-course meal began.

Anne wasted no time furthering the dinner conversation. "Bonjour, Monsieur John the américain, did you have a good trip to Paris?"

Without waiting for an answer, Anne continued, "Please tell us about the men of America today, are they full of love and affection?"

Anne had a uniquely vivacious style, not waiting one second to fire off the first shot for a lively and humorous dinner party.

John laughed at her forward thinking, and was up to the task and quick to respond. "Well, I would think that there might be nothing more controversial for a *Paris*ian dinner party at a posh hotel than beginning the conversation with *sex or politics*, is that a fair assumption?"

"Oooh, Mr. John, I like your style," chimed in Laura, never too far from commenting on a thought for any topic that might arise.

"Oui, John," agreed Anne, "you know that us *Parisienne* soul mates are *in love with love*."

"I have noticed that," agreed John, "even if the object of your affection might change the next day."

"Hahhaha!!" agreed Anne, "we have a Live one here, and what is the focus of your great manhood in American life, Mr. américain Johnhood?"

"Well, I would rather lift a book than lift weights," quipped John with a smile. "And there are some mornings that I do not shave."

"Yes, yes, yes," cheered Laura, "now this is the type of man that we have been looking to have dinner with. Who needs muscles when you can have a real man?"

"Class, humor, and a bad boy, eh?" agreed Anne. "This is the type of fashion model that we look at for photo shoots."

Anne continued, "Clean, but not too obvious, hahahah."

"Fancy, and a bit dishy I might add," agreed Laura.

"Maybe you are two of those magnificent *Parisienne* that always wear their sunglasses, even when it is raining outside?" teased John.

"Oui," agreed Anne, "as my northern sister might say, mysteriously posh, ideal and undefined."

"By all means!" agreed Laura, "you know me well la soeur. It is the something special that makes it seasonally interesting."

They were having their fun with John, who took it well and enjoyed returning their creative banter.

Sophie reveled in the humor, taking it all in, "*I love the love of love*," she surprisingly stated, "and sometimes we girls of France are just in love with the idea of love I think, ready to buy the special lingerie that nobody will ever see."

"Oh, my goodness," stated Arne, not sure what to make of this raucous start to the dinner party, but loving every minute of it. "Our Amsterdam girls have a different flair than this, but you *Parisienne* do know a good party when you see it."

"The cake is in the frosting," agreed Laura. "You start at the top, and then see where it leads, hahhaha."

Gabriel returned to the table with the aperitif and began setting up for the hors d'oeuvre. Clearly the guests had settled in nicely since just the short time that he suggested an aperitif.

"What is the great mystery about love in Paris, anyway," continued John, "Sophie is right, maybe you are just *in love with idea of love*, simple as that."

"Yes, it is somewhat true, Monsieur John, even with love, we know that the phone call from the perfect man may never come," lamented Anne, "and our current man may not be perfect, but we know that he really does exist.... *at least until tomorrow*, hahaha."

John snickered at the response and further fanned the flame. "I am fascinated by the prospect that the *Parisienne* can up dream up a life and relationship with someone who doesn't even know her name."

"Oooh, Mr. John," chimed in Laura again, "you have a way with words, you *américain ace*."

Laura was fluent in French, but classically British with a strong command of the English language. She spoke both languages so well that she could easily cross back and forth between the two, often in a way to stem her boredom from those less skilled with communication. Even so, she loved the British and French slang, and enjoyed any chance to repartee thoughts back and forth with people she found lively and interesting.

"Hey Arne, they don't make girls like this in Amsterdam, do they?" humored Anne. "Well, maybe some in the district of *lumieres rouges*."

"No, no, no, you girls are much too complicated for me," agreed Arne. "I am a banker and my thrill for the day is taking the taxi to work."

The Tuesday night in Paris continued into the next topic at hand, as the menu proceeded through its third and fourth courses. There was a light green salad between the first and second courses, and a sorbet mixed in between the second and third courses.

Anne was a famous fashion guru on the Paris scene, enjoying her life and turning the fashion trends upside down with a new wave of fresh but classic Parisian designs.

"I've seen your work, Anne," stated John. "My daughter introduced me to your company with some online links a couple of months ago, very inspiring work indeed. I had no idea at the time that I would be seeing you here tonight."

"Merci, John! You know that we never discuss work at our dinner parties, but since this is a special *Bienvenue diner,* we can make some exceptions to our visitors from the north, south, east and west."

Anne realized after she said this that her table guests had strangely come from four different directions to all meet in Paris.

"Très beau travail!" agreed Laura. "The best fresh new fashion designs that anybody has seen for a very long time. You will go down in *Histoire de la France* as a very great trend setter of your day, *mon Anne*."

"You are all too kind, but beneath it all, I am only just a girl, and a mom, trying to create and live a life that I love. All the same, you are much too kind," said Anne.

"You are a mother?" asked Sophie. "You look so amazing, and I would have never have guessed it."

"Certainly, you make a very magnificent mummy," agreed Laura as a matter of fact, "but I agree nobody would ever have guessed because you look so *magnifique* and could not have possibly been carrying a child with that sleek figure. And you do have such a great attitude and time for everything that is important, it is amazing that you can also work and enjoy your friendships while raising a child." Laura was a dear and loyal friend to Anne.

"*Merci mes amours*, but you are much too kind, I stayed independent and single until the day I walked into the delivery room for my *Belle Lucie*," said Anne.

"And you came well out of the other side, bravo my dear girl, with the *Belle Lucie*," cheered Laura.

"Yes, well, you know that I did *wear my high heels into the delivery room*, didn't you?" asked Anne, with a jokingly sweet smile on her face.

"By all means, my dear *la soeur*, and that is one of the reasons that you will go down as one of the great fashion icons in French history, hahhaha," joked Laura. "A real *Parisienne original! The maternity girl with the high heel shoes!*"

"Come to my studio on the *Avenue Montaigne* someday my dear new friends, I would love to show you around and have you meet my lovely staff and the people that really make it all happen," offered Anne.

"*Oui la soeur*, you are in the heart of the luxurious and high end fashion stores, right where you belong my remarkable friend," summarized Laura. "We shall all make a mockery of ourselves and visit you at once!"

"You have already been there my dear friend, but there is nothing I would love more than to see the rest of you show up for a studio tour," agreed Anne.

"And Monsieur John," Anne continued, "you should come and meet my main assistant Olivia, she knows everybody in town and can help guide you to the best places in Paris while you are in town! She knows all the great local French artisans, and can give you an inside look at some great creative minds in Paris. I will make sure that she clears her schedule to show you around!"

"How very nice," replied John. "I will most certainly plan to come over for a studio tour."

The next meal course arrived, and Gabriel continued to impress with his subtle but effective waiter skills. He was a very skilled restaurant professional, and was not about to interrupt the group as they continued their innocent but sensitive topic about life, love and romantic relationships, between people who have just met each other.

"*Only in Paris,*" thought John, "*Seulement à Paris.*"

In America, he would have steered his clients completely away from a conversation such as this before it began. There was something refreshing about people being able to speak their mind without concern that someone might take it the wrong way or as an infringement to their personal rights. The dinner conversation was innocent and creative, and everyone knew that it would stay at the table and not be a threat to anyone after the dinner was finished. The difference with this dinner is that everyone had a sophistication of humor, and were simply having fun with the ideal of dancing around a normally sensitive topic. Everyone was in fact a well-respected professional, and everyone knew from the start that the bantering was all in good fun and not meant to have anyone leave the room with an uneasy feeling.

In a typically *Parisienne* manner, Anne moved the topic off motherhood and children, and into the sphere of politics. She threw out a new controversial topic for everyone to thrash about, beginning with the latest liberal and conservative rumors of local politicians that were serving her beloved French city.

John took note of the simple but elegant table display. The plain silver cutlery sat on a white table cloth with a simple and plain pattern, elegant but understated. The plates were uniquely designed with a rare curved form, but still had a plain white surface that set off the food in a special way.

The main course had been elegant and easy, a *bouillinade*, made of potatoes and fish baked together with herbs and butter. The quality of the food was exceptional, and the cooking had all been done using fresh ingredients. At the *Grand hotel de lucarne*, the chefs clearly took great pride in their work.

Between the glasses of wine and the courses between courses, John tried to recall if they might be well into their fifth or sixth dinner course for the evening. It is in the evening, for dinner, that the great French restaurants pull out all the stops. Even on weekdays, such as this Tuesday evening in the *lumiere Room*, eating out in the evening can often be a long-drawn-out affair, and diners can easily spend between two and three hours at the table. Dining out, in France, is an evening's event.

The conversation moved further into the evening with coffee and chocolate mousse, as the group made their way to the fire warmed courtyard area. The city still clamored in the distance, but the sounds had diminished as the hours moved further into the evening. The *le grande patisserie*, the *cafe*, and the additional deserts continued to be served by the faithful Gabriel. A night out in in Paris was an event to remember like no other.

After a full three hours of dinner, wine, coffee and conversation, the group began to gather their things and say goodbyes at the door. Anne reminded John to come and visit the fashion studio tomorrow afternoon. The evening has been a great success, and everyone left with large smiles on their faces. To be sure, the conversation would continue between Anne and Laura, for long into the evening hours.

"Drink a half gallon of water, everyone, you will feel much better in the morning!" encouraged Anne. It was the *Parisienne* trick after a long evening of champagne, aperitif and wine, so that they might not wake up with a painful hangover.

Everyone met at the hotel lobby to pass along their cheerful goodbyes. There were kisses by everyone on both cheeks, and John made the rounds to his newly found friends.

Anne handed John a small card with her company info on it, as he turned back toward the hotel interior.

"Come see me tomorrow!" shouted Anne. *"Viens me voir demain"*

John looked back and acknowledged the invitation, as he headed toward the elevator, *"je te verrai demain!"*

Anne and Laura jumped into a taxi and raced down the streets of Paris.

In the corner, waiting for everyone to depart the gathering when they were finally ready to go, was Enzo with a large smile extending from one ear to the other.

CHAPTER 13

Hidden in the Streets

John rose out of bed, and the streets of Paris were alive and well just outside of his window. In this boutique hotel, you could open the windows wide over the street, and lean out into the masonry opening as if you were planning to use the window as an exit.

Looking out from the third floor, the view angled down through the winding streets and John could see the wide array of quaint shops lining the street below, and the 17th century domes and urban structures in the background to the southwest.

With it being spring time in Paris, the balconies across the street and lining down the boulevard were full of plants and flowers, and the entire street area was fully in use and with barely an inch to spare. History oozed from the old cityscape and roof tops, and the building facades tightly undulated and interlocked with the sidewalks and street areas, adorning itself with classical French nouveau architecture.

The bathroom was a marvel, with the built-in bidet as one of the options along the wall area. The shower and the bathroom area was surprisingly tight, at least as far as American standards were concerned, but for the center of Paris it was commonly appropriate.

In this beautifully renovated hotel room, small but elegant, the glass shower and bathroom were one of the main room walls. Only glass separated the two rooms, so the experience of taking a shower was really one and the same with being in the main room.

The sleep was much needed, and the shower was refreshing. The half-gallon of water suggested by Anne also did the trick, as John was surprisingly well rested after a late evening of food and beverage consumption.

John hit the sidewalk with energy, and made a right turn out of the hotel. Bouncing down the street like a teenager going to his first college class, he had a light backpack across his arm and was armed with his water, phone and book. A good park was never very far away in Paris, and if he became tired he could just stop for a short read or a few shots of water on one of the classic Parisian benches.

Coffee was the first order of business, as he headed down the old nouveau corridor. '*New*' was a relative term over the centuries, and a curious study in French life. What was modern in its day had consistently progressed in compared to what is now considered modern in this century. Centuries from now, the idea of modern will redefine itself again and again, but it was hard to image that this street would not somehow remain the same through all the future changes to come. The French had a special way of both embracing the new, while simultaneously retaining the old.

As John strolled down the avenue, the words *café* and *le patisserie* became noticeably etched into the glass windows on the right, and John turned immediately at the next colonnade and into the busy lower level space.

The café buzzed with energy of the morning, which was John's favorite time of day. He found a small table toward the side wall area, and made himself quickly at home.

"Bonjour," said the waitress, flashing a brief smile as she approached John's window table. With a packed house, she was saving time by beginning the conversation early.

"Bonjour, Un café au lait s'il vous plaît?" asked John, ready for some morning coffee.

"Oui très bien," and off she went.

John observed the crowd and contemplated the various roles that they might be playing in life. Among others, there was an artist, a couple of business people, a young entrepreneur, and a group of retired locals. The café scene was quintessentially European, with no American drive thru windows, and no grande latte' to go. This was the type of café where you grabbed a seat and became part of the urban fabric of city life, much like the cafés across other parts of Europe and the older cafés of Greenwich Village in New York.

He purchased a local newspaper and did his best to follow the headlines of the day. There was something comforting about filtering through the local newspaper, even if much of the text was undecipherable. He was solidly planted in Paris, at least until such a time that it was time to depart. It would take several days before the locals would remember him entering the shop as a recognizable figure.

Settling into the classically French café chair, John checked the local maps on his phone and charted a course for the day. He could see that he was on the right bank of the Seine River, only a short distance from the *Cathédrale de Notre Dame*. After the Cathedral, he would generally plan to make his way to the west, along the Seine River, with the eventual goal of ending up near the Avenue Montaigne. John was a geography freak and loved the adventure of finding a new path or uncovering a new adventure. Simply walking the streets and grasping the local flavor of the area would be enough to make the entire day worthwhile. He would weave himself through the streets, stop in some shops, have some lunch, and then make his way toward Anne's studio in the afternoon.

John read through a few chapters of his fictional book, which made him feel like he was truly on vacation. He then paid the billet and darted for the exit. There were many adventures to explore on this first day in Paris, not the least of which was examining the local neighborhood that Janey had placed him in.

John bounced onto the sidewalk area with the same energy that he had left it, and continued down the boulevard.

This was a good time to send Janey a thank you message, and share his appreciation for placing him in an outstanding boutique hotel in the heart of Paris. He leaned against the urban façade and put together the brief text message. It was still the middle of the night in California, but she would receive it when she woke up the following morning. He noticed all sorts of other notifications on the front of his phone, and checked to see if any were from Jordan. He ignored all the remaining inquiries and continued down the sidewalk area.

Morning in Paris was a special occasion. As Anne had mentioned the prior evening, spring time in Paris did bring a special energy to the city, and the plants and flowers were in full bloom. People were out on the streets, many with a light coat or scarf, and the effects of winter were slowly being removed from their faces.

Paris was of course the capital of France, and a major European city. It was a global center for art, fashion, fine cuisine, and culture, and its 19th century cityscape had a unique way of crisscrossing between the streets, boulevards and Seine River that cut through the center of the city.

The distinct and famous landmarks were already known by most across the world, including the Eiffel Tower, the Louvre Museum, and the Cathedral.

Beyond the landmarks, however, was an interesting mix of cafés, culture, and designer boutiques, including shopping strips such as the Rue du Faubourg Saint-Honoré. The Latin Quarter had always been a favorite neighborhood for John, along with the Le Marais where he was staying. There was also the 18th century Montmartre, the Montparnasse as a haven for artists with great cafés and bars, and the many other neighborhoods weaving throughout the heart of Paris.

John had packed and worn the shoes that Jordan recommended for his last trip to New York, which were dress shoes on the outside but had tennis shoe inserts on the inside. This gave John great confidence that he could walk for a long time through the urban streets without gathering blisters on his feet.

John quickly checked his phone map, as a reminder of the cross streets that he should be looking for. In the next block, he passed by the Le Pavilion de la Reine, which was a luxury hotel facing the large Place de Vosges. He continued down a few more blocks, turning left on Rue Pavée. A quaint shop caught his interest as he split the Y intersection, continuing down Rue Malher, and looking for the Rue de Rivoli which would lead him toward the Pont Saint-Louis bridge and the Cathedral.

The streets in this part of town were narrow, with cars parked on each side of the street and a thin lane of way one traffic down the center. John relished the various shops along the way, and there was some street activity along the Rue Malher that caught his attention.

As he approaches the wider boulevard of Rue de Rivoli, a black awning and green storefront jumped out at him on the left as in a science fiction movie, with the words *"Hotel Emile"* pasted in several concentric circles on the front of the awning. John felt chills pass through his body as he stopped to make sure of the lettering on the awning. Sure enough, it was a modest five-story hotel with balconies across the front, and a sixth-floor penthouse which was set back into the roofline above the main five-story building.

John gazed at the surrounding shops and streets, taking in this newfound location. It was a surprise that had hit him not ten minutes into his trek across the city, in the very neighborhood that he had stayed in during the previous evening. His mind immediately took him back to the *Vintage Rags* store, and the girl Amelie who had hauntingly filled his mind since that first day with the mannequin on the sidewalk. Now, he was standing in front of a hotel by essentially the same name.

John crossed the street and leaned against the storefront of the adjacent building, mouth open as he looked back toward *Hotel Emile,* and absorbed the hotel location.

He examined each floor level, and the way that the hotel building sat on the corner lot and directly connected to the building next door, leading to a full wall of buildings that extended back in the direction he had just walked. It was not an elaborate hotel by any means, but its name was a sight that he could hardly believe.

John looked around to see if there were any other mannequins in the storefront windows of the neighboring shops.

He made a mental note of the location, and turned right to head down Rue de Rivoli, which was the wider boulevard that he had been looking for. As he moved further down the avenue, he looked back again and again to view the corner *Hotel Emile*. He wondered about the history of the hotel, the neighborhood, and the origins of this intersection.

The chills continued up and down his arms as he took another look at the corner hotel, before proceeding further west down Rue de Rivoli.

He had been in Paris for less than 18 hours, and already the images, words and feelings from his recent experiences in California were suggestive of what had occurred over the past week. He thought of his discussion with Charley, and he contemplated if there was any greater meaning to this than just a hotel by the same name as a girl that he had not actually met. Maybe there was nothing to it. He needed Jordan or Charley's input to understand if they thought this might have any transcendent or spiritual meaning.

A bit further west, John took a left turn that would lead him toward the Pont Saint-Louis bridge, which was a crossing that would connect him between the two islands that merged together but did not touch in the middle of the Seine River. The Île de la Cité was the larger island to the north, and a natural island in the Seine. Home to the origins of Paris, the Cathedral sat on its eastern end at the southeast corner.

Crossing between the two islands on the Pont Saint-Louis, the views and details were spectacular, typically French, and especially beautiful with the morning light ringing down on a calm spring Paris morning.

The *Cathédrale de Notre Dame*, with its twin vertical towers rising each over 200 feet tall, sat impressively in the center of the second island between the outer banks of the Seine River. Originally constructed in the mid 14th century, the remarkable French Gothic cathedral had been a shining example of French architecture since medieval times. John marveled at the history and longevity of the structure, and had been reading in the café the way in which the church building needed some renovations following some destruction that occurred during the French Revolution in the late 17th century.

John finished crossing the second bridge in front of the Cathedral, enjoying the extraordinary structure and historical significance of the church. Large numbers of people had already begun assembling on the front courtyard.

John took it all in, and then headed toward the left bank of the Seine River. He angled toward the corner of the front courtyard, and then crossed to the side of the cathedral. He noticed some large vinyl banners, which were mounted against a fence that was separating some construction activities at the corner of the site. The text was in French, and the large title in the center had something to do with an upcoming evening celebration that was to take place at the Cathedral.

As he studied the text and tried to catch the meaning, he noticed a bird at both the upper left and upper right corners of the banner, just like the one that he had seen on his backyard fence. This was also the same bird figure that had appeared in his dream at the ocean front palisades park.

Chills shot up and down his arms again, having nothing to do with the brisk clean morning. He focused on the eyes of the bird figures, which seemed to be strangely real. It was the type of figure that was looking directly at you, and would follow your eyes even as you moved.

John read through the text heading again and noticed the main phrase "Viens rejoinder le vol de la colombe." The sign was asking for people to come and join them for some event at the church.

John grabbed his smartphone and searched the French dictionary for the word *colombe*.

That was it! The bird was a dove!

The banner was asking the congregation and the public to "Come join the flight of the Dove."

John could not take his eyes from the feathery figure on the banner. He noticed that it had something on its shoulders, just like in the dream, which he now realized were oversized wings.

Albeit not real, the bird was stoic and calm looking, just like the real one on his fence at home, unruffled by any activity surrounding it.

While this bird was simply a figure on a banner, it had a life of its own. The wings were much larger than might that be needed for actual flight, just like the bird on his fence, and the feather and wing part resembled the pattern of an angel type figure.

As the bird sat in front of the Cathedral, it was all beginning to fit together.

John looked around and took in the larger context of the church, the river, and the island city in the middle of the Seine. He wondered what parts of the city were there when the Cathedral was first built, and then how it might have changed before the days of the French Revolution.

John remembered what Charley had mentioned in *BP's* back in California, the way that sometimes an angel might be represented by a dove. Charley had somehow connected for John the idea of an illusion with the idea of a spiritual messenger.

In short, Charley had speculated that a spiritual being, represented by a dove, could possibly be acting as an agent or messenger of God. Charley had gone so far as to suggest that maybe Amelie was some sort of a saint, sent here as a messenger to speak with him.

The whole idea of an intermediary was supremely fascinating to John, and Charley had seemed certain that there was a message of some sort in this for him.

John's mind drifted back into *BP's*, with Charley sitting across the table.

The words had seared themselves into his John's mind, and he could hear the voice and inflection coming from Charley on that day when he said, "someone is trying to communicate with you through this clothing store experience." Charley had then paused and continued, "*Maybe even Mia.*"

The idea that Mia could have ever been directly involved with the clothing store experience was beyond fascinating. It was hard to believe, but nevertheless fascinating.

Did Mia also send the dove to his fence?

Was Mia also involved with the dream, or in direct communication with Jordan?

Jordan was right to recommend and push for John to take this trip to France.

John contemplated what additional secrets might be lying for him within the streets of Paris.

First, *Hotel Emile* just minutes from his hotel, and now the dove represented on a fence, just ten minutes later and directly in front of the Cathedral. He could only imagine what kind of a spiritual message was being sent. The increase of occurrences, along with the repetitive symbolism, had seemed to extend beyond mere coincidence and into a category that he was far less versed.

Whether he found Mia or not was a long shot. The way in which his life would be changed forever, however, was becoming a certainty.

The messengers of Paris had been hidden in the streets.

CHAPTER 14

The Scarf

John turned and headed up the left bank of the Seine River, when the urge hit him to shoot across to the Latin Quarter for a look. His mind was racing as he tried to remember more details about the dove from his dream, and he wasn't really paying attention to where he was walking.

His sudden change in direction had startled a large group of pigeons who were being fed by some locals on the benches. The locals looked up and laughed, as three birds banged across his leg and fluttered for safety. Surely these birds had nothing to do with the flight of the doves.

The streets continued to twist and turn as John made his way to the south and southwest, into the district known for its student life, bistros and night life. He had not intended to take this route, but this impulse had sent him toward the place that he remembered from long ago. The Latin Quarter was home to several higher education facilities, including the old Sorbonne, which was one of the first universities in the world dating back to the 13th century.

This was one of his favorite places back in his college days, given his age at the time. It was also a considerable plus that it was off the beaten track of tourists going to museums and national monuments. It was a busy and well-known neighborhood, drawing in all types to experience all that it had to offer. He remembered that the area received its name from the Latin language, which was once widely spoken in and around the University, since Latin was the main language of learning in the Middle Ages in Europe.

John disappeared into *La pâtisserie* to sit down for a minute and gather his thoughts. He pulled out his smartphone again and began to look up the origins of the dove as a messenger. It was, in fact, what Charley had said, often serving as a symbol as a messenger of God. The stories described how sometimes people would see birds appear before them to deliver some type of spiritual message. The folklore also described people having encounters with angels that had manifested in the form of a bird.

Where was this dove leading him?

As he considered the thought, John realized at that moment that it had led him right here, to Paris, to the very area that he was presently experiencing. If he just continued to follow the signs, he might someday find the answer that he'd been looking for.

John knew that birds had inspired humans throughout history, with their ability to soar through the air and rise above the Earth. It was something that stirred the souls of humans, even motivating the Wright brothers to create flight for themselves. But it was more than the literal soaring that connected with many people, it was the possibilities beyond our Earth, both in space and with the spiritual world, which motivated people to look beyond themselves and try to understand the larger picture of why they were placed on this planet.

Some find it through religion, and some find it through a more general description of a spiritual connection.

John pondered the way that this spiritual connection was the intersection of birds and angels, of angels and doves, with the dove being the symbol of this spiritual connection. In texts throughout history, doves and angels shared a special bond, with both symbolizing spiritual growth.

Reading further, it was apparent that angels were associated with birds more than any other type of animal, and when appearing to humans in their heavenly glory had very often featured wings. Wings were both the symbolic tie between spiritual covering of care, as well as the freedom and empowerment that can be gained from spiritual growth.

Even more interesting, thought John, were descriptions of how the angels may appear in the physical form of earthly birds, conveying the message that was meant to be delivered.

John finished his pastry and exited the shop. He thought about the airplane from the dream, the traditional travel trunks, and the messenger that approached him at the station.

The neighborhood had a variety of shops to explore, including a quirky bookstore, an eyeglasses shop, a mini ski chalet, a travel shop, and a florist. There were some marvelous little boutiques of all types.

He thought about Jordan, as he slipped into a small women's clothing store that had elements for her age group. Jordan was weighing heavy on his mind at that moment. Not only was she his only remaining direct link to Mia, but she was also the main reason that he had decided to pursue this adventure.

John had remembered that the European stores had a knack for pouncing on the customer when they first walked into the store. He had especially remembered this occurring in Italy and some other countries, but couldn't specifically remember how it was done in France. John had always hoped that he could at least take a few steps into the shop before they offered him help, after all, if a customer does not know what is in the shop, how will they know what they are looking for? Not everyone goes into a shop with a specific purchase in mind, thought John.

With his guard pulled up, John walked through the front doors of the shop.

This store did not attack back. It was much more relaxed than he had anticipated. John wandered up and down the aisles, and filtered between the clothing racks. The clothes were mostly for women, and the shirts and jackets had a look of minimalist construction. The jewelry racks were creatively simple, with a range of gorgeous rings, bracelets, and earrings, all in various shades of metal.

John saw a scarf that reminded him of Mia, which was soft, beautiful and entirely unique. It appeared to have been made by a local artisan, from a small French town by the sea. He tried to understand the remaining print on the label, and had not remembered any stores in the USA that had given such an in-depth description about the artisan that had created the apparel product. Maybe they did exist, but he was not aware of any stores like this that existed back home.

The larger clothing lines would of course never approach it in this way, since they were mostly high volume manufactured apparel. This clothing shop was a unique and interesting find, almost as if the owner had created his or her own products and then just opened the doors to sell their designs.

John continued appreciating the clothing on the racks, and it became clear that most of the items in this shop had been handled this way. There were a variety of options to select from, but they were each very customized, unusual, and tailored with a unique style. It was a one-of-a-kind shop.

The scarf was incredibly unique. It was handmade and yarn dyed, with a beautifully simple pattern. John realized that he had still been holding it as it moved between the racks. Once it had been caught in his grasp, he had never intended to let it go. It was going to be his, no matter what the cost, even before he went to the counter to pay for it.

A girl had been alternating between two areas as John toured the store: some work behind the counter, and displaying some items on the nearby racks. John was so intent on not being bothered by a sales clerk that he must have given off a message to be left alone, and the girl respectfully complied with his wishes.

Recognizing that this had been an entirely different experience than expected, John finally looked up and acknowledged the girl near the counter. He was nearly shocked when he saw how similar she looked to the girl at *Vintage Rags*, and did a double take looking back at her – it was not the same girl, but they looked so much alike in their facial features that his head nearly exploded. He was relieved that she had not seen him looking at her, as she may have been frightened by his reaction.

John looked the other direction and tried to gain his composure. She saw him turning back toward the clothing racks, and continued refining the display.

This girl in the shop was maybe five years older than Jordan, and just a bit younger than Amelie at *Vintage Rags*. Her hair color, eyes and shape of her mouth were nearly identical to Amelie, but she had her hair worn a bit differently. It was a similar medium long cut, but she was wearing it in a pony-tail tied high up on her head. John examined the features again, which were precisely like Amelie. Black bangs fell over her eyebrows, and she had a lightweight jean jacket over a white blouse. She was very relaxed in her black jeans, and had some very sophisticated black ankle boots that he recognized from his wife's closet as being Chloe'. Her jewelry matched the style that was being sold in the store, and her face had a peaceful and composed look on it. This was a person that was very content and extremely comfortable with herself.

John neared the counter area again, only partly looking at the jewelry designs.

"Bonjour," said the girl, without looking up.

She must have known that John was looking at her.

"Bonjour," replied John.

Finally looking his direction, with a calm and serene smile, "Did you find something that you like?"

It was a lesson in humility. John was in a mild state of shock. He did not want to come back the next day and find out that she had never really worked here.

"Yes, I did," responded John. "You have a wonderful store."

"Merci, monsieur, vous passez plus de temps ici que la plupart des hommes." This was beyond his French. She was somehow comparing him to other men.

"Pardon?" asked John.

"I said, you spend more time here than most men," responded the girl.

"Oh, oui, I really love your store," said John, "and I have some special women in my life that would also love your store."

"*I knew that about you,*" she stated, turning back toward the display.

The sales clerk was re-introducing John to himself. How did she know?

John was slow to respond.

"Oui?" he finally asked.

"Oui," she continued. "I am pretty good at analyzing what is best for others, but sometimes I am unable to see my own needs," she said with a confident smile.

She was not really that way at all, but she had a fully self-deprecating humor that was very interesting to John, especially in a French accent.

"Are you the designer of these items?" asked John, looking up without raising his head.

"Oui," said the girl.

"I knew that about you," said John.

He smiled, and turned back toward the jewelry rack.

John looked through the necklaces, rings, pendants, and other beautiful artisanal metals. There were glossy stones with an intriguing matrix, along with turquoise and silver pieces. He found a lariat necklace with a semi-precious stone in silver that he thought Jordan would like, and added it to his grip on the scarf.

He went back to the clothing rack and picked out two more blouses that he had eyed for Jordan, and brought the bundle to the counter. The girl continued her early morning routine of hanging up new designs on the displays near the check out.

John placed the four items on the counter, and indicated that he was ready to pay.

"Combien?" asked John.

The girl rang up the goods, and placed them in a special tote. John grabbed the scarf from the bag, which belonged in his hand.

"I didn't catch your name," said John.

"I didn't say it," replied the girl.

"Oui," laughed John. Smiling, he continued, "and what would you tell someone your name was if they didn't ask?"

"I would tell them it was Alaïa," said the girl.

CHAPTER 15

The Waiting

John exited the clothing store and browsed the shop windows as he strolled down the avenue. He didn't realize the continuous smile on his face, until he saw some passerby's look at him and smile back without saying any words.

His mind was still on the jewelry display, and the encounter at the store.

The unusual shop of eyeglasses and sunglasses came up again on the right, as he made his way back toward the west. It was modest in size, but had an extraordinary design interior with a long winding counter top. The counter almost looked as if it were shaped in the curve of some elegant elastic sunglasses, with a glass top, and with stainless steel inserts that had backlit lighting along the upper rim.

He thought about the airplane from the dream, and the girl with the French shopping bag. He remembered that she had several people around her, all gathered for the adventure that was taking place.

As John walked along to the west, it gave him time to think about the evolution of his faith development recently. He realized that he had become more relaxed about trusting the process, and allowing things to work themselves out with the proper time perspective.

He had thought so much on the idea of hope back in California, near the ocean at his favorite thinking spot at the flats. Hope was a critical part of getting his mind properly set to be happy, and to progress to the next level of his spiritual development.

But as he walked along the streets and boulevards of Paris, he realized that it was faith all along that was the ultimate warrior for him. Faith was the vehicle that was allowing him to trust the process, enjoy the moment, and enjoy how life's answers were slowly but consistently being revealed to him.

Waiting can be difficult for humans. They want answers solved immediately, especially in this fast food era with high internet speeds. Most individuals don't even like to delay their day in a doctor's waiting room, let alone wait for answers to life's larger questions and challenging situations.

But many of life's answers do not come so fast, thought John, and life's answers tend to evolve in their own time. Quite often they do not come until we are ready to receive them. Life's answers can be working themselves out while we are waiting for direct results, but we don't see the progress that is being made until the situation has played itself out.

This process of waiting, trust and faith, was beginning to emerge deep inside of John, finally understanding that not only can he not control everything, but that he was *not meant* to control the outcome.

The spiritual forces felt alive and at work in his life, possibly solving many things as he ate, slept and traveled, without him directly knowing it at the time. He just needed to activate the faith.

The encounters with the doves, the angels, and the various individuals put in his direct path, were surely a part of helping him understand to trust the process. It was telling him to have faith in the process, and continue moving forward in a positive and joyful manner.

The Cathedral, the dove on the fence, and the elements in his dream all stirred in his mind, combined with the conversations with Charley and Jordan. He had come across a hotel in the neighborhood where he was staying, that had the same derivative name as the girl at *Vintage Rags*. This was the girl that was working at the store, and then had suddenly never worked there. Now he had experienced a second shopkeeper that looked nearly identical to the first, each with names that began with the letter 'A', but in completely different countries. These were all part of the same message, he thought, somehow collectively leading him to Mia.

For the first time, as he continued thinking about it along the boulevard, he felt nearly certain that he would find her someday. Too many coincidences were taking place for them to be mere coincidences.

Yes, the spirits inside of him and the messengers in the streets were aligning and telling him that his path would someday cross with Mia.

This was not rational, but John was beginning to understand that the unseen world was not always rational. The spiritual world happened in its own time, and on its own terms. The answer would eventually be revealed, and all he needed to do was to trust the process and to follow through on the messages that he was receiving.

When and where he would locate her, was uncertain. Waiting was always the most difficult part, and always tested a person's patience.

But there was an energy in the universe, whatever you might call it, and however it worked, which was tied into messengers and angels, and which was leading him to the conclusion that he was on the right path. He felt it deep inside that he should continue forward in faith

- steadily, patiently, trying to enjoy the process, and embracing the messages that were being sent his way.

John thought about Charley's words at *BP's*, when he said, "you will hear it in your spirit before it will come to pass."

Maybe this is what he meant.

CHAPTER 16

The Bistro

John had walked for nearly three miles, not quite realizing how far he had gone. His map showed close to 4.5 kilometers from the Latin Quarter clothing store, but his legs were still feeling fine. He had been absorbed deep in thought, while simultaneously experiencing the sites of the city and the shops along the way.

When he finally looked up, the Eiffel Tower was directly in front of him on the Champ de Mars.

The Eiffel Tower, with its picturesque wrought iron lattice tower named after the engineer Gustave Eiffel, was the entrance to the 1889 World Fair. It has become one of the most recognizable structures in the world. It was hard to believe, thought John, that this beautiful structure was initially criticized by some of the leading artists and intellectuals for its design. This was the tallest structure in Paris, equivalent to about 81 stories, and was the tallest building in the world until the Chrysler Building in New York was completed in 1930. John had always appreciated great architecture and great art, and this structure was certainly one of the most iconic structures that he had ever seen.

While absorbed deep in thought, John had overshot his mark and had continued much further west than intended. He would need to reverse course somewhat, to get back on track for connecting across to the district where Anne's studio was located.

The morning had passed quickly, and he was hungry for some lunch. Walking all the way to the Eiffel Tower had worn him out, and he needed to temporarily take a seat.

John turned back down the side street to the north, and located the nearest bistro. He grabbed a table by the window, and ordered up a lunch plate consisting of a salade verte, fruit, cheese and escalope.

He checked his map again, and saw he was not too far from Avenue Montaigne, in the neighborhood where Anne had her studio.

John noticed along the way that the city had put up more resistance to the retail colonization of Paris than some other cities such as London and New York. Yes, there was Starbucks, Zara and Nike, but the Parisians clearly still loved their little neighborhood vendors selling one specific thing and selling it very well.

In most cities, these small shops may not survive, but in Paris the unique and quirky retail experience was alive and well, pushing the retail confines far more boldly than the typical international company.

He had noticed that shops included all types of different specialties, quite often with a singular focus and specific target audience. He observed stores focused only on spices, honey, stuffed animals, photographs, and there were perfume shops intending to match you with a specific fragrance. There were locations for sensitive skin cosmetics, and special types of house plants. You could even experience shops that were street level support locations for creative artisans, which held workshops and classes for several of the artistic trades. Collectively, each individual shop left the public with the idea of individual creativity and value, and presented a nice change from the standard clothing and shoe shops found in many international shopping districts.

As he prepared to head toward Avenue Montaigne, he knew it would be much more of a high-end international shopping experience, and a backdrop for the international fashion icons.

This would be in a district representative of a different class of wealth than many of the streets he had just maneuvered, including the political influence of the haute bourgeoisie, and increasingly with the bon chic bon genre.

In modern terms, the bourgeoisie was a sociologically defined class in France, referring to people with a certain cultural and financial capital means and belonging to the middle or upper stratum of the middle class. It was an affluent and often lavish stratum of the capitalist class. In its original sense, the bourgeoisie was linked to the existence of cities defined by their urban charter, so this class only existed within the walls of the city. The original meaning was to define those that lived in the borough, as opposed to those in the rural areas, and this distinction had begun to grow in the 11th century and further developed during the Renaissance period of the following century.

John read a few more chapters of his book, relaxing at the table by the window. It was just past noon, and the people were filling the streets in full force. Scooters angled through the traffic, and the sidewalks had filled with pedestrians.

The interior of the bistro was quaint and full of light, with a rustic neighborhood feel. It had a very efficient table layout, maximizing floor space to fit in all the customers. It appeared that it had been in operation for several decades, with a loyal group of patrons.

John's book became more of a backdrop for his lunch and rest period, as he found himself observing the locals in the bistro and the appealing characters in the streets. He was in the heart of Paris, and enjoying every minute of the authentic Parisian lifestyle.

His mind could not help but drift in and out of the unusual experiences that had been taking place over the last week, continuing into this morning. The encounter with Alaïa was especially thought provoking, as he ordered a café au lait and continued staring through the glass.

Suddenly, a girl approached him in the aisle near his table.

"You have a *Capelle*!" announced a girl that had passed in front of his table.

"Pardon?" answered John, as he turned to see who was speaking to him.

"You have a *Capelle*," repeated the girl, with a large smile on her face. "We are scarf twins!"

John looked at the scarf that he had purchased at the clothing store where Alaïa was working. He didn't even know the name of the store. He also realized that the scarf had become a permanent part of his grip, which he had been holding with his book.

"Oiu," agreed John. "I just purchased my scarf this morning."

"These are very rare, only made in small batches," continued the girl. "My best friend bought me a scarf just like that, it is made by a local artisan from a small French town by the sea."

With another large smile, she summarized, "we are scarf twins, *jumeaux d'écharpe*."

"Yes," agreed John, "I read that on the label about the artist."

"Scarf twins," he continued with a smile, nodding his head up and down as he looked at her.

"Oui," said the girl as she raced off. "You have very good taste, Monsieur."

Scarf twins, thought John, he had never been somebody's scarf twin.

CHAPTER 17

Avenue Montaigne

John left the bistro, cut across a small side street, and then continued back to the north along the large boulevard of Avenue Rapp.

John was at the western end of central Paris, still on the left bank of the Seine River. He was making his way toward the bridge that would take him back across the river to the right bank of Paris.

The left bank, called La Rive Gauche, was the smaller section of Paris, and historically known as the artistic part of the city. John knew that many of the famous writers and artists had once called this part of Paris home, including Picasso and Matisse. He had a special connection to these neighborhoods, with its artistic focus, winding streets, unique shops and great cafés and bars. The left bank had become pricier over the years, but still maintained a distinctive artistic flavor.

Historically, the right bank, or La Rive Droite, was the larger bank that was north of the river, and the more traditionally upper class section of Paris. Back when the left bank housed the struggling creative souls with inexpensive rent, the right bank was where the city's wealthy residents lived and worked. The right bank was still the main location for many of Paris' large banks and businesses, as well as most of the big tourist attractions, although some of the neighborhoods on the right bank were no longer considered affluent.

As much as he enjoyed and appreciated the left bank, John was excited to cross back over the river and catch up with Anne at her fashion studio near Avenue Montaigne.

John cut across the Pont de l'Alma, landing back again into the right bank of the Seine River. Crossing the large intersection just past the bridge landing, he veered right and plunged immediately into the high-end section of the city along the Avenue.

Avenue Montaigne had become the home for high fashion and accessories in Paris, surpassing the importance of rue du Faubourg Saint Honoré. Several established clothing designers had set up here, particularly *Louis Vuitton*, who brought investment and international attention to the street.

John walked down the avenue, noting some of the high-profile hotels and theatres in the area, along with the numerous stores and shops specializing in high-fashion. *Armani* and *Prada* greeted him to the right, with *Valentino* across the street to the left. Further down, he would be able to look at *Christian Dior, Hermés, Chanel, Céline,* and *Chloé,* not to mention *Yves Saint Laurent* and *Versace.*

The area was an absolute gold mine for stylists and fashion designers across the globe, to view the latest trends.

John weaved in and out of the stores and storefronts, appreciating the great design and articles that Mia and Jordan would have loved to peruse. The two of them could have spent several hours meandering back and forth between the incredible stores, matching one style to another, and listing out their favorites in each category of clothing, handbags, sunglasses and other accessories.

There was the black crepe pant by *Armani*, and a black cashmere turtle neck by *Gucci*.

Max Mara had a faux rabbit and wool vest, for both warmth as well as softness and comfort, and you could grab a pair of heels from *Jimmy Choo*.

John came up in front of the *Louis Vuitton* store, which stopped him in his tracks.

There it was, the interlocking '*LV*' logo from his dream, prominently displayed on the front of the *Louis Vuitton* leather handbags, the first brand emblem to be trademarked in France. The LV monogram stared at John with a supernatural presence, familiar now from his dream at the flats along the ocean in Santa Monica.

In the left display window, facing the street, and conspicuously displayed in a stacking pattern, were the famous luggage trunks that had sent Louis Vuitton on his way to become one of the world's most valuable brands. These were the trunks that had appeared in his dream with the airplane and the French travelers. John stared in amazement to see the rectangular trunks that had preoccupied him for over a week.

This was how it all began for Louis Vuitton, when he was only sixteen years old. He had designed and become a trunk maker for the elites in Paris. These innovative trunks were stackable, and were designed to keep out water during the turbulent ocean voyages. They were the original items that led him toward becoming one of the world's leading international fashion houses that now operate in over 50 countries.

John walked through the store and noticed how the LV monogram had appeared on most of their products, ranging from luxury trunks and leather goods, to ready-to-wear, shoes, watches, jewelry, accessories, sunglasses and books.

John's adventure had come full circle, from the mannequin at the shop in California, to the fashion icons along the Avenue Montaigne in Paris.

John exited to the street, and slowly moved along the avenue. He was contemplating all that had happened over the prior two weeks, and the events that had led him to this moment. He wanted to take it all in, and appreciate the fact that he had trusted his friend Charley, his daughter Jordan, and his own inner voice, to carry through on the mission and see where it all might lead. He was appreciative of the presence of Amelie, whether she was real or not, the insight from Dr. Gregor, the ducks, the flats, and all the other messages and messengers that had come across his path.

John continued up the avenue, past *Christian Dior* and *Givenchy,* and then crossed back to the other side.

Chanel could fix you up with a great pair of sunglasses, along with great fragrances and fine jewelry. Next to that was *Yves Saint Laurent,* which was extraordinarily creative.

Just past *Céline*, John saw the name *Anne Avé*, the store owned by his newly found friend from the dinner party at the *Grand Hôtel de lucarne.*

He walked into the impressive *Anne Avé* store, enjoying the entry colonnade and high open ceilings out front, as he passed through the lavish vestibule. The initial main room was full of luxurious fabric, and had an enormous steel fountain. The lighting was magnificent, and the rooms were large but comfortable. The room had an air of tasteful luxury, with marble floors and special seating areas tailored from velvet fabric. There was a story being told of high fashion clothing and accessories, as you linked between the associated rooms. The store displayed a variety of unique but classic designs, from the runways of Paris, New York and London, to the shops in Los Angeles, Rome, Milan and Barcelona. Large video boards displayed the runway scenes, as if they were separate web sites all showing a different web page in each subsequent and adjoining room.

John noticed how the store of *Anne Avé* would attract a unique buyer, a sophisticated woman that enjoys noble materials as much as luxury. There were gorgeous looks and styles, with a store design to match. Her ensembles were very creative, but simple and elegant, with much to take note of by the fashion icons. There were also items for the everyday girl, looking to dress up for a formal event or just add a signature piece or even a special accessory. She had handbags, shoes, formal dresses, blouses, boots and jewelry.

Anne had done very well for herself, was incredibly talented, and there was a flair of fun and joy that permeated the store. John was delighted to see the successful enterprise of his newly found friend.

John checked the business card that Anne had handed him the prior evening, and looked up the address on his smartphone. From Avenue Montaigne, he just needed to go one and a half blocks back to the south, and then turn west on the side street.

As he came upon the studio building, he passed under the awning and toward the main exterior entry door. The entry was understated and modest, but also elegant and well designed. The studio building had her business name on the glass entry doors, and in large steel letters at the face of the awning covering the entry.

John checked in with the security guard and took the elevator to the 3rd floor.

Coming out of the elevator, John proceeded directly ahead to a set of double glass studio entry doors. The name *Anne Avé* was set in block letters beyond the glass, at the top of a dividing wall that separated the entry from a space behind it. There was a large amount of natural light that was filtering through the area. As he passed through the studio entry, the receptionist greeted him with a warm smile, and offered to bring him some water or coffee. He could hear Anne's voice in the background laughing about something that had just occurred. She certainly enjoyed her work, and gave the aura of being exceptional at handling the high stress that much surely rest on her shoulders in running such a high-profile fashion enterprise.

The receptionist brought John a bottle of fresh spring water, while he toured the lobby area. John finally took a seat under a large stylish fashion photograph, and looked around at the fabulous runway photos gracing the lobby area.

He also noticed some large black and white shots of a young girl in the corner hall, in the area leading toward the back offices. John wondered if these were possibly photos of Anne's daughter *Lucie*. The girl was beautiful, with a wide smile, and wearing a soft dress that barely touched the sand on a beachfront in the French Rivera. The girl had bare feet, with her toes buried in the sand. There was a small bracelet on her left wrist, and the sun grazed across her forehead.

"Monsieur John," came a voice from his side. "I am so happy that you came to visit my studio! I did not know for sure if you would come today!" shouted Anne, very pleased to see John.

"Oui, of course," said John. "I would not miss it for the world."

"Come meet my staff," continued Anne, as they kissed on the cheeks and she grabbed his hand. Anne was thrilled that John had followed through and arrived.

Anne took John into the main studio area, which had a flurry of activity taking place by people that clearly enjoyed their work.

"Bonjour, Mr. John," came a voice up ahead. It was Laura from the dinner party of the prior evening.

"Bonjour Laura! Nice to see you again, I didn't know that you would be here today," replied John, as they kissed on each cheek.

"Oui, I almost live here, Monsieur John," answered Laura. "I am so glad to see you again."

The studio was well organized but very busy, with fabrics and designer elements laying across the large counter areas. Sketches and ideas were posted across a variety of vertical wall boards. There were glass rooms toward the outer wall of the space, one for a large conference area, and a handful of private glass offices. There were multiple racks of clothing, in all types of colors and designs, that were also used as dividers to the various interior work areas. The far corner area to the left had full length mirrors with multiple rows of shoes and heels, and there was a large wall display area next to that with necklaces, bracelets, cuffs, and several other jewelry items. A large storage room toward the back area housed a variety of fabrics and studio supplies, for implementing the targeted designs.

Dresses, coats, vests, pants, skirts and blouses all graced the numerous racks, with belts, purses, handbags, and sunglasses organized in various locations. A small lounge seating area with a small group sitting area appeared to be a lively spot for open design discussions, with a glass table in the middle.

The glass top at the small group work area was completely covered with lap top computers, coffee cups, purses, water bottles, smartphones and catalog clippings. The narrow dividing walls surrounding the mini work areas were full of photographs, sketches and design ideas which covered the area in vertical arrangements from floor to ceiling.

Smiles were all around, as Anne introduced John to her staff beginning with Olivia. Olivia was her right-hand personal assistant for all company matters, both design and business.

"John, it is my pleasure to meet you," said Olivia. "Anne has told me what a great time she had last night at the hotel *bienvenue diner*. You all must have talked well into the evening hours."

"Your wonderful leader is quite a trendsetter and story teller," replied John, "and yes we had a magnificent time at the tasty dinner last night."

Anne and Olivia continued to show John around the work studio.

In the designer area were Michel and Christian, her main designers in charge of implementing the details of the main visions, and they showed John some of the new and cutting edge designs coming forth.

Lina and Jade were working in the corner, and came over to greet John. They were her office assistants, assisting Olivia with a variety of matters on the business and marketing side of the company.

"And this is Lucia," introduced Olivia, "one of our main models, who is with us in the studio this afternoon to try on some of the new designs." Lucia was tall and blonde, with short hair and an engaging smile. She was modeling an amazing long silver beaded gown that was under development. Lucia was very professional, and you could tell she had been a fit model for years.

John noticed some of the branding and advertisements under development in various part of the studio. Since the evening before, he had been intrigued by her surname *Avé* , and asked Anne about the origins of her family name.

"The name is so beautiful," continued John, "and I was wondering about its descent."

"Oui, Mr John," my name is an Old French name, but it is also Galician, which is where my father was born. My mother was

French, but my father was a Galician Portuguese from the northern end of Portugal."

Anne continued, "the name *'Avé'* is from Latin extraction, and comes from the Galician word that means 'bird'."

"It is a beautifully simple name, and has a great designer ring to it when they interview you and call out the full name *Anne Avé,* added John.

John thought about the 'bird' meaning of her name, and the way that these feathery creatures had continued to repeat themselves with the events and people that he had continued to encounter.

"And Monsieur John," Anne continued, "Olivia has cleared her schedule to show you around, do you have some more time after our studio tour for her to show you along the Avenue?"

Olivia knew most everybody in town, or so it seemed, and was a great source and guide for anyone looking to undercover some of the most interesting people and the best places in Paris.

"She knows all the great local French artisans," continued Anne, "and can give you a history of some of the great creative minds in Paris."

Olivia was mildly embarrassed at the complement, but was very pleased to be so warmly spoken about in public. Anne had a great love and appreciation for Olivia, as well as her entire staff.

Anne and Olivia continued walking with John through the studio, and toward a second work table that had some of her latest designs. John was surprisingly able to provide feedback and comment on many of the outfits, the mix of color and fabrics, the classic simplicity, and how the accessories had so marvelously been chosen to accent the different ensembles.

"Very impressive," responded Olivia at his insightfulness.

"Oui, John!" agreed Anne. "How do you know so much about the latest fashion trends?"

"Well, I have two family members that taught me well," responded John, "including my beautiful daughter Jordan, and they would be so envious if they could see me taking a tour of your wonderful studio today! I will be sure to tell them all about it and how well you have treated me these past two days."

"Oui, you are a father!" chimed in Laura, who had just joined the conversation.

"Oui?" said Anne, nodding her head in unison. "How lucky is this girl to have a father like you!"

"What is her name?" asked Olivia.

"Her name is Jordan," replied John, as he reached into his wallet and offered a picture of Jordan.

"Oh, belle fille Jôrden," replied Anne. "Wait here Mr. John, I have something for you to take back to ta belle fille."

Anne reeled off about twenty words in French to Olivia at lightning speed. Olivia nodded her head in agreement, and took off toward the back of the studio.

"You must take home a *souvenir spécial* from *Anne Avé*," agreed Laura, "one of the best designers in all of France."

Anne had no greater support than her dear friend Laura, who was an enormously talented woman in her own career.

Olivia returned with a small silver box, and handed it to John.

"Merci," said John, surprised at the gesture. He opened the lid, which contained a gorgeous bracelet.

"Oh, my goodness," continued John, "that is so beautiful." His words were elongated and grateful. He was clearly touched by the kind gesture. "Merci, you are much too kind to think of my Jordan with this gift, she will cherish it to be sure."

"Oui, oui," said Anne, "de rien Mr. John. It is our pleasure to have you here and to be able to place a memory in the heart of your wonderful daughter Jordan."

Anne had a way with words. They were romantic, intelligent, and always full of kindness.

"Très bien merci." John thanked her again with full sincerity in his eyes.

Anne and the girls continued to show John some of the latest designs, and one of the articles that Laura had written about the company.

John was very impressed with the article, and Laura handed him a copy of the fashion magazine to take home with him.

"How about if we go have a glass of Bordeaux at the hotel?" offered Laura. "I know that Anne has a meeting now, but Olivia and I will show you the Plaza Athénée."

"Oui, génial," responded John. The three of them prepared to exit the studio.

"Monsieur John, you will keep in touch, no?" asked Anne. They kissed on the cheeks.

"Someday I want to hear more about your life in Los Angeles, and about your *belle fille Jôrden*. You should bring her to Paris next time for a visit," continued Anne.

"She would love that more than anything in the world," said John. "I shall surely have her come along on the next trip to Paris."

Anne was a remarkable human being. Incredibly talented to be sure, but her best quality was her selflessness, her joy of humanity, her sincerity to all that she touched, and her loyalty to all that deserved it. It was hard to imagine anyone not enjoying their interaction with *Anne Avé*. She was quite different than her *Parisienne* style at first glance, and she had a genuine kindness that meshed perfectly with her unique creative flair.

The wonderful staff all said goodbye, as the two girls and John departed the studio for some Bordeaux.

CHAPTER 18

A Bordeaux

Laura, Olivia and John took the elevator down to the building lobby, and exited to the street. They were heading back toward Avenue Montaigne, and would walk the avenue to the hotel for some drinks. It was a lovely French afternoon, and the smell of flowers permeated the quaint side street.

As they hit the Avenue, they turned toward the *Anne Avé* store and crossed in front of it. Olivia had great pride in walking past their flagship store, and looked toward the windows to see who was working this afternoon and how busy the store might be today. She had spent many hours planning and coordinating the development of the store, and always kept in tune with any changes or additions that might be required to the layout or presentation.

They continued down the Avenue to the southwest, walking directly in front of the *Céline* store. They all noticed an amazing pair of black sunglasses in the window, with a bold geometric shape, and with acetate frames. The glasses had a timeless elegance, with well-defined lines and minimized logos. The oversized frames were sophisticated, inspiring, and visionary, and the design incorporated the smooth edges with Polarized lenses.

"Bring me some of those tomorrow!" laughed Laura, as she salivated at the sight of the eyewear.

"Striking," agreed Olivia. "Such a talent."

Next up was *Yves Saint Laurent*, with its incredibly inventive designs, styles and tall boots. The designs were stunning, elegant and creatively original. John especially loved the tall boots and the one-piece leather shift dress.

The next store down the avenue in the path toward the hotel was *Chanel*, which John had toured just an hour earlier. The window display had a stunning gold *lame'* goddess dress, with an empire cut and great lines. All three of them slightly held their breath as they looked at the lines and details of the design, which were simply magnificent.

They continued another two long blocks to the southwest down Avenue Montaigne, talking and looking at the window displays along the way. The walk was uplifting and enjoyable.

The *Hôtel Plaza Athénée*, the famous international luxury hotel and part of the Dorchester Collection, was located directly on the Avenue Montaigne, toward the southwest end of the Avenue. The street façade of the building had a lavish stone facing, red awnings, wrought iron railings, and balconies that covered the building facade with red and white flowers.

There was a friendly doorman in a white coat, with a white hat, red tie and red coat trim, who opened the doors for them to enter. The doorman knew both Olivia and Laura, and greeted them with some kind French words and a genuinely wide smile. They were all part of the same tribe, each of them deeply connected to the neighborhood and its people. The three of them took a right under the metal and glass awning and into the nicely scaled entry.

The interior lobby was modestly ornate, with marble floors, natural wood, a large crystal chandelier, two story high marble columns, a large central light cove, and a large bouquet of flowers at each vertical column face. The main dining room was extremely opulent, with white furniture, crystal chandeliers, silver table settings, and marvelous tall white fluted Corinthian columns.

There was a beautiful indoor bar area that wrapped toward the main dining area, slightly curved with wood backed stools, fresh flowers, gilded local artwork, and a piano area just adjacent to the space.

They bypassed the indoor bar and continued toward the exterior courtyard area. This outdoor area was exactly what John had been longing for, a decorative natural seating area where he could catch the fresh air of the afternoon.

The exterior dining area was an interior courtyard of the hotel, with hotel rooms wrapping above on all four sides. Red umbrellas and candles accented the space with some bright color, mixed in with the mostly green setting of small trees, plants, and flowers set into movable planters. White linen table cloths set off the space, with metal backed chairs. There were round tables in the open areas, and some low backed booths and rectangle tables set in a linear fashion along the central area.

Laura chatted with the server, who she appeared to know well, while Olivia said a quick hello to some friends that she spotted at a corner courtyard table. John enjoyed the setting, looking around at the couples, friends and business associates that had gathered at the various tables.

Laura finished her greetings and ordered a *tartine of Camembert*, accompanied by a bottle of excellent Bordeaux.

Olivia returned and dropped into her chair with great excitement. "That was *René* and *Luca* from the *Rafael House*," she said, "they are traveling to Milan next week to meet about some new boutique locations."

Olivia had a natural flair for the fashion business. She was comfortable and at ease with most everyone that she came across or interacted with, a natural communicator and socially oriented individual. There was never a smile too far from her face, and she was a perfect match as the primary assistant to Anne.

John commented on how much he respected and admired what Anne has accomplished, along with the design talent and the individual respect and care that she showed to all her employees. Both girls nodded in agreement.

"Yes, she is very good to us," agreed Olivia, "she has always has been very generous to her staff, and is supportive of our individual contributions and open minded to our ideas."

"Exactly true, *la soeur,*" agreed Laura.

Laura and Olivia described the way that Anne has supported so many charitable events, without anyone really knowing that she had been involved with financing them and offering support assistance behind the scenes.

"You would never know it," said Laura, "she doesn't mention it to anyone outside of her main staff, but she is a true giver who selflessly donates without looking for any public acknowledgment or reward for it."

"Oui," agreed Olivia, "her personal joy of doing it and quietly helping others is her sufficient reward."

Olivia moved the topic toward Laura, who was extremely accomplished in her own right.

"You are such a great writer," said Olivia, "and it is amazing to see how much you have done to support the *Anne Avé* product line."

Laura is appreciative, but modest about the compliment.

"Well, merci, my dear *la soeur,*" said Laura, "but it is easy to support Anne and write great things about her because she is so incredibly talented, and I do not need to fabricate any exaggerated tales about her or her design work."

"So, nice," said Olivia.

"She is also a great person," continued Laura, "with a big heart for children and for others needing her help."

Laura had climbed to the top of her profession and was a well-respected fashion writer. She had combined her insightful fashion observations with her extensive journalist background, writing online and print media articles that described the elegant fashion trends around the globe. She was great at research and turning that data into descriptions, but also had a creative mind and an eye for great fashion.

Laura was very well read, and a natural linguist in English and French. She also had a great imagination, which you could tell by how she responded to most any topic that was raised. Her discipline was quite apparent, even in the way that she walked, and she could spend entire days in the various fashion houses across France, not to mention the fashion shows, store visits, and reading and researching both online and through print media. She loved her job, but was not afraid to treat it like a job. Like Anne, she was very passionate about her work. Although British by birth, she had also become a true *Parisienne*, and had crossed over into wearing both ensembles seamlessly. She loved a good story, but could tell a better one.

Laura, like Anne, was quick to change the topic when she felt that too much attention was being lavished on her.

"*Livi,*" as Laura called her, "how is everything with your family?"

"They are doing fairly well," said Olivia, who described to John how her father had recently passed away.

"Oh, I'm sorry to hear that," replied John.

"Merci," said Olivia, "it has been a very difficult time for our family, but I had a very unusual episode last weekend that made me feel better."

Olivia was always searching for the bright side of a situation.

"What was that?" inquired Laura.

"It is hard to explain," continued Olivia, "but I had two things happen to me over the weekend that were very comforting to me. The first was late on Saturday night, and then there was another unusual occurrence the following morning. Some people might think that I am crazy for thinking this, so don't judge me too harshly," she said with a self-conscious smile.

"What?" said Laura, "about your father?"

"Oui," she continued, "he has been sending me messages through some dreams and other sequences, but then this weekend I was out in the province and the sky was very clear, and I noticed a very bright star in the sky to the east. I swore it was my father, trying to send me another message of love, and that he was going to be OK. My eyes could not move off this single bright star, and my mind began thinking about the words that had come in one dream saying to me 'I'm never gone, I'm never gone.' There was something eternally pleasing about that bright star on the eastern horizon for me, and now I will look for it whenever the sky is clear for many years to come."

"Oh, my dear *la soeur*, how nice that is for you," commented Laura, "I am so happy that he is helping you feel comfort for your great loss."

"Then after that," continued Olivia remembering, the next sequence, "I had this thing happen in the early hours on the following morning, as I was sleeping."

"Really?" said Laura, "you are a mystical soul my dear girl."

"Yes," continued Olivia, "it was quite remarkable".

Olivia paused, thinking about how to explain what had happened, without making it sound too surreal. John and Laura gave her time to remember the event and formulate her words.

"Yes, you may be surprised at this, but I believe that my father came to me at my bedside the following morning," said Olivia. "I woke up to see him. It must have been before 5:00, in the early dawn, and he was telling me that everything was going to be alright. He was a faint image of light, and he was accompanied with another white spiritual figure of some sort, as if he were in very good hands and wanted me to know it."

Olivia was very pleased that this event had happened, and even more so to get it off her chest. She was very comforted by the thought that he was going to be alright, and appreciated that she could share it with her friend without fear of being laughed at.

She must have deeply trusted John to include him in the story, which made him feel honored by her trust. After all, thought John, they had just met an hour earlier at the studio. But Olivia felt she knew him based on the positive things that Anne had communicated earlier in the day, about their great evening at the hotel dinner. It was a testament to Anne, really, the way that Olivia trusted her insight and understanding about John.

Laura was happy for her friend. "Oh, my darling Livi," said Laura, "you had quite an eventful weekend in the country, and I hope your entire family can work through the difficulties of your loss."

Olivia was deeply appreciative of Laura's support, and always cherished her great friendship and ability to be a good listener.

"Yes," agreed John, "how nice to have a strong and comforting message come to you like that, that is incredible that he came to your bedside."

"Oui John," agreed Laura, "what a miraculous experience for you, Livi, to have your father come visit you in the early dawn. It is your receptiveness and spiritual connection to it that makes it possible!"

The girls continued to chat about food, fashion, and what they were planning to do the next weekend. The conversation moved quickly from one topic to another. They were both excellent communicators, and did not need to overstay any topic. John loved the fast pace of discussion, and was much the same way in any conversational setting.

Laura and Olivia moved to a discussion about some of the great artisans in the city.

As Olivia was describing to John some of the fashion schools and artistic neighborhoods across the city, she noticed the scarf.

"By the way, John, I have noticed this great scarf that you have been carrying around, it looks very familiar to me, can I have a look at it?" asked Olivia.

"Yes, of course," and John handed her the crumpled-up designer scarf.

"Oh, yes, of course!" shouted Olivia. "This is a design by my good friend Alaïa!"

John tells her about the girl at the shop, the way that she had black bangs that fell over her eyebrows, with a medium long cut that she had been wearing in a pony-tail high up on her head.

"Oh, I can't believe it!" said Olivia. "You met Alaïa today?"

"Yes," said John. "I was in her boutique today and bought some things for Jordan."

"Alaïa is a good friend of my family," said Olivia, "and has been involved with French fashion, local artisans, and the college scene for quite a while. Her mother was a fashion icon and professor at the University for a decade, and her exceptional language skills had put her mom in charge of the University's work study program, and had done this for many years following her own work study experiences back in her college days."

Olivia continued, "Alaïa has continued the tradition, not as an educator, but as a fashion designer herself who has been connected to the local University system. That is why she had located her small boutique in the Latin Quarter."

Good lord, thought John, the spirits were hard at work in making him a believer. A smile came across his face, as he sat back and took in the great experience. It was as if he was watching it all unfold as a spectator, amazed at the sequence of events and cheering on the developments as they occurred. He was pleasantly surprised at each successive event, and began to truly enjoy the process. The more he trusted it, the more it was revealed to him. It was an indescribable experience that he could only sit back and smile about.

John thought about the experience at the store, and began to describe his interaction.

"Alaïa was a very interesting character, to be sure," observed John. "Not only was she clearly talented, but she had a no-nonsense type of demeanor and was nobody's fool. I was impressed with the design talent, but also a bit surprised that she was directly involved with the operations of the boutique."

"Yes," said Olivia, "she usually does not work in the boutique except for a few days each week, and only in the early morning hours. She likes to stay in touch with the pulse of what the people are interested in wearing, so that is the reason that she spends a small amount of time in the boutique each week."

"She does lovely work," added Laura.

"Yes," Olivia continued, "her focus is her design work, marketing and promotions to some of the larger buyers, but she feels the small boutique helps to keep her grounded to her small home town upbringing and making a very personal and individualized experiences for her favorite neighborhood customers."

Olivia continued, "She also does a small set of special items, and this scarf is one of those smaller special runs, which she does in a limited supply to make them unique and customized. They are very detailed and exceptionally well crafted, yet skillfully simple at the same time."

This description of Alaïa all fit perfectly for John. This was exactly the personality of the person that he had experienced in the store. However, he had wondered how a person of such talent was able to have time for both design and running a boutique. She was not there to oversell him on any of her clothing or accessories this morning, which also made more sense now after hearing Olivia's description.

"She is truly a talent," confirmed Laura. "I did a story on her once, connecting her to her roots in Saint-Émilion. Her background story and family history was a very interesting research project, and gave me great insight into how she became such a great designer, and blends *la province* into her designs."

154

"Saint-Émilion?" asked John.

"Oui, she is from a small province in southwestern France, a small town near Bordeaux, like the wine!" said Laura, pointing to the bottle on the table.

"Oui, John," said Olivia, "you have an original *Capelle*! And very good taste my new friend!"

"I had a girl say that to me earlier today, in the bistro!" said John. "Why do you call it a *Capelle*?"

"That is the name of her company, my dear John," confirmed Laura. "Her last name is *Capelle*, and her boutique is called *la capelle*."

"Alaïa Capelle," repeated John. "Of course. I have a *Capelle*. I never looked at the name of the boutique!" John had done the same thing at the clothing store in California.

"And you won't let it out of your grip!" chimed in Laura, laughing in admiration of her newfound friend's commitment to his scarf.

"Like no other!" added Olivia. "I think you have already worn it out, and it has not yet gone around your neck even once, hahaha!" They enjoyed the way that John was embracing his new *Capelle*.

"Yes, it's for Jordan," clarified John, "but I guess I got a little carried away in my connection to it. It reminds me SO much of my wife Mia, that I just haven't wanted to part with it all day."

"Your wife Mia?" asked Laura, never missing a beat.

"Yes, my wife Mia," said John, "but she has disappeared for over two years, and I am still trying to find out what happened to her. It is part of the reason that I am in Paris, to possibly find her. It is a real long shot, but she has been on my mind so much the last two weeks, and it has led me here to be with you today."

"Oh, my good lord," said Laura, looking toward Olivia with disbelief. "I had no idea that you were going through such an adventure, but I did have a feeling about you last night at the dinner that you are right on time with where your life was supposed to be going. We just had no idea about the framework of your journey."

"I admire your courage, John," said Olivia. "I don't know how I might handle something like that in my life. You handle it so well, nobody would ever know that you were going through such a difficult time, you have such a great attitude about life, and give off a great aura of wishing everyone else their success."

Olivia slowly added, "And here, all the while, you are going through such a devastating and strangely confusing set of circumstances."

"How do you handle not knowing?" asked Laura. "That would be the most difficult part for me."

"I know," said John. "I have learned to live with it."

John paused, looking down at the stem of his wine glass, then continued, "but I believe she is still alive, and all the clues continue to tell me that I am on the right path to finding her."

"Bravo, dear John, and yes you will find her," said Laura. "I believe it in my heart, you should keep searching until there is no tomorrow. There is no other way to approach it."

"Yes, my goodness," said Olivia. "It gave me shivers up and down my arms as you were telling us this situation."

The three of them had already started their second bottle of Bordeaux, and the cheese was long gone. The waiter had brought out an additional two rounds of hors d'oeuvres, as they continued to bond in a way that they had never quite expected.

"You are truly an *américain ace*," said Laura, remembering her words to John last night at the hotel dinner.

"But this adds new meaning to my comments last night," she continued. "I had no idea how romantic you really were Mr. John. This story about the great love for your wife that you will not let die, it is the stuff of legends! I am very inspired at your continuing pursuit to find her."

Olivia agreed. They were both silent for a moment as they thought about how that might even be possible. Suddenly, their worries and concerns in life had paled in comparison to what they were hearing from John.

Laura, the consummate journalist, just had to ask, "Have you checked with the local police?"

"Not yet, but I was planning to do that tomorrow," confirmed John, "just in case they might know something about her."

Olivia had been so touched by the story, and was also still thinking about how unusual it was that John had met his good friend Alaïa.

"I will arrange a gathering with Alaïa sometime soon!" announced Olivia, expressing out loud what she had been mulling over in her head. "We shall all get together as friends and laugh at the small world that life can be sometimes, and maybe you will be able to meet someone who can help."

"Oh, yes, my darling *la soeur*, what an excellent idea, let me host it at our gathering place in Le Marais, we shall have a caterer and invite some of our mutual friends to gather for the evening."

"That sounds great," said John. "I would love to meet more of your friends and get together again soon."

"How about next week on Tuesday night?" asked Laura. "I must travel back to London for the long weekend, but will be back straight away early next week for the gathering."

They all kissed on the cheeks and said their goodbyes at the courtyard.

John jumped into a taxi and headed back toward the hotel.

CHAPTER 19

The House Call

John returned to the *Grand Hôtel de lucarne*, and was greeted by Enzo at the door.

"Bonjour, Monsieur John!" said Enzo, with his wide signature smile. "Did you have an enjoyable time in Paris today?"

"Oui," said John. "It was quite magnifique. How are you doing today, Enzo?"

"Very well, sir, merci," replied Enzo, with an additional nod of thanks and his prolonged natural smile.

John had always been a person to notice and care about most everyone he met, especially the daily laborers such as the waiters, the clerks, the construction worker, and others just trying to make ends meet. He was as comfortable speaking with an elevator repair man as he was a chief executive of a company, and always appreciated those that gave great effort and attitude toward the most basic of jobs.

It was 5:25pm, as John headed up to his hotel room for a short rest.

John exited the small elevator, and proceeded down the hallway toward his room on the third floor.

As he reached to locate his hotel card key, his phone began to buzz in his pocket. John picked up the call and said hello.

"Hello, John," said the Doctor. "It's Dr. Gregor, did I catch you at a good time?"

"Yes, Doctor, it is good to hear from you. What's new with you?" answered John. He closed the door and threw his small backpack on the hotel bed.

"Very well, thank you," said the Doctor. "I wanted to follow up from our meeting last week. I spoke with Charley again, and he gave me some additional background information on Mia. I didn't know the full extent of what you have been going through, and Charley gave me a better context for what might have happened to Mia. He mentioned that the police had speculated that she might have been taken against her will in some way, or been through another traumatic experience of some sort, is that your understanding of the matter?"

"Yes, Doctor," said John. "They did give us those thoughts, but they never put it in the police report because there were no concrete facts to back it up. There were some clues that led them to a hypothesis about it, and they did tell me that cases they had investigated with this type of fact pattern had often led to that type of conclusion, but they just did not have all the pieces in places to confirm it for certain."

"Yes, I see," said Dr. Gregor. "Well, based on that possibility, I did do some additional research for you that might be helpful."

"Thank you for considering it further," responded John. "What did you find out?"

"Of course," qualified the Doctor, "not knowing exactly what happened makes it very difficult to project a medical reason for it, but as a friend I wanted you to be aware of the three possibilities that may be applicable, at least until you are able to gather more accurate info about what actually may have happened."

"Yes, I understand Doctor, it is very difficult to speculate on what may have happened, but I thank you for thinking it through and considering the possibilities," replied John.

John took a seat near his hotel room window, the one that he had become his favorite spot earlier in the morning to sit and relax.

"My pleasure," said the Doctor.

"Of course," he continued, "we previously discussed the possibilities related to epigenetics. Without any DNA samples, it is still difficult to project an outcome from this situation, but whenever possible we want to avoid any damaging genetic triggers. There is always a possibility of an inadvertent alteration to your genes, if you don't take care of them. We know that there can be negative effects from radiation, from second hand tobacco smoke, as well as many chemicals and some insecticides, which are all general factors that could damage the DNA of an individual. These examples are most likely a longer-term effect than what Mia may have experienced, but nevertheless are factors that could change a person's genome if she was previously exposed to these types of negative effects."

"I understand," said John.

"However," the Doctor continued, "after gathering more information from Charley, I think there may be two other possible explanations that might be more applicable in this case."

"I see," replied John, listening intently.

"Yes," said Dr. G, "if there was an injury sustained as part of a kidnapping or other physical impact that may have taken place, like the police had speculated, then there could have been a head trauma situation that either led to possibly amnesia, or to a PTSD condition. I believe we touched on PTSD at the office last week."

"Yes, we did," agreed John.

"Yes, as we discussed, with post-traumatic stress disorder, this could happen to someone who has been kidnapped, stressed, escaped, or in some cases could even cause memory loss from the anxiety of a rare situation," said the Doctor.

"But I also researched this third prospect," continued the Doctor, "given the chance of the head trauma aspect, since amnesia can be connected to head trauma. Although amnesia is a rare condition, it is still a possibility and would explain her inability to remember past events and previously familiar information. This impairment could lead to the point where she might not even remember you or Jordan."

"No kidding," said John, as he thought about Mia and watched a young couple holding hands and walking on the sidewalk below.

"Yes, like I said," continued the Doctor, "it is a very rare condition, but if there was head trauma involved and maybe a brain injury, or if she had a highly traumatic experience of some sort, then amnesia could have been a contributing factor for her current condition. Other symptoms related to this could include confusion or disorientation, problems with her short-term memory, and typically refers to a large-scale loss of memories that should not have been forgotten. These may even include her forgetting about important milestones in life, memorable events, key people in her life, and vital facts that should has been told or taught."

"I see," said John, "that would explain why she may not be able to locate us again, even if she had escaped from some sort of violent situation or had originally been taken somewhere against her will."

"Yes, it would," agreed the Doctor. "If that situation did occur, and then she escaped from it, it is possible that the head trauma might disable her from knowing how to re-gain back her regular life. Therefore, she may be alive but not know how to find you, or not even know that you exist."

"If this is the case, would it be possible for her situation to be reversed?" asked John.

"Yes, it can, and that is the good news if it were amnesia. First, it can be removed over time, since a person would be able to regain memory as their neurons rebuild," continued the Doctor, "and many cases can be resolved without treatment, so if you can locate her, it is possible for her to recover over time and eventually return to normal."

It pained John to think that something like this could have happened to Mia, but at the same time gave him great hope that maybe there could be a silver lining someday.

"That is excellent information, Doctor, thanks very much. I really appreciate the research and follow up information. I am in Paris now, and I will give this some more thought," said John.

"Oh, you are," said the Doctor, "that's excellent, enjoy your trip. It's morning here in California, so feel free to give me a call back today if you have any more questions, or sometime later this week if needed."

"Thanks again, Dr. Gregor, your additional research is very much appreciated," said John.

"My pleasure," replied the Doctor. "Goodbye."

CHAPTER 20

Mia Michelle

John stretched out on the hotel bed and stared up at the ceiling. The cool evening breeze fluttered the curtains and left a fresh sensation in the room. The sounds of the city rang throughout the room, but his mind drifted off to a different place and time.

John's mind crossed over a variety of perspectives. He thought about his evenings at the flats, the palm trees, the ocean horizon and the calming of his mind. He thought about how far he had come in his thinking over the years, especially recently. John enjoyed his perspective of deciding how he would feel about things, rather than waiting to see where his feelings might lead him, and loved the idea of a person fighting for themselves, even against all odds. He liked the idea that he could drive away negative thoughts through positive thoughts, words and actions, even though he could not necessarily stop them from showing up. His faith had grown, and he knew that something good was going to happen to him. He wanted all the blessings that were meant to come his way. He wasn't looking to be greedy, or to undermine any that were meant for others, but simply had reset his mind to receive the blessings that were meant for him.

John could see the sky in the distance, through the wide flung windows and over the buildings across the street. The city of lights was in full hue tonight. As he considered the distant sky, he thought about Olivia's story about her father. The lights of the city were too bright to see any stars on this night, but he loved the idea that she had found her comfort through them.

He thought about the dove on his backyard fence, that very first morning following his episode with Amelie at *Vintage Rags*. The dove was a mystery, calm and confident, sent specifically by someone to see him. It was there when he woke up on the veranda. It was there in his dream at the flats. Now it had shown up again this morning in Paris. It had appeared in three versions with the same quills - in person, in a dream, and at the Cathedral on a banner.

John wondered if the girl in his dream was meant to be Mia, or Amelie, or even Alaïa. Or maybe the dream was representative of French women in general, that he should come here, enjoy his stay, and maybe find his path toward Mia. He tried to remember how the girl in the dream was dressed, what she trying to convey, and the type of personality she exuded. The whole experience was becoming quite intriguing to John, rather than making him nervous. Jordan, Charley and Doctor Gregor, along with Anne, Laura and Olivia, had all helped him find comfort in this journey.

With all their help, John was beginning to trust himself, his inner voice, and follow the messages and events as they were unfolding. It was a feeling of extreme liberation. He was choosing his own path, by following the natural and unbridled path that was being laid out for him. He could not control it, but he could embrace it. He was following the signs, the dreams, the messages, and the advice from friends, as they were all part of the process of where his life should be leading. This new information from Dr. Gregor was also encouraging, and had reinforced some things about Mia that Jordan had said to him, including the way that maybe she was wanting to be found but didn't quite know how to do it.

Maybe Mia was indeed sending a prayer that she knew she was lost but didn't know where she was or how to be found, as Jordan had speculated. Jordan had a way of knowing things, sometimes without knowing how she knew them. It would be just like Mia to do that. She had a willpower that would enable something like that to occur, strong, influential, and commanding, even if she was not discernably attempting it. Maybe Mia sent the dove, or maybe someone or something sent the dove on behalf of Mia.

The power of the mind was an amazing thing to consider, and the power of the spirit was even greater. How many people just use a fraction of their capability, let alone tapping into the power of their subconscious, thought John.

John enjoyed having the windows wide open and the sights and sounds of the city rushing in with the air. It reminded him of his many years of living in New York City, especially in the late spring and early summer, when he would open wide the windows to his loft in Tribeca and let the sights and sounds of the city be absorbed into his existence. New York was the city where he came of age, went to law school, and learned how to be an adult. It was engrained into his constitution, had become part of his permanent life disposition, and gave him his elevated street smarts. It was the city where he roamed the streets of Greenwich Village, SoHo, Tribeca, Little Italy, and the upper west side, in both the early morning and late at night, and gave him the exact same sensation as he was currently experiencing in Paris. It was a very similar urban fabric, with similar thoughts and experiences, but with a different language, history and culture. Most of all, New York was the city where he married Mia, on a beautiful day in the early summer, and that forever will be his best memory of the city.

His mind settled into the day that he married Mia, and how wonderful their life had been. They were two peas in a pod, a match made in heaven, and he did not want it to end. He thought about their long journey over the past twenty-two years, with twenty of them together, and where this current search had brought him. After all, thought John, he would not be in Paris right now were it not for Mia, and he would not be growing so much spiritually, emotionally and intellectually were it not for Mia. She was the beginning and the end to his current chapter in life. Where it went from here, nobody knew, but she had been instrumental in bringing him all this way to this point without even saying a single word of English or French over the past two years. The language now had become much loftier, indescribable, even ethereal. He trusted her more than ever, and he was beginning to count on the idea that maybe she could help him find her. It was a strange and bizarre thought, but somehow it made sense to John.

Mia had a one-of-a-kind personality. She was born Mia Michelle Girard, living on an American military base in France until she was two years old, and was a beauty from the start. Her father was an American serviceman, with some French, English and Welsh ancestry. Her mother was born and raised in France, and then moved to America after his days in the service. She had died at a young age, but still had relatives somewhere in France that did not speak English. Her mother was a very creative individual, and had raised Mia with a mind toward grace and style. Her father had also died several years later, and had left her a great legacy to carry on, especially with his great compassion and service oriented personality.

Mia was very artistic, and always viewed living from a perspective of visual beauty and a balanced existence, much like her mother. She was spiritual, full of faith, and effectively used both sides of her mind. She could be moved to emotions with her family and creative endeavors, but was never too far from a logical basis to making sound decisions. Mia never let emotions get the best of her, but was a real person with love and loss, and felt deeply about the elements of her conviction.

Mia was welcoming to all nationalities and personality types, and was very supportive of those simply trying to find their way in life. It is the reason that she went into educational training, to help all types with the basics of reading and literature, but in a new and creative way. She could also teach art and fashion design, and had a personal interest in reading history and biographies.

She was very stylish, had a good sense of fashion, and could throw together a fashion ensemble with very little effort and a minimum of cost. Mia had a way of mixing materials, colors and styles, and could put together a unique mix with a simple signature piece and simple jewelry accents. She was interested in finding unique costume jewelry, or could wear the top of the line items from the top fashion houses, but would never wear a fake version of a designer item. She wouldn't be caught dead with a knockoff item on her body. Mia loved her ankle boots, her handbags, and interesting jewelry, but would mix them very cleverly. Her closet was full of *Chanel, Hermés, Dior, Céline* and others, but she selectively mixed them into her daily ensembles. Her daughter Jordan had inherited this trait, and could put together great ensembles with very little expense, although she also did like her special designer items when she had a chance to wear them. She was a great mother, as demonstrated by her daughter Jordan.

Mia loved to laugh, and was a loyal friend to her many admirers. She had a way of disarming and not competing with her friends, or being a threat to their existence. She was completely comfortable with herself, so she never had a need to compete. This allowed her full attention to her friends, unconditional love, and extended help to whoever needed it at most any hour of the day. It was a lovely thing to watch, because very few people operated so selflessly in life. She knew her worth, but had no desire to prove it to anyone.

John was clearly drawn to these female personalities that were positive and secure with themselves. He thought about how well Anne had done this naturally, and Laura, and Olivia, not to mention the mirage of Amelie at the store. They all had the same spirit and positive outlook as Mia and Jordan. He also felt, however, with these recent activities, that there was something greater at play, something spiritual that was directing him toward finding Mia. It was both fascinating and welcome. His mind skipped to what Charley had said at *BP's*, that "you will hear it in your spirit before it will come to pass." It was a piece of advice that had stayed with him for two weeks. Maybe the experiences with these people of similar aura to Mia were leading him to the answer, and his spirit was directing him toward these revelations that Mia may somehow be led to him, or he to her.

He ran his mind back through the dream, or at least the parts of it that he could remember: There was a rolling terrain behind the bird in the far background, which was similar but different than at his home, and appeared to be a European setting. There were flat fields in the foreground, with something being grown on rows and rows of parallel stakes. There was the Paris shopping bag, the Louis Vuitton handbag, and there were travelers all around, all of which have materialized since he arrived in Paris. He could see the interlocking LV logo on one of the handbags, and was given the marching orders to fight for himself and fight for his family.

John thought about the man in the dream that handed him an envelope with a message inside, but he could not see any print on the card.

Maybe time, or a new circumstance, would help this ink flow to the surface.

CHAPTER 21

la Préfecture

John left the hotel early the next morning to stop in at the local police department, the Préfecture de police de Paris, a unit of the French National Police which provides the police force for the city of Paris and the surrounding three suburban areas. It is headed by the Préfet de police. John didn't expect that much could be found out by meeting with the police, but nevertheless he believed he had to at least give it a chance, and make an inquiry to them in the slim chance that they knew something about Mia or her situation.

The department was extremely busy, with people coming and going in all directions. The French police's equivalent to the missing person's unit was tied up that morning with some active cases, and John was asked to set up an appointment and return in a couple of hours. He was required to fill out a Missing Persons form regarding the matter, and allow them to make a copy of his passport. The form was nearly four pages long, and took him about fifteen minutes to complete.

John departed the building and found a local café in the neighborhood. He read through the local newspaper, or at least the parts that he could comprehend. He then turned to his book, in a vacation type of mindset, and ordered a breakfast of fruit, a baguette with jam, juice and café au lait.

John had all the time in the world, and just let the events of the day unfold as they desired. This French café did not mind people coming and hanging out for as long as they desired, provided they ordered food and drinks, and John left a healthy tip of Euros for the nice young girl that was serving his table.

He returned to the department at the scheduled appointment time, just under two hours later. After a small wait in the lobby area, a fully uniformed police officer called out his name and asked John to come with him.

John exited through a set of double doors with the officer, and proceeded along the corridor at the edge of a large open room. The officer opened the door to a small conference room, and motioned for John to enter. The Officer did not speak English, but John gathered that someone would be in shortly to see him. His name tag said *Bernard*, and Officer Bernard nodded and closed the door behind him.

John waited in the small conference room, which consisted of a medium small round conference table and four chairs. There was a small office desk against the side wall area, and an additional chair had been placed in each of the two back corners. A dry erase board was mounted on the wall above the desk area. A half-height wire glass window covered the remainder of the wall next to the door, and John could see out into the main police unit work area from his seat at the table.

This was not an interrogation room, but appeared to be a room in a row of three or four small conference rooms that lined this section of the main adjoining space. The larger open room next to it had about twenty or thirty desks laid out in the main area, back to back and in efficiently organized rows, much like was done in an old American newspaper company. This was the first French police unit that John had ever visited, so he didn't know if this was a typical way of how they organized their police units. It was a very large building, with multiple floors, departments and units, as it served not only the local police units but was home to the French National Police. He had gathered that he was probably brought into a section that was connected to the larger national operation.

John waited in the room for about five minutes, and then heard a short knock and saw the door open. Two police officers entered the room, a male and a female. They were not dressed in full police uniforms, but had a special attire that was more akin to undercover police officials of some sort. The officers each greeted John with a handshake and a slightly forced smile, and introduced themselves as Officer Lambert and Officer Moreau.

Officer Lambert, a medium sized male with a stocky figure with thin brown hair, took a seat across from John at the round table. Officer Moreau, a slightly shorter female, had her hair tied in the back and remained standing at the side of the table. She was holding a clipboard, with some papers attached to the front, and a pen in her hand.

Following the greetings and basic introductions in French, Officer Moreau switched quickly to English. She appeared to have a much better command of the English language than Officer Lambert, although it appeared that he did understand a moderate amount of English. John was not sure if they normally handled an inquiry like this with two officers, or if she was primarily in the room to assist to a greater degree as an interpreter. Officer Lambert sat at the table across from John and listened intently.

Officer Moreau asked John to help them understand what was the nature of his inquiry. As John spoke with the two Officers, he explained the background situation regarding Mia, the length of time that it had been a cold case, and the basic summary of the police report that was on file with the Sherriff's office in California. They each had a copy of the form that John had filled out, and each of them spent time reviewing it as John described his circumstances. Officer Moreau kept detailed notes as he spoke, while Officer Lambert listened and nodded as he explained the history. They took an approach of being cautiously helpful, and spent more time listening than asking questions for the first fifteen minutes.

Each of the officers had a look of concern as John described the history, but did not readily give away any thoughts about what they were thinking, or if they knew anything about the case. They asked to see his passport identification, and looked at his personal identification page and the pages with visa stamps. They already had a copy of the passport, but wanted to see the original. They handed the passport back to John, and continued to listen to his overview and review the form that John had filled out.

Officer Moreau continued to take notes following his descriptions and answers, and continued reviewing the file. They could tell that John had a strong understanding of the law and the operations of a police unit, and were very patient in gathering all the facts before commenting on any of his descriptions.

The officers began asking several routine questions about her physical description, her habits and personality, her style of clothing, her overall health and condition at the last time he saw her, and potential people that he might contact. These were many of the questions that he had answered with the California police officials, so John was well versed with this type of questioning.

John answered all their questions, and reached a point where he had finished the factual description as he knew it, including the specific dates of her disappearance and the details of the police report on file. He then described some additional information that his local police had speculated about the case, that had not been officially added to the police report.

After about twenty-five minutes of discussion, they moved to their next area of interest. Officer Moreau again flipped through the small file of additional papers that were attached to the clipboard, and asked a few additional questions as she reviewed it.

"And we see from your form that your wife's maiden name was Girard, and we see the year that she was born," said Officer Moreau, "do you know anything about your wife's mother's family, and do you happen to know their family name?"

John paused and searched his memory. He had never met Mia's grandparents on her mother's side, and only generally knew of them.

"Mia's mother died at a young age," John began. "I know at one point that Mia had relatives from her mother's side still living somewhere in France, but they did not speak English, and because we live in America we never crossed paths with that part of the family. We knew her father's family much better, the Girard side. Mia was heartbroken at her mother's death, and lost touch with that part of their family as she was raising our daughter. I believe her mother's maiden name was Guerin."

"Did your wife stay home to raise your daughter or did she have a profession?" asked Officer Moreau.

John was intrigued by these latest questions.

"Yes, she was trained as a teacher, and served for many years as an educator in our local school district, but once Mia was born, she stayed home to raise her and did some volunteer work at the local charities," answered John.

"Did she have any other professions?" continued Officer Moreau.

"Well, not really, although she studied fashion in Paris and was a stylist and fashion consultant for about one year following her first college degree, so I guess that was her profession before she went into education, yes," answered John.

The two officers looked at each other in silence.

"And what is your understanding of her college days when she was in Paris?" asked Officer Moreau.

"Only that she studied in a work-study program here in fashion for a year, and then worked for short time with a local fashion house before returning to America," said John.

They waited for more details.

John continued, "That was right before we were married, so I don't know much detail about what occurred during her work-study days in Paris."

John paused, "Why do you ask, do you think there is a connection?"

The officers just looked at each other again, not giving anything away.

"We don't know, monsieur," responded Officer Moreau, "we are just trying to gather the background facts now."

John had been through this before, at work and with Mia, and had the distinct impression that they knew more than they were revealing.

The two officers thanked John for his cooperation. They asked him if he wanted something to drink, and indicated that they would return in about ten minutes.

John watched through a wire glass window and the department continued to have people coming and going from the unit. The activity had settled down a bit from two hours earlier, but it still was a very busy operation.

John knew that this line of questioning was standard fact finding. It was also a way for them to help confirm that John was who he said he was, and had the motives that he had communicated. There are cases where a wife may enter a foreign country to get away from an abusive or otherwise difficult marital situation, so a police force would always use caution before offering too much information. They also may not have much information about a missing person request, and may need to do some further checking before offering any thoughts on the case.

The questions that they asked about her physical appearance, habits, personality, and style of dress were a typical line of questions. However, he did find it slightly unusual that they had not asked any questions about her citizenship. They also appeared to place some extra importance about her maiden name. Maybe they had cases where women had disappeared on purpose, and reverted to their maiden name by choice, or maybe there was something more that they were holding back for now.

John pulled out his smartphone and looked up the main duties of the Préfet de police. It noted that the unit operated under the Minister of the Interior, and were responsible for the security of Paris, issuing identification cards, traffic control, protection of the environment, and management of the police and firefighters, among other things.

After about ten minutes, the two officers knocked on the door and entered the conference room.

"Thank you for waiting, monsieur Marcomb," said Officer Moreau. "We have met with our Officier supérieur and he has reviewed your file."

"Yes, thank you," responded John.

"We wish to do some further checking," continued Officer Moreau, "so we will contact the American embassy, and see what was on record with the FBI, the state and local police. Please make an appointment to come back in about ten days, and we will let you know at that time if we have more information to share with you."

"Oui, merci," responded John. "Thank you for checking on this, and I will make an appointment to return soon for an update."

They smiled more broadly than at the first introduction, and made their way out of the room. They led John back toward the lobby area, and said goodbye.

This might take some time, thought John, but I can wait.

CHAPTER 22

Extension de réservation

John extended his reservation at the *Grand Hôtel de lucarne* in Paris for an additional two weeks, and made the third floor of the hotel his new temporary home. He used the time to check into the office at home, and catch up with some friends in California that wondered where he had been.

The neighbors at home were watching over his house, and his partners had picked up his client load and had been seamlessly managing his business affairs. Other than some vacations with Mia and Jordan when she was younger, it was the longest period in over a decade that he had taken off work to rest and relax.

John spent considerable time in Paris touring the museums and local sites. He went to the local theatre for two different shows, and checked in often with Jordan. John and Jordan texted or spoke on the phone most every day, and John kept her up to date with the latest information and escapades involving his new friends in the fashion industry. He promised Jordan a trip to Paris soon, and passed along the special invitation for her visit Anne's studio.

"I am so happy for you, daddy, your voice sounds happier than you have been in a long time," she would repeat every other day.

John's French was improving, and the locals at the café down the street were beginning to recognize his face and say bonjour in the mornings. He was effortlessly mixing in a few words of French in his daily conversations and text messages with Jordan.

The catered dinner party with Laura and Olivia had been moved back an additional week, due to some business travel that arose for the girls. John was fine with that, which gave him time to sink into the French culture and further enjoy others that he met and spoke with at the hotel. He had spent considerable time enjoying the city, attending the theatre, going to museums, and visiting the local shops. He had attended a church service at the *Cathédrale de Notre Dame*, to extend his great appreciation for his faith development and continued grace and inner messaging over the past month.

John had made a full two-day trip to the French Riviera, along the Mediterranean Sea, including time at the beach resorts of Saint-Tropez and Cannes. He then did a separate full day trip to Calais, the Old Town of Calais-Nord, and points further north along the shores of the English Channel. It was as close as he could get to England, without hopping on the ferry and crossing the channel.

During the second week, John made a return stop into Anne's studio to see progress on her latest line of clothes, and sat in on another *Bienvenue diner* plus two other special impromptu dinner parties at the hotel's *lumiere Room*. John was in continuous contact with Anne, Laura and Olivia by text message, along with Jordan, Charley and several of his other old friends. He had seen Arne again at the hotel, and they got together one evening for some dinner and a bottle of wine about two blocks from the hotel.

John was becoming a *Grand Hôtel de lucarne* favorite, and he appreciated their friendship, smiles and continuous great service. The laundry and dry cleaning was delivered in excellent condition, and the meals were like having a special chef in his very own kitchen. John had spared no expense to order top of the line wines, and shared his blessings with all who had become dear to his friendship.

Enzo was an exceptional assistant, and reliable source for anything that John needed or requested. The reservation desk and the hotel staff did everything possible to help John have an enjoyable stay at the hotel. The chief chef had come to know his name, and on occasion would send him a special dinner, course or entrée of some sort. With this extraordinary restaurant on the ground floor of his temporary home, he was never far from a great meal and an exceptional glass of wine.

John enjoyed the sounds of the city bouncing through the rear courtyard, the central fountain area, and the long narrow skylight. He even sat in on a couple hours of conference sessions that were being held at the hotel, learning about entrepreneurship in one and the latest cutting edge technology in another.

This occasion away from the daily grind of life enabled John to continue looking for the unseen, the deeper spiritual balance, and in a sense also helped him refine and reinforce his roots. His personality was already largely formed, but his outlook on the world and his balance in life had been given a chance for much greater depth and refinement. He embraced the opportunity and enjoyed the days as they unfolded. He began to enjoy the simple childlike items as well, such as watching it rain or sitting in the park as the locals fed the pigeons.

John was an authentic American, with English descent and a mix of Welsh, Scottish and Dutch. Born in California, he was given the name Jonathan James Marcomb. His grandparents had arrived at the port of New York in the 1880's, and his father grew up in Manhattan. His mother was from the western part of England, and met his father while she was attending New York University.

The Marcomb's had always been a family of travelers and adventurers, going back to the 18th century, and he was named in part after the Anglo-Irish writer Jonathan Swift, the author of Gulliver's Travels. His middle name was given to him in honor of his grandfather James Marcomb, who had led the difficult voyage and transformation to America.

This current trip to France had touched something deep inside of John, something that he had not expected. He was appreciative of so many different cultures and styles of living, and was enjoying his current time exploring this area of the European continent. Europe, which was essentially the westward-projecting peninsulas of Eurasia, and part of the great landmass that it shared with Asia, included the country of France which was situated as part of the westernmost section of this great landmass. Considering it was neither a peninsula nor an island, France was bordered by a considerable amount water, including the English Channel on the north, the Mediterranean Sea on the south, and the Atlantic Ocean on its entire western border. John had connected with two of these three bodies of water just this week.

John was also rediscovering his interest in the arts, spending time at the Louvre Museum with the Mona Lisa by Leonardo da Vinci, and the sculpture of Venus de milo. He also spent time visiting museum works by the French sculptor Auguste Rodin, the Spanish painter Pablo Picasso, and many others. He spent a few evenings drinking wine under the courtyard skylights at the hotel with local regulars, meeting new guests and engaging with the hotel staff.

John had some definitive classic English traits, and was a blend of his American work ethic, an innovative spirit, and moderated by his more relaxed California mindset and personality. He had a clever sense of humor, and an ability to mix in a fair amount of sarcasm. He loved to search for bargains, but could also not waste a moment making a large purchase for his wife or daughter. He enjoyed asking people about their journeys, and following the details of how it had impacted their lives. Although he had inherited a slight inability to express his emotions, this recent period in Paris and before over the past month had done a great deal to change his mind set about this topic, as he continued his greater balance of blending an emotional balance into his life.

Above all, John had retained his admirable DNA trait of achieving against all odds.

This trip to Paris was the test of a lifetime.

CHAPTER 23

The Small Dome

Enzo assisted John in locating a taxi.

John left the hotel, and raced off to the special catered event that was being arranged by Laura and Olivia. The entire morning in Paris had seen rain, but the afternoon had cleared off and the sun was coming out in plenty of time for the late afternoon event.

The gathering was to be held at a location in the Le Marais section of Paris, in the same district as John's hotel. Le Marais was a historic district in Paris, home to many great buildings of historic and architectural importance. John had walked the streets of this area on many days the past two weeks, weaving through the streets in the 3rd and 4th arrondissements in Paris, visiting museums and cafés.

The Le Marais has long been the aristocratic district of Paris along the right bank of the Seine. It had become the temporary home for John, and except for the late afternoon traffic, would be a very short taxi ride from his hotel. John handed the taxi driver the address for the event.

John arrived at the event location in short order, paid the taxi fare, and entered the building that had a large classical arch above the entry passage. It had a second story arched window above that, with a metal railing in front of it. There was a large classical pediment at the base of the third story roof line, directly symmetrical to the entry. A third floor continued across the building on either side of the pediment, with a steep mansard roof and windows protruding through the slope along the facade.

The open arch brought John into an open-air courtyard, as he passed under the stately passage. Sun filtered into the courtyard from above, with the stone building enclosing it on all four sides. Old cobblestone pavers covered the entire courtyard hardscape area, and landscaping was integrated along the back and two side walls of the courtyard, with windows lining the building wall areas.

"Bonjour." A French gentleman in a black coat greeted John in the courtyard, and took him through an opening along the left face of the courtyard. His name on the lapel said Noah, and John greeted him by that name.

They passed through the arched opening at the left face of the building, which had two doors open wide to the space beyond.

There was a small greeter table just outside the double doors, with name tags laid out on it and a stack of small cards describing the event. John was given a pre-printed name tag with his full name on it, and one of the small white event cards that had black scripted lettering across the front. The card looked familiar to John, as if he had seen it before, but he was occupied with the greetings and enjoying the setting and architecture of the open courtyard and spaces beyond.

Once he had attached his name tag, Noah took John through a small ante-room that had small arched niches surrounding the small room in a segmented circular pattern. Past that, he entered the room which had a nicely scaled medium sized dome at the top. The dome filled the entire room, square at its base, and ending in the perfect circle at the top.

There were some server trays that had been set up around the back-perimeter wall, and some staff in waiter's uniforms preparing a tray to the right-side area that held wine glasses in rows across the top. There were tall, thin tables with rounded tops that had been mixed throughout the main space in a random pattern, so that patrons could set down their wine glasses or plates as they were milling around the room.

"Merci," said John to Noah, after he had fully entered the room. Noah smiled and nodded in approval, and then fanned out his right hand toward the space. This would be the location of the catered event.

John stared at the small white card that was still in his hand.

The print on the card had been centered in a symmetrical layout, and the largest line printed in the middle said *Le petit dôme d'originaux*, in semi-bold italic text.

The main name must have been the name of the room. John thought it extremely interesting to be called *'the small dome of originals'*. This must have been a common gathering space for groups, parties, openings or private events, to gather in with restaurant tables or to get together for small talk.

The small card also listed the building address and city in smaller print below the space name, and the caterer name was stretched below that at the bottom in slightly larger print than the address but smaller than the main name.

John observed the stately room, which was nicely scaled and very unusual. It was large enough for a private standing room only gathering, but not too formal or large to make people feel uncomfortable.

He could hear two girls to the left talking about their favorite breakfast items. The French did not typically eat a large breakfast. There was usually some fruit, a baguette with jam or butter, and coffee or tea, such as what John had ordered on many mornings, but rarely included meat or a heavier breakfast plate such as the English or Americans might prepare.

"Yum," said one girl, about eating croissants for breakfast.

"Yes, but no self-respecting French girl would eat butter on their croissants for breakfast," said the other girl.

"Oh, no, but jam is good, and buttered toast also," said the first girl, "my favorite is having slices of baguette with the freshest jam that you can possibly find."

They mutually determined that it was not the best breakfast for a weight loss program, but they had to be able to justify their indulgence in it for at least one morning each week.

The room was setting up in sort of a *néo-bistrots* setting, but without the formal tables for sitting down like a bistro or bistrot might be arranged. Given that this was a catered event, they had it set up for milling around and eating during small talk. The domed room probably was utilized for a restaurant type table setting for certain events.

Paris, of course, was famous for its dining options. Even a seasoned resident, however, could find it difficult at times to narrow down where to go to dinner some evenings, whether choosing from a neighborhood or area, let alone ranking and narrowing it down to a specific restaurant. Their minds could wander amidst the thriving dining-out neighborhood choices across Paris, including the Montmartre, Le Marais, Bastille or the Grands Boulevards, as well as the Canal Saint-Martin or the Champs-Elysées if there were limitless funds.

John could begin to sense the seafood smells coming from the room beyond the space, as well as a grilling smell of some sort that made you hungry upon first breath.

A waiter brought across a tray with some glasses of champagne, and John selected one from the tray.

John continued looking up and around at the ornamental detail. The building appeared to be from the early to mid 16th century, and the domed room was a beautiful two story structure that concluded with a small dome at the top. Windows were all around a cupola area rising above the small dome. This was a period when the Kingdom of France had been involved in wars in northern Italy, and had brought back to France not just the Renaissance art treasures but also some stylistic ideas. The Renaissance ornament had been draped across the French facades and cornices, which was coming out of the Gothic period in central Europe at that time. France eventually developed into its own unique French Mannerism style, under Henry II and thereafter, as the focus on architecture continued to thrive in France over the many centuries.

A crowd was beginning to form in small pockets across the room, as the late afternoon sun filtered through from the courtyard and the beautiful small dome above. Laura and Olivia had chosen a magnificent setting for a small gathering of this type, and John felt honored to be their friend. The catering activity was in full swing beyond the perimeter tables, with much activity taking place beyond the walls.

The *Parisienne* girls that he knew, of course, were typically late, but John was fine with that. He was one of the primary guests, and didn't want to be the one who was not present when everyone arrived. He was fine that they were delayed, and they had all been sending text messages to him that they were on their way. As usual, they had been delayed by a meeting, or a traffic jam, or some other this or that.

There were a variety of conversations beginning to take place around the room. John was observant of each name on their tag, as he filtered between the small gatherings with his thin flute of champagne.

Sarah and Corrine were determining where the best crêpes could be found in Paris, which are a specialty in the Brittany region of France, according to Sarah. Most locals in Paris had their favorite places for all types of specialty food and other items.

Victor, Nathan and Simon promised themselves a weekend in the countryside. They determined that it was fine to travel to the provinces for work or holiday, but not to live.

Louane was looking for a new place to cut her hair. Her hairdresser had unexpectedly flown off with a wealthy businessman, and she needed to find a new stylist.

The room had almost instantly filled over the next five-minute span, and waiters were bringing across the trays of champagne to the newly arriving guests. Noah had kept his eye on John, and made sure that he felt welcome and had plenty of champagne in his flute. Olivia or Laura must have asked Noah ahead of time to look out for John.

He saw Laura and Olivia entering the domed room, and making their greetings to Noah and some other friends near the entry. Noah pointed across the room in John's direction, and brought the two ladies across to the area that he was standing.

"Hello, John!" said both ladies, and they all exchanged kisses on the cheeks.

"How do you like our quaint *Le petit dôme d'originaux?*" said Laura. "Is it not *magnifique?*"

"It is absolutely perfect!" said John. "You are two of the most creative minds in all of Paris."

"Yes, we love this room," said Olivia, "and decided to have our favorite caterer come to this location today! It is the first time that we combined an event here with catered food. It is one of our favorite gathering places!"

"It is absolutely brilliant, and your guests are having a great time!" responded John. He had noticed that the guests throughout the space were greatly enjoying the setting, as they talked and laughed with most anyone that came into their vicinity.

Suddenly from the left, John was tapped on the arm.

"Bonjour, monsieur, is it you? You are my scarf twin!" said the girl from the bistro.

"Foulard jumeau!" she repeated in French, looking at her girlfriend in amazement.

"You called him your *scarf twin* at the bistro?" asked Alaïa. "Hahahah." It was Alaïa from *la Capelle* in the Latin Quarter, standing next to the girl from the bistro. John could hardly believe that they knew each other.

"You know each other?" asked John in amazement, pointing between the two.

"Yes, we do!" said Alaïa.

"I can't believe you called him your *scarf twin* at the bistro?" repeated Alaïa.

"Yes, she did!" said John, "it is my first time to be a *scarf twin*, and I was truly honored by that distinction!"

"Hahahah," laughed Laura, "I will surely use that phrase in one of my future fashion editorial pieces."

"I am Juliana Dubois," said the bistro girl, not waiting to be introduced.

"Nice to meet you…. Again," said John with a smile.

Juliana was a very creative individual, who loved good humor and always had a unique way of phrasing experiences.

"You are one-of-a-kind, my dear friend," said Alaïa, "and a loyal promoter of my fashion line, although I never knew you were doing it with complete strangers at a bistro full of tourists, hahahah."

Alaia was much more talkative than she had been at the boutique two weeks earlier.

"Yes, you know me, my dear friend," responded Juliana, "I will speak to anyone that will answer me back, hahhaha."

John truly enjoyed these two fast friends, Juliana and Alaïa. On the surface, they had nearly opposite personalities, but their humor, creativity and disarmingly open social banter were exact matches.

"John, it is my distinct pleasure to introduce to you my good friend Andréa," said Juliana. "Andréa is originally from Saint-Émilion where my family is from, and the two of us grew up together."

"Andréa, this is John, a friend of Anne, Laura and Olivia, and my scarf twin!" said Juliana. "We first met in a bistro on the left bank, but John was very surprised at my formal introduction on that day, hahhaha," said Juliana.

"Nice to meet you John," said Andréa, "if you know Juliana and Alaïa, you must be quite a character…. and I mean that only in the best way possible!"

Andrea was cut from the same mold as Juliana and Alaïa.

"I am learning new social graces with these two," laughed John, "and wondering if they all went to the same school as my new friends Anne and Laura!"

"Yes, my dear Andréa", said Laura. "We had quite a dinner party with Mr. Johnhood last week, and he is no saint himself I must tell you, a man of great passion and romanticism is lying beneath that calm and logical exterior!"

"Yes, you are caught again!" said Anne Avé, sneaking up behind John and giving him a hug and kisses on the cheeks.

"John, this is a business associate and dear friend of mine, Louis Durand, he is a financier and fashion consultant," said Anne.

"My pleasure, John, I hope you are enjoying Paris?" asked the stately gentleman.

"I certainly am!" answered John. "It is impossible to not have a good time in Paris with these lovely ladies spicing up my days."

"Yes, indeed, my dear *la soeur*, Mr. John is no saint," continued Laura, getting back to their discussion at the *bienvenue diner* two weeks prior, "and I must tell you, my dear Andréa, we found out what an *américain ace* this gentleman can be, to be sure."

"Where is Arne when I need him?" laughed John. "He would be much better at commenting on my current state of embarrassment."

"Oh, no, mister *dishy*, it is all in good fun, and you wear it very well with a cut of bad boy and a clever mind beneath that calm exterior. We have thoroughly enjoyed getting to know you these past few weeks, and now we have a place to visit in California when we come there very soon after you locate your lovely wife," continued Laura.

193

"Locate your lovely wife?" asked Andréa. "Where is your lovely wife?"

"Well, my dear *la soeur,*" continued Laura, this interesting gentleman is on a romantic and mysterious quest to locate his missing wife, and I am certain that he will find her! I can feel it deep in my spirit!"

"Oh, my goodness," said Andréa, as all three girls stood there with a look of amazement. Juliana, Alaïa and Andréa all collectively asked at the same time what had happened.

Olivia explained for John. "Oh, you have no idea what John has been through, and you would never know it! He is trying to locate his wife who has been missing for over two years, and his search has brought him to Paris!"

"Yes, indeed, my dear Livi," said Laura.

"I heard about your evening at the Plaza, monsieur John," added Anne. "Olivia and Laura told me all about your adventures. I am so impressed at your quest, and we would all like to do anything that we can to help you find your dear wife Mia."

"Amazing," said Louis.

"Yes, indeed," confirmed Laura.

The three friends of Alaïa, Juliana and Andréa stood in amazement, trying to absorb the situation. "How completely stunning," said Alaïa. "You were shopping for some articles in my boutique for your wife, with her missing all the while."

"Yes," said John, "and for my daughter," he continued.

"Was the scarf for your wife?" asked Alaïa.

"Yes, it was," said John.

"I knew that about you," said Alaïa with a smile, remembering the day that John had visited her store. "I knew you had some special women in your life, from the minute that you walked into *la Capelle*," she continued.

"You certainly did," agreed John. "But you didn't spend too much time speaking with me, how did you know?"

"You didn't want anyone speaking with you!" responded Alaïa. "When you came into the store, you looked like you were avoiding an attack."

"Yes, that's true," said John. "I was keeping to myself on that morning."

"Yes, you were," agreed Alaïa. "But I knew all along, you had a look about you that you were on a special mission, and that you had placed part of your life on hold, so we are happy that you are here with us today to support you in your romantic quest."

"Here, here," said Laura, "a toast to John, in his quest to find his Mia Michelle!"

The glasses, which had switched to red wine, all met in cheers and smiles. Juliana and Andréa were supremely intrigued by the news story being laid out by Laura and Alaïa.

"Your wife's name is Mia Michelle?" asked Juliana, never too far from an inquiry.

"Yes," said John, "Michele is her middle name, she is Mia Michelle Girard Marcomb, originally born in France, but has lived with me and my daughter for twenty years in America, at least until two years ago."

"Girard," said Andrea, looking at Alaïa, "don't we know some Girard's?"

"Yes, we do," said Alaïa, "my mother knew some Girard's going back to her days at the Sorbonne, we should check with her if she knew anyone by the name of Mia."

The brochettes and bouchées made the rounds throughout the space.

There was also a selection of verrines and cuilléres.

The *small dome of originals* had a wonderful group of people attending tonight.

Alaïa's business partner Lucas had joined the group, along with Olivia's friends Luca & René which he had seen from across the room at the Plaza Athénée. Michel and Christian had also arrived, the designers from Anne's studio, along with Lina and Jade a few moments later. Anne, Laura, Olivia, Louis, Alaïa, Juliana and Andréa were there, along with Juliana's friend Samuel.

The red wine continued flowing strong, as the group mixed in their delicious finger food and roamed about the room.

"Is your mother still teaching?" asked Olivia to Juliana. "She was always such an accomplished educator."

"Yes, thanks for asking," said Juliana. "She is with St. Catherine's school, and still involved with all her educational and charity work."

"Yes, I know Christine," said Louis. "She is a tireless supporter of children's fundraisers, and a delight to work with on those projects, a real professional with a large heart."

"Those girls are a real dynamic duo, your mums," said Laura. "I always enjoyed getting together with Danielle and Christine for a night of fashion and learning."

"Danielle is a real pro," said Anne. "So many great years at the Sorbonne, she should have her name etched into the building façade. I always loved her symposiums and conferences, even after she stopped teaching full time."

"Thank you," said Alaïa. "My mom is my best friend in the world," she paused, "besides all of you!"

"We have an event coming up this weekend," said Louis. "It is for autism support, along with donations and communication tools for the family, it should be an outstanding opportunity for families dealing with these effects."

"Simply wonderful," said Anne, "and your recent efforts with underprivileged youth put a lot of smiles on their faces. It is remarkable how you have been able to set up an ongoing effort to support those families and children in need. They are learning how to build confidence, and I heard that one found a new position with the skills that they learned? Quite wonderful!"

Anne and Louis could talk all day about the educational charity events and study programs, and Juliana and Alaïa had grown up with it for years watching their mother's careers and working directly with both gifted and special needs children.

Alaïa's business partner, Lucas, shared some humorous stories about customers that had come into the boutique, and Laura recounted some unusual happenings during her trip back to London.

Andréa circled back to the topic about John's wife. Both Juliana and Andréa had been touched by the story, and had their antenna up about what they had heard. Olivia filled them in further about the history of the search, and the three of them gathered for discussion about it.

"Have you checked with the police," asked Andréa.

"Yes," said John. "I went to the police recently, but I need to return and see what they found out and might be willing to share"

"I need to check with my mom and some people at the school," said Juliana.

"That would be great," said Olivia. "Maybe your mom would know of some Girard's or others that may know them."

"I shall give her a call tomorrow morning," said Juliana.

"I also wonder if my mom would know something about it," said Alaïa, still listening into the conversation. "The name Girard caught my attention, and my mother may be able to help me remember how I know the name."

"It is worth an inquiry, to be sure," agreed Olivia.

"What are you discussing, my dear Livi?" asked Laura, joining the group.

"The same topic that we were discussing after our Bordeaux at the Plaza," said Olivia. "Alaïa and Juliana are going to check with their mothers about the school, and Andrea may also have some ideas of people that she may be able to contact for information."

"Saint-Émilion had come up in a couple of different conversations," said John.

"Yes", said Olivia, "and maybe Andréa will be able to inquire with her family and friends this next weekend when she is back home for a few days."

"Yes, I sure will," said Andréa. "French roots run deep, and you never know who might know some family members or friends that could assist with some information."

"Thanks so much!" said John. "I appreciate all of your thoughts and the courtesy of checking with your families and old friends."

"We would love to help, John," said Olivia. "That is why we wanted to get together tonight to meet some new friends that maybe could help."

"And have a couple of good glasses of Bordeaux!" shouted Laura, knowing the importance of both. "But it is our pleasure," continued Laura, "and it was also a good excuse for us to get together with some dear friends that we do not see enough during these busy days of our lives."

"We have enjoyed meeting you, John, my one and only scarf twin!" said Juliana.

"Oh, my goodness," said Alaïa. "I shall never forget your vivacious nature, my dear girl"

"Like no other!" agreed Andréa. "She has been this way since she was about two years of age!"

"Some things never change, thank goodness for that!" said Andréa, who smiled and extended a large hug to her longtime friend.

"I must go," said Alaïa, "but we will all speak again soon. And I will look to see you in *la Capelle* again soon Mr. John, but you should have no worries that I will attack you when you arrive!"

They all kissed on the cheeks, and said goodbye to Alaïa.

Juliana and Andrea moved across the room to speak with a couple of friends and co-workers, and Laura was laughing with Anne and Louis about something that had happened earlier in the day at the studio.

Olivia said to John, "I wanted to tell you, John, but not in front of the crowd."

"What's that?" asked John.

"Well, you know after our get together at the Plaza recently, I ran into a friend the next day that got me thinking about your story. The following night, I had a premonition about her being somewhere nearby. I'm not sure what it means, but I'm usually not wrong when I have thoughts like these come to me. You said that you discussed the case with the police?" confirmed Olivia.

"Yes," said John. "I did meet with them, but they were very protective of releasing any information until they checked with the American Embassy."

"Right," said Olivia. "That is not surprising, but something tells me they know much more than they are telling you. I had a male figure come to me in a dream a few nights back, and he was asking about some woman. You were in the dream, but you were silent and just sort of waiting in the corner. The figure in the dream kept holding up two fingers to me, so I asked a friend of mine with the police force named Philip what he thought that might mean. Philip said that the Préfecture oversees all identification, including passports, and that you should check with them about the records from when she was born. She was born in France, correct?"

"Yes," said John.

"Well," continued Olivia, "he said they will have records from her birth, but they may also have information on her dual citizenship, and maybe this will lead to more information about if she is actually in the country. Philip wondered if the two fingers pointing toward me in the dream meant that you should ask them about her dual citizenship."

"That's very interesting," said John. "I will definitely do that. I had contemplated the fact that she may be a dual citizen, but did not consider that it had any impact on the events that transpired near our home in California. I am scheduled to return to them next week for a follow up meeting."

"OK, good," said Olivia. "Like I said, it may be nothing, but I am usually not wrong when I get a premonition like this."

Olivia continued, "I also have a strong feeling about your conversations tonight with Alaïa, Juliana and Andréa. I could hardly join into the conversation because I was experiencing such a strong vibration about what they were saying. Maybe their families will have more information for you once they check into it."

"You are one magnificent person!" said John. "I am truly honored to call you my friend, and I wish nothing but the greatest of continued success to you and all that you hold dear in life."

"That is so very sweet," said Olivia. "I shall keep in touch with you and shall continue our hope to figure this out."

John made the rounds to say goodbye to Anne, her staff from the studio, and Louis.

He also made a special stop to thank Laura for the special evening and her hard work in setting it all in motion. "You are a dear person, Laura, and may your life continue to be filled with the greatest of successes."

"My pleasure, my dear John," said Laura with a look of deep gratitude, "and I told you from the first moment I knew of it that you shall indeed find your lovely wife, I can feel it in my bones."

"You are a very special person," said John, "and we shall continue to be in touch."

They all kissed on the cheeks, and walked John to the exit.

"I will follow up with Juliana and Andrea tomorrow, and we shall be in touch soon," said Olivia.

"Thanks so much, my dear friend," said John, as he grabbed both of her hands and look her straight in the eyes. "You are a delight!"

Olivia waived toward John and added, "Stop over at the studio tomorrow morning if you want to talk, and maybe I'll have more information by that time."

John had exited through the small entry portal and back out to the open building's open air courtyard.

"I will", said John with a smile, turning back toward Olivia. "We will talk soon."

As John passed by the greeter table, he noticed again the stack of small cards describing the event. He pulled out the card from his pocket and took a closer look at it. This was the card from his dream at the flats in Santa Monica, when he could not read the print. He now knew that the black scripted letters had risen to the surface and said *Le petit dôme d'originaux.*

CHAPTER 24

Saint Catherine's

The morning sun filtered through John's hotel room window, as it had done on many prior mornings in the Le Marais section of Paris.

John had rested very well overnight, although it had taken him a long time to get to sleep the prior evening. His mind had been running through the conversations at the small dome with Juliana and Alaïa, and how they were planning to contact their family members to inquire about the Girard name. He had also been surprised at the introduction to Andréa, and how the trio of families had deep roots together in Saint-Émilion, which was a town that had continued to come up in conversations around John.

John dressed and headed toward the elevator. Exiting into the hotel lobby, he saw Enzo and Zoé chatting near the main reservation counter. Zoé was his favorite reservation desk attendant, and had been the person who kept extending John's reservation at the hotel. She always made a special effort to notify him of special dinners and events that would be occurring at the hotel.

"Bonjour, Mr. Marcomb," they both said in unison, as John entered the front desk reception area.

"Bonjour!" replied John. "Isn't it a beautiful morning!"

The sun was filtering through the doors and windows along the street, and the sky had cleared early on this morning. Both Enzo and Zoé always enjoyed his enthusiasm in the morning, and appreciated the way that he had always treated them as special individuals.

"I'll be back shortly," continued John with a smile. "Can I bring you anything?"

They both knew that John was getting ready to walk down the street to his favorite café, which was part of his normal daily routine.

"Merci, no, Mr. Marcomb," they replied. "But thank you!" added Enzo.

John turned right beyond the hotel entry doors and made his usual walk down the sidewalk to *le patisserie*, saying hello to the locals on his way in.

"Bonjour, Monsieur John. The usual?" asked Nicole, the waitress that had often served him at the café.

"Oui, merci!" said John, "and a petit baguette with jam?"

The usual was a café au lait, extra hot, with a second refill very soon.

John took up his seat near the window and pulled out his smartphone. The streets outside the café window were alive and bustling with activity on that morning, but John was focused on his small device.

He pulled up his maps on the electronic device, and searched for the town of Saint-Émilion.

It was a very small town, located in the southwestern part of France, not far from the Atlantic Ocean, and just outside of the town of Bordeaux.

"Here you are, monsieur," said Nicole.

"Thank you, Nicole," said John.

He began reading about the small town of Saint-Émilion, which was not far from the Bay of Biscay, and slightly inland from Bordeaux.

It was nearly a six-hour drive from Paris, and a total of nearly 600 kilometers. This equated to about 370 miles in America, thought John, trying to get his metric conversation straight in his mind.

John considered the travel possibilities, and searched the internet to see how to best travel to this part of the country. If he were to take the train from Paris to Bordeaux, he could probably rent a car from there and be in Saint-Émilion in about 40 minutes or so after arriving in Bordeaux.

He looked at some train schedules from the Paris stations to see how that might work. The Paris Montparnasse Train Station provided service for intercity TGV trains traveling west and south-west of Paris, and if he were to take this high-speed train, he could be there in about 3 hours, or nearly half the travel time.

That would be the best approach, thought John, to take the high-speed train to Bordeaux and then rent a car and drive the twenty miles east to Saint-Émilion.

Bordeaux was the hub of the famed wine-growing region, and a port city on the Garonne River. It was known for its Gothic Cathédrale Saint-André, the 18th century and 19th-century mansions, and notable art museums including the Musée des Beaux-Arts de Bordeaux. They had beautiful public gardens lining the curving river jetties, as the Garonne River fed into a larger bay, which then connected to the larger Biscay Bay and Atlantic Ocean.

As John was reading about the history of Bordeaux, he received a text message from Olivia. She was updating him that Juliana had placed a call to her mother, and Olivia should know more soon.

John responded to the text message with his thanks, and asked if he should stop over to the studio in a couple of hours.

Olivia responded, "Oui, of course, I will be at the studio 11am."

John looked up to see his coffee refill, and continued reading about Saint-Émilion and looking at the map. Nicole knew his regular routine, and always left him undisturbed when he was deep in thought at one of the café window tables.

John redirected his reading interest toward Saint-Émilion. The small town and surrounding area appeared to be exceptionally beautiful, and the region was one of the principal red wine areas of Bordeaux. The region was much smaller than the Médoc, but was also near the Graves area and directly adjoined the Pomerol. Together, these four regions were the primary red wine areas of Bordeaux. Evidently, the primary grape varieties used were the Merlot and Cabernet Franc, with smaller amounts of Cabernet Sauvignon being used by some châteaux.

John was fascinated with the small town, the Bordeaux region, and its history. He read about how Saint-Émilion's history had gone back to prehistoric times, with attractive Romanesque churches and ruins extending along the steep and narrow streets. The Romans had planted vineyards as early as the 2nd century. The town was named after the monk Émilion, who settled into a hermitage in the 8th century, and it was the monks who followed him that started up the commercial wine production in the area.

John considered a trip to southwest France. He had already been to the Mediterranean Sea and the English Channel recently, so why not check out the Bay of Biscay near the Atlantic Ocean? As Jordan had said, at least he would get in a good vacation while in France.

Saint-Émilion appeared to be a place with great character and charm, a deep history, and some very interesting medieval architecture. John had always enjoyed visiting the vineyards in California, and this would be a very fascinating region to explore.

John said goodbye to Nicole, waived toward some of the locals, and departed for the hotel. He always left Nicole a large tip. She was a young mother, and could use the extra income to pay her bills and take care of her little girl.

John passed into the hotel lobby, and confirmed with Enzo about the best way to travel to the Bordeaux region. He returned to his hotel room to continue reading his mystery novel, and settled into his favorite chair by the window. The glass casement windows were fully open, and the morning sun continued to filter throughout the room.

At about 10:30am, John departed the hotel and landed in a taxi, where he headed toward Anne's studio near Avenue Montaigne. He arrived at the studio, passed by the Anne Avé name on the glass entry doors, and took the elevator to the 3rd floor.

"Bonjour," said the receptionist Elisa. "Please go in, they are all gathered at the design table this morning."

"Merci, Elisa," said John, as he made his way into the main studio room.

Anne came over with shoulder hug and kisses on the cheeks.

"You have become a regular part of our team!" said Anne. "If you don't watch out, I will hire you directly to help us with our business affairs and you will need to become a permanent French citizen!"

John waived at Olivia across the room, who was talking on the telephone.

"That would probably be an offer that I couldn't refuse," said John, with wry grin toward Lina, who had just joined them. John knew that Anne was a great promoter.

"No, really!" repeated Anne. "I don't say too many things that I don't mean, my new friend."

Lina looked at John, and tilted her head forward in agreement.

"That's very nice," said John. "Maybe someday that could work out. You would certainly be a magnificent person to work with and for."

Anne gave him another side hug, as she latched both hands to his upper right arm in a manner of kind friendship as she smiled toward Lina.

Olivia hung up the phone and came scurrying across the office toward John.

"John, I have more news, both Juliana and Alaïa have been able to connect with their families. Christine and Danielle were both very surprised at the stories the girls were telling them, especially when they mentioned the name of Girard, so both Alaïa and Juliana thought maybe you should go over to the school and speak with them directly about your family."

Olivia filled in the group with the latest news. The ever-social Juliana had called her mother Christine about John first thing that morning. Also, Alaïa had been sending text messages to her mother

Danielle, while she was setting up this morning at the *la Capelle* boutique.

"That's wonderful!" said John.

"Yes, according to Juliana," Olivia continued, "Christine was a little confused, but maybe it is because they don't get American visitors very often. The good news is that she was open minded to meeting with you and seeing if she could help."

"What else did they say?" asked John, wondering how they might have described such an event.

"That's about it," continued Olivia. "Alaïa told her mom that you were a great guy. She also told her that you were friends with Anne and me, and that you could be trusted to meet with her."

"That's very nice," said John. "Where is the school located?"

"I'll get you the name and address. Why don't you go over to the school and meet with Christine, and I will be there soon after I meet with Anne and the team on some new design concepts."

"Sounds great," responded John. "I will do that."

Olivia located a piece of paper of sticky backed paper, and wrote down the school name and address for John.

She also added a phone number for Alaïa's mother Danielle on the back of the paper, and handed it to him.

"Many thanks to you all," said John. "I owe all of you a very exceptional dinner, some theatre tickets, and many hours of pro bono work for all that you have done for me!"

"Not to worry, my dear John," said Anne. "We are happy to help. Go over to the school, and be sure to let us know what you find out!"

"Yes," agreed Olivia. "I will stop over to see you after we finish our team design meeting."

Olivia and Anne gave John kisses on the cheeks, and Anne grabbed his upper right arm again in a friendly manner. "Good luck to you," she said, "we shall be praying for your safe journey, and know that somehow this will all work out for you."

"Merci," said John, appreciating this great kindness from Anne.

Anne was a person who was busy with many things, but always took the time to extend an extra level of kindness to everyone she knew. She could make most every individual feel as if they were the most important person on earth. Like all humans, thought John, Anne probably had her flaws, but this was not one of them.

Olivia walked with John toward the studio exit.

"Alaïa will take care of everything with Danielle," said Olivia.

She briefly paused, and then continued, "Christine can get a little nervous sometimes if she doesn't understand what is going on, but she is very nice and a great educator."

John listened intently to the personality descriptions from Olivia.

"But Danielle," she continued, "is both very calm and intelligent, and will know how to handle the situation. If you cannot find anyone to speak with at the school, be sure to use this number and call Danielle, and I am sure that she would meet with you based on Alaïa's recommendation. I will also try to give her a call after my meeting here."

"Many thanks, my dear girl," said John, "I'll meet you over there later."

"Oh, and one more thing," continued Olivia, in a softer voice than before, "I didn't want to mention this in front of the entire group, but Alaïa just told me that there may be a girl with the last name of Girard that works at the school. Maybe this will be a connection of some type to your family. You might ask Christine about her when you get to the school."

"Oh, my goodness," said John, looking through the double glass entry doors and beyond into space.

They looked at each other in amazement.

"Thank you, dear," were the only words that John could find to respond with. Olivia's kindness, insight and resolute determination to help him was extremely touching.

"I'll be there soon," said Olivia, nodding her head forward.

John took the elevator back down to the building lobby, and walked two blocks toward the main avenue. He jumped into a taxi along Avenue Montaigne, and headed across town toward the school. It would be about a 35-minute drive to the school. John settled in to enjoy the scenery.

They crossed over the Seine River, and took the Boulevard Périphérique ring road around Paris toward the west. They were heading toward the Hauts-de-Seine, which was a middle and upper class group of neighborhoods directly to the west of Paris, covering the western inner suburbs.

As they approached a tree lined street near a residential area in Hauts-de-Seine, John saw a sign up ahead with the words *Saint Catherine's Catholic School*. It had been placed on the corner of the residential street intersection, and was surrounded by lavish landscaping and some trees draping above it. Saint Catherine's was a private school, and sat on a large acreage of land within this beautiful western suburb of Paris.

The taxi pulled up into the main circular drive of the school. John paid the taxi fare and closed the door.

The school contained a variety of buildings extending across and into the site, with a uniform architecture and two story scale to most buildings. There were quaint walkways and landscaped areas between each of the buildings, with tall light poles along each of the sidewalk areas. John could see a building toward the right side that appeared to be a chapel, and there was a centrally arranged set of administration offices directly in front of him at the front of the property.

John continued observing the attractive school setting. He noticed a statue of *Saint Catherine* to the right side of the main entry, in front of the main administration building. It was stationed within a well-trimmed landscaped area, and had a small waterfall in front of it. There was a large metal gate just beyond the statue area, with a wider sidewalk that led toward the chapel building beyond.

John looked at the first main building, and entered the door near the sign that said *Administration de l'école.*

"Bonjour," said the woman at the front administration desk. "May I help you?"

"Oui," said John. "I was hoping to speak with Christine, is she here today?"

John signed the sheet on top of the front counter, which was required of all visitors to the school.

"Christine is teaching a class right now, is there something that I can assist with?" responded the girl.

The woman's name on her desk plate said Adrienne Malveaux.

"Do you know when she will be free?" asked John. "Her daughter, Juliana, suggested that I come and meet with her."

"Oh, I see," said Adrienne. "Let me check with Christine, and I will see what I can arrange."

"Merci," said John, with a warm smile.

Adrienne exited to the back of the space, and through a door to an adjoining hallway.

John took a seat in the reception area, and looked around the room. There were some old black and white photographs stacked together on one wall, and a school trophy case covering a second wall.

Adrienne returned to the front office area. "Christine says that she will be done in about twenty minutes. Would you like to wait for her?"

"Yes, of course, merci," said John.

Adrienne had an interesting look on her face. John was not quite sure what it meant, but was happy to hear that Christine was available for a meeting.

"You are an American?" asked Adrienne.

"Yes," said John. "I am."

Adrienne continued to stare in his direction, as she sat in her desk chair just beyond the front administration counter.

"Can I get you some coffee?" asked Adrienne, still checking him out.

"No, I'm fine, merci," said John. "I will just read my book until Christine is free."

John absorbed himself in his book. A couple of people came and left from the administration reception area, as Adrienne periodically looked over in his direction. The time passed quickly, as John read his book and patiently waited.

"Hello, my name is Christine." A voice had come unexpectedly from his left side.

"Oh, yes, hello Christine. My name is John Marcomb. We seem to have some mutual friends, and I wondered if we could meet for a few minutes," said John, as he stood to greet her.

John continued, "They thought that you might be able to help me look for a family member."

"Sure," said Christine. "I don't have much time to meet today, but is there anything that I can answer for you now?"

Christine did not seem to be interested in offering a private room to discuss his questions, and did not seem to mind that Adrienne was listening to their conversation.

John looked over at Adrienne.

The front door of the administration building suddenly opened, and they saw Louis Durand entering the reception area. It was Anne's friend from the small dome party.

"Bonjour," said Louis in a bellowing voice.

"Oh, John!" Louis also added with a surprise in his voice. "What brings you here?"

"You know him?" asked Christine.

"Oh, yes," said Louis. "We met at *Le petit dôme d'originaux.* John is a friend of Anne, Olivia and your daughter Juliana."

Louis was a positive influence on Christine's skepticism. He was a stately gentleman, who appeared to be well-respected at the school.

"So, what did you need from me, monsieur?" Christine asked. "I have another class that I need to teach now."

John looked around and noticed that everyone was waiting for his answer.

"Juliana told me that you wanted to inquire about a family member?" she continued, with a somewhat protective and impatient tone of voice.

"Yes," said John, looking toward Louis, who was still listening to the conversation.

John was not sure if he would ever have a chance to speak with her again, so he just decided to come out with it.

"Yes," he repeated, "I am looking for a family member, and her maiden name is Girard. Olivia had mentioned that you might have someone working at the school by that name? Her first name is Mia."

The room went quiet for a moment, as Christine looked over at Adrienne.

"Well, yes, we do know someone by the name of Girard, but her first name is not Mia," continued Christine with her protective tone. She had crossed her arms and was trying to understand where John was going with this.

Adrienne had been sitting quietly and not saying much.

Christine looked toward Adrienne. "Is Aimee here today?" she asked.

"Aimee?" asked John.

"Yes, we have an Aimee Girard that works here," said Christine, "but I've been busy all morning and haven't seen her today."

"Why are you searching for her?" continued Christine.

"She left on vacation," said Adrienne, "and she won't return for a while I think."

Christine looked toward Adrienne with a slight look of bewilderment.

John tried to assemble the messages.

"That's funny," said Louis, "we just spoke on the phone yesterday about the charity event this weekend, and she said she would meet me here to today to go through some details."

"Are you sure she left for vacation?" Louis inquired of Adrienne. "Where did she go?"

Adrienne confirmed to Louis and Christine that Aimee had gone on vacation, but was not offering any additional details.

Christine asked John again, with a protective voice, "Why are you searching for her?"

"Well, I'm confused by the name Aimee," said John. "Maybe this is a distant relative of the person that I am searching for."

"Yes, maybe," said Christine.

Christine excused herself for a minute, and went to the corner of the office to make a phone call.

After a couple minutes, she returned. "I need to get back to my classroom now, but I spoke with Danielle. She could meet you at the local coffee shop to maybe help you with your inquiry. Would you like to meet with Danielle?"

"Yes, of course," said John. "Where is the café?

"Adrienne can get you the information," said Christine. "Good luck to you, John." Christine swiftly left the administration building for her classroom.

Adrienne wrote down the coffee shop name and address for John, and reached for the telephone to call a taxi.

"I can drop you over there," said Louis. "Come with me, John, it is not too far from the school."

"Thanks, Louis," said Adrienne, as they departed the administration building.

"That is so confusing," said Louis, as John closed the car door on the passenger side. "I just spoke with her yesterday about meeting me here today. It is unlike her to miss a meeting, without letting me know that the schedule has changed."

Louis dropped John at the coffee shop, and continued back to Paris.

CHAPTER 25

Michel's Café

John walked into Michel's Café, and took a table by the window.

Olivia sent John a text message that she had spoken with Danielle, and will also plan to meet them at the café. She had been delayed with a new meeting, but was on her way now.

Michel's was a small corner café, serving breakfast, a light lunch, and a casual dinner. It was a place for locals to meet, hang out and work. It was part of a two-story building on a light commercial corner, set mostly in a residential neighborhood. Vines were growing up the two sides of the building facing the streets, and small metal chairs and tables lined the sidewalk in each perpendicular direction from the corner. A small canopy covered the entry, and the local café was beginning to get very busy with a lunch crowd.

John continued texting with Olivia, who was making her way around the Périph in the company car service.

He updated her about the somewhat bizarre meeting with Christine, and hoped that the meeting with Danielle might go better.

John ordered some coffee, opened his book, and waited for Danielle to arrive.

A small group of college students had taken a table next to John, which reminded him of Jordan. He decided to update her by text message with some of the latest events of the day. She would receive the updates when morning arrived in California.

"Are you John?" a voice came from his right side and slightly behind him, in the aisle near his table.

"Yes," said John, as he raised up from the chair. "You must be Danielle."

"Yes, I am," she said. "It is a pleasure to meet you."

"Merci," said John. "I am honored that you have agreed to meet with me."

"It is no problem, John, I am happy to assist," responded Danielle.

Danielle ordered some coffee from the waiter, waiving toward him from across the room as if she had done it a hundred times at this café.

"I appreciate your time," he continued, "and I believe you know that Olivia is also on her way here."

"Yes, I spoke with Olivia," confirmed Danielle.

"I really don't know if there is anything that I can help you with," she continued, taking a seat directly across from John at the table, "but you certainly have developed a loyal following during your short time in Paris, and I wanted to come and meet you."

Danielle took a moment to study John from across the table, as the waiter arrived without delay. She stirred in her cream, and watched his response to her arrival.

Danielle began with some small talk, seemingly wanting to know more about his background before Olivia arrived.

"Where are you from, in America?" asked Danielle.

"California," responded John. "Southern California."

"And what is your last name?" she continued.

"My surname is Marcomb," he responded, trying to be as cooperative as possible. "My full name is John James Marcomb." These were all natural questions, thought John, and less intimidating than being a trial witness.

Danielle appeared to be interested in his life, and continued asking John some detailed questions about his background. She was very inquisitive, much like you would expect a good educator to be, but in a more social way than some might approach it. She appeared to be focusing on understanding more about his character and mindset. John was very patient with her inquiries, and assumed that she may have some reason for asking. He answered by describing some of the adventures and day trips that had taken place since he had arrived in Paris, what he did for a living, and what the neighborhood looked like in the area where he lived.

"Bonjour, sorry I am late!" said Olivia, bouncing into the seat next to John near the window. Kisses all around, and both John and Danielle were truly happy to see Olivia.

"You have such an infectiously wonderful spirit," said Danielle. "I am so happy that my daughter knows you, and appreciative of the way that you have always been a blessing to our family."

John smiled toward Danielle, and looked at Olivia.

'How sweet, my dear Danielle," Olivia responded. "You know how much I love you and your family. You and Alaïa have always been there for me, whenever I have needed your support. I think the world of you both."

John sensed that Danielle had always trusted Olivia.

Danielle and Olivia spoke about Alaïa, her morning at *la capelle* boutique, and that she had called Danielle that morning for her to consider meeting with Olivia and John.

"She is an incredible girl, and supremely creative," added John.

"I would trust Alaïa with my life," said Danielle. "She has spoken very highly of you, John, and she is rarely wrong when she makes a recommendation about someone."

"That's very nice of her to say," responded John. "She certainly does have a sixth sense about many things."

"There's nobody better," agreed Olivia. "She is talented and intelligent, just like her mother!"

Danielle smiled toward Olivia, with a look of quiet appreciation.

"So, what can I help you with today?" asked Danielle, looking generally in the direction of both John and Olivia.

"I don't know any Marcomb's," she continued, "so I am not sure how much help I can be, but I am told that you wanted to discuss your family?" The second question was directed more toward John.

"Yes," said John, "we wanted to check with you about my wife's family, and ultimately I am here in France to try and locate my wife. She disappeared from us about two years ago, and we didn't know what had happened. The police could not solve the mystery, and it continues to be a cold case in America. I had nearly given up on it, but a series of recent experiences and clues has led me to Paris, in a final effort to see if she is maybe alive and living somewhere in this country. Olivia, Anne, Laura and others have been extremely instrumental in leading us to this point today, when I went to the school. My wife's maiden name is Girard, and they said that someone by that name worked there, but she had a different given name and she had suddenly left on vacation, so I had no way of speaking with her. Alaïa had suggested that I meet with you about this. Christine seemed distracted and too busy to meet today, so she apparently also called you about getting together."

"Well, my goodness," said Danielle. "That is quite a journey. I am very touched by your commitment to locate your wife, and it must have been a terrifying two-year period of your life. You have such a calm demeanor, on the surface nobody would ever know that you are going through such an experience."

"I know!" agreed Olivia. "Laura and I discussed this same thing last week at the Plaza. John is a special person, indeed."

"Thank you," said John, looking toward Olivia and then back to Danielle.

John continued with his quest, "To put it simply, the girl that I am looking for is my wife, and her name is Mia. Her maiden name is Girard, and I was hoping that the Girard girl from the school might be a distant relative of some sort that could help me with my search."

Danielle listened in silence, absorbing the romantic tale.

"Now I understand why Olivia, Anne and Laura have been so interested in helping you," Danielle finally conveyed.

John looked at her with appreciation of her understanding.

"It is a remarkable situation," said Danielle, looking toward John with respect, "and I admire your courage and resolve for following through on it to a place that is very far from your home town." She glanced toward Olivia in amazement.

Olivia looked back toward Danielle and nodded her head up and down.

John reached into his pocket and showed Danielle a picture of him with Mia and Jordan.

"This is my daughter, Jordan," he said, "and this is her mother Mia, my wife."

John noticed a small teardrop coming down the left cheek of Danielle. "You have a daughter also," she said, more in the form of a statement than a question.

"Did Christine see this photo?" asked Danielle after a long pause.

"No," said John. "She didn't seem terribly interested in meeting with me, or maybe she was just too busy today, so we never got around to looking at any pictures or describing the situation. Anne, Laura and Olivia have seen the photo, but nobody yet at the school."

Danielle continued to have new tears rolling down her left check, slightly more than before. Olivia and John looked at each other, and then back toward Danielle.

"Are you OK, my dear?" asked Olivia.

"Yes," she said, trying to compose her words.

After a long pause, Danielle said, "I have known Mia for many years."

"Excuse me?" asked John, with a puzzling look on his face.

"I noticed that you called her Mia?" he continued.

"Yes, continued Danielle, "I know her by that name. When she was in college, she had been given the nickname of 'Ami' by someone, which was just the letters 'Mia' flipped around. We were being silly one night in a café about it, but the nickname stuck, and people began knowing her as Ami, and in some cases spelled it Aimee. That is why they didn't know her given name at the school, very few people here know her full history back to college."

John stared at Danielle in a shocked state of silence.

"Wow," said Olivia, "so that IS her!"

"Yes, said Danielle, "that is Mia Michele Girard who works at the school, the person in your photograph."

They all sat in silence, as Danielle wiped away the tears.

"You see," she continued, "I didn't know that Mia was married until just now. Mia had come back to France one day a couple of years ago. At the time, we figured that she was just wanting to live in France, and to reconnect with her old friends. I found her a job at the school through my friend Christine, and Christine allowed Mia to come and live with her in a separate house on their property. I suspected after a while that Mia had confronted some difficulty in her life, because she was having trouble with large parts of her memory."

John and Olivia let her continue.

Danielle had become a fashion icon and professor at the University, who had led the University's work study program for several years. This had followed Danielle's own work study experiences back in her college days, when she first met Mia as a fellow student and friend.

"We originally knew each other during her work study program here in Paris. I didn't know much at all about her life after she left France, so I didn't know that she was married with a daughter. I just assumed that she had returned to live in Paris because she liked it, since she did not mention having any spouse or family. We ran into each other at a school charity event nearly two years ago, that had been sponsored in association with the Sorbonne, where we attended school together. Her memory of our life in college was as if we had never lost a minute of time, and we reminisced and talked about the old days in college. It took me a long time to realize that maybe she had some type of traumatic event, because there were large sections of her memory that had waned. It took Mia over a year to try and explain it to me, and she would always say that she didn't know how to get it back. She had even lost her basic identification papers, and couldn't remember where they had gone, so we had to help her get a new French passport. Since she had been born in France, we were able to get her the proper paperwork so that she could work at the school with Christine."

"Oh, my goodness," responded Olivia, "you just never know when you get up in the morning what a new day might bring!"

John was still sitting there in silence. He was mulling over the incredible news that Danielle had just delivered. He was extremely happy that she was verified to be alive, but also somewhat concerned that she might not remember him. Why had she left town so suddenly?

He finally got out a question. "Why didn't Christine admit that she knew the name Mia?"

"I don't know," answered Danielle. "When I spoke with her earlier today, she was scared and confused. Juliana had called with so much excitement about somebody looking for a Girard family friend, but Christine took it in a very different way. She didn't want her life to change, and more than that, she was afraid that Mia might be in danger. Christine is a good person, but not very good with change. Mia has been living with her for two years. When you came to the school today, she must have been protective and concerned about her safety, so as a result was reluctant to admit her real name. Nobody else there knows her by the name of Mia."

"So, you spoke with Christine about it this morning?" asked Olivia.

"Yes," said Danielle, "I had heard from Alaïa that John was from California, and I knew that Mia was from California before she came to college in Paris, but I didn't know anything about the rest of the story."

"Mia had never mentioned the name Marcomb," Danielle continued, "but now I see why. Maybe that whole period of her life had been compromised as part of her traumatic experience. I also never knew she had a daughter. I would love to help get all of you reunited."

The tears continued more fully down both of Danielle's cheeks, as John and Olivia grabbed some new napkins for her use.

John gave her some extra time to absorb everything and gather her emotions.

"Christine did not seem to be aware that she had left town on vacation, did you know anything about that?" asked John.

"Yes, why did she suddenly leave town?" asked Olivia, wondering the same thing.

"Christine was so upset and full of concern after speaking with Juliana, so I called Mia to speak with her about it," responded Danielle. "I was the one that informed Mia, and suggested that maybe she should travel out of town for a while until we could determine who might be looking for her. I think Christine was teaching her morning class when I spoke with Mia, so she might not have known what happened next."

"I do feel like I know you," said John, letting Danielle further wipe away her tears.

Danielle looked across at John with some curiosity.

"Yes," continued John. "I realize that there is no way for you to know me, but I do feel like I know you."

Danielle appreciated the earnest tone in John's voice, and continued to listen.

"Mia used to speak about you," continued John. "She would talk about the Sorbonne, the year of work following graduation, and how much love and respect she had for you."

Danielle looked over at Olivia, as both continued to listen.

John continued, "I believe that the two of you lost contact right before Mia and I met in New York. She always spoke very fondly of you, and often mentioned how she wanted to return to France someday soon for a return visit. As it turned out, the work careers got in the way, and then we had our daughter Jordan, and life tends to get in the way even with the best of intentions."

"Yes," agreed Danielle. "That can happen."

"So, she never could get that trip scheduled," continued John, "and eventually a person begins to wonder if the original friendship could ever be the same, and maybe the friend had moved on and would be less interested in getting together again."

"I understand that," said Danielle, nodding her head up and down.

They both sat in silence for a moment, as Danielle remembered back to an earlier time.

"As you are aware, I have a daughter of my own," said Danielle, breaking the silence. "She is a few years older than Jordan, but I remember how difficult it was during the early years, trying to figure out how to be a mother and still get everything else done during the day."

"You have done a magnificent job, and what an enormously talented person she is. I enjoyed seeing her boutique in the Latin Quarter. Little did I know where it would all lead," said John.

"Yes, it is a very small world," agreed Olivia, looking toward John. "I just couldn't believe that you had met Alaïa and then also ran into Juliana on the very same day!"

"Like I mentioned earlier," said Danielle, "Alaïa has spoken very highly of you, and she is rarely wrong when she makes a recommendation about someone. I was somewhat concerned about what Christine had been saying this morning, but Alaïa is the reason that I agreed to come here today."

"That's very nice of her. Such a talent, and very creative," said John. "When I saw the scarf that she had designed, it reminded me so much of Mia that I put it in my grip and would not let it go for the entire day," he added with a large smile.

"Yes!" laughed Olivia, "It was all crumpled up in his hands, but it looked so familiar and I wondered where he bought it. Had he not been carrying around Alaïa's scarf all day, we might never have connected the two of you together."

"Olivia is a very humble person," commented John.

"Yes, she is," agreed Danielle.

"I might have been carrying around the scarf, but Olivia was the one that noticed it and then miraculously knew the designer!" said John.

"That sounds like Olivia," said Danielle. "She is so talented and so humble about it. Anne has a real gem in her, and is lucky to have such a loyal and talented girl running the operations."

"You both are too kind, and don't forget that I am sitting right here while you are embarrassing me!" said Olivia.

"It is all well-deserved," said John. "You have a selflessness and a great joy in helping people succeed. I hope that those blessings are returned to you seven-fold during your lifetime."

"Without a doubt," agreed Danielle, "you are an authentic and cherished friend."

"Oh, enough about me!" said Olivia, more than a little embarrassed at the kindness lavished on her.

"Tell me about Jordan, would you?" asked Danielle with a smile, changing the conversation back to the photograph in John's hand. "Is she as sweet and creative as her wonderful mother?"

"They are exactly alike," said John, "both are beautiful, intelligent, kind and creative. Jordan has the same fashion sensibilities as Mia, and I am very proud of her hard work and the way that she builds and maintains friendships. She dearly misses her mother, but she is one of the main reasons that I decided to come to Paris."

"It is quite an escapade!" agreed Danielle, "you are full of faith, a prisoner of hope, and a constitution of courage!"

"Yes, he is," agreed Olivia. "His story to Laura and I one evening left us talking about it for hours, and that is when we planned the party to have Alaïa attend. It is remarkable to me that we are sitting here today with you Danielle, and you have known Mia for over twenty years!"

"Life has an interesting way of working out," said Danielle, "but it sounds to me like we would not all be sitting here today if it were not for your kind soul, my dear girl," she said, looking at Olivia.

"Here, here," said John, raising his empty coffee cup for a toast. "That is the absolute truth. Olivia's connected to people and to her own inner spirit was the pivotal link in bringing us all together."

"Merci," Olivia said modestly.

"And it was Anne Avé, at the hotel dinner party," continued John, "who invited me to the studio to meet Olivia, so she was also instrumental in bringing us together today." John was always willing to give credit where it was due.

"I've known Anne for years," said Danielle, "and there is nobody better than her for extending a kind and generous helping hand."

"Without question," agreed Olivia.

"Can I ask one more thing?" John requested.

"Of course," said Danielle.

"At the risk of inquiring about the obvious, do you know where Mia went?" said John.

There was a long pause by Danielle, who had surely anticipated that this question would eventually be coming her way. She looked out through the café window near their table, and slightly squinted her eyes, as if the spirits were guiding her to an answer. Maybe she had to be fully sure that she trusted him, thought John, before she would share this final detail. Her eyes eventually came back into the café, as she looked toward Olivia, and then across to John.

"She left for Saint-Émilion," she finally stated, in a short sentence with full conviction.

John sat back in his chair and looked up toward the café ceiling.

"Saint-Émilion!" repeated Olivia. "Why of course! That would be a natural place for her to go."

"Yes," agreed Danielle. "She has family there, and of course Alaïa and I come from a long line of people with connections to the area."

"What do you know about her family in Saint-Émilion?" asked John.

"Not much, really, we have never met," said Danielle. "But I do know that it is the group on Mia's mother's side of the family."

"The Guerin family?" asked John.

"Yes, that's it, the Guerin's," said Danielle.

John thought about his meeting with the two police officers, and that they had asked questions about this side of the family.

"The police had asked me about the Guerin's, but I didn't make the association at the time that they would be connected to this event in any way. I never met her grandparents on her mother's side, and only generally knew about them," he said.

Olivia thought about her friend Philip at the police station, "Maybe Philip will be able to help us out with some more information about them," said Olivia.

"Yes, that would be very helpful," agreed John.

"I spoke with Andréa's mother about two days ago," offered Danielle, "and she mentioned that Andréa might be down there this weekend. Have you met Andréa?"

"Yes, I met Andréa," said John. "She is a very nice girl."

"Yes," said Olivia, "she did mention that at the small dome party, but I will confirm with her again about the trip for this weekend."

"Andréa will be able to help you if she can," said Danielle. "She is a very dependable girl, and been a close friend of Alaïa for many years."

"That would be fantastic," said John. "I will plan a trip to Saint-Émilion right away to look for her," continued John, "and will plan to check in with Andréa this weekend."

"Good luck, John, and please let me know what you find out. You have my phone number, correct?" asked Danielle.

"Yes, I do," said John, "and thank you so much for your insight today and trusting me with this critical information about your long-time friend. I can assure you that we have a positive mutual interest in finding her, and I am so greatly appreciative of your support and understanding of the situation."

"It is a pleasure to assist," said Danielle, "and yes, I do trust you."

"I also want to thank you," said John, as he rose from the chair, "from the bottom of my heart, for helping her when she needed you most. Your assistance in finding her a job, helping her to get a passport, and most of all being there as her cherished friend. I cannot thank you enough for all that you have done to love and support her."

"That is very kind, my dear man, and I wish you safe travels in locating her this weekend. I will be here to help in any way that I can, and if I happen to see her before you do I will arrange for us to all get together at once," said Danielle.

"Merci, Danielle." John kissed her on both cheeks, and then gave her a long shoulder hug with both hands gripped tightly toward her upper arms.

"Bless you," said John into her ear, as he prepared to exit the café. "My daughter and I are greatly appreciative."

"Goodbye, my dear girl," said Olivia to Danielle, as they kissed and embraced at the table.

John and Olivia found a taxi nearby, and headed back toward Paris.

Danielle had planned to stay behind for a few minutes to collect her thoughts. After John had mentioned his daughter again, a new strand of tears began to form down her left cheek area.

CHAPTER 26

Officer Moreau

John and Olivia rode in the taxi through Hauts-de-Seine, winding through the back streets of the western inner suburbs, and connecting into the Périph to the east.

"When are you scheduled to meet with the police again?" asked Olivia.

"Not until next week," said John.

Olivia grabbed her smartphone, and filtered through the directory. She located what she was looking for, and pushed on the screen.

"Philip, it's Olivia," she said on the telephone. "How are you today?"

John could only hear one half of the phone conversation.

"Can you do me a favor?" she continued.

"Oui, oui," she said, "for the case I spoke with you about, oui, oui. It is John Marcomb. Can you call the officer on John's case, and see if he can speak with her today? Oui, oui, we have some new information about where she might be, and he needs to travel to the province right away. Oui, oui, he could use a police update as soon as possible."

She pulled her phone to the side, and looked over toward John. "What was the case officer's name?" she asked John.

"Officer Moreau," he said.

"It is Officer Moreau," she continued, "Could you arrange for John to call her today? He needs to leave town for a few days, and needs to know if they have found any new information."

"OK, merci," she said, and ended the call.

"Philip will call me back," she said to John.

John loved her spirit and initiative.

He watched the cars weaving on both sides of them, as they raced down the Périph toward the east. John and Olivia recapped the meeting with Danielle.

The phone rang and Olivia answered.

"Oui, yes, oui," said Olivia. "Magnifique! Oui, I will have him do that, what is the number. She scrambled for a piece of paper and a pen in her small designer purse. "OK, go ahead," she said, as she scratched down some numbers. "Oui, merci Philip! You are the best. Oui, oui, merci." Olivia ended the call.

"OK, John, Officer Moreau will be back at her desk in about 45 minutes, so that would be about 2:30pm, and you can call her directly and find out if there is any new information. Philip says that they have finished their initial review and believes that they have some good new information that they can share with you," she said.

"That's wonderful," he said, looking at the time stamp on his phone. "Merci, I will call her at 2:30pm. We should be at the hotel by then."

They continued discussing Danielle, and how much they both appreciated her assistance. Olivia recounted her extreme surprise when she heard that the girl at the school was Mia, and was very happy for John.

"You must be thrilled!" she said.

"Yes, I still can hardly believe it!" responded John. "I just hope that she remembers me," he continued.

"Isn't it a blessing! agreed Olivia, focusing on the positive part of the message. "You will find her! It will all work out!" confirmed Olivia, without the slightest doubt in her voice.

"Yes, I am thrilled beyond words to know that she is alive, and where I might find her!" said John. "That is about the last thing that I expected to hear when I woke up this morning!"

"It is SO exciting," she agreed. "When are you leaving for Saint-Émilion?"

"Probably early tomorrow morning," he said. "I will let you know."

"OK, please do, and let me know what Officer Moreau has to offer," she said. "I am sure that they will be of assistance if they are able to do so. Philip will make sure of it!"

"I will," said John, "I will. Thank goodness for Philip."

Inside his mind, John was also thinking, "thank goodness for Olivia."

The taxi crossed back over the Seine River and into the heart of Paris, finally turning down the street of the hotel. John prepared to exit.

"Call me!" said Olivia, as they pulled up in front of the hotel. "You can rent a car when you get to Bordeaux," she advised, "and then drive across to Saint-Émilion."

"OK, Olivia, I will call you later tonight, merci beaucoup!" They kissed and John closed the taxi door. A large wave came from John at the sidewalk, as he turned and entered through the automated hotel entry doors.

"Hello, Enzo!" you could hear him say, before the automated doors had closed.

John returned to his hotel room on the 3rd floor, and located the piece of paper that Olivia had handed to him.

He checked the time, and took a seat by the window. There was some hotel stationary and a pen on the table near the chair, which John hoped he would need.

He looked at Olivia's notes, and pressed in the telephone number for Officer Moreau.

"Bonjour? C'est Officier Moreau," said the voice on the other end.

"Bonjour!" said John. "This is John Marcomb. Officer Philip mentioned to my friend that I could speak with you today about my missing persons case?" he asked.

"Oh, oui, monsieur John, I spoke with Officer Philip and I have your file in front of me. How are you today?"

"Very well, merci," said John.

"I recognize your voice, monsieur John, but it is department procedure to confirm your identity before I share anything further by telephone. Would that be OK with you?"

"Oui, of course," said John. "What would you like to know."

"Merci," said Officer Moreau. "First, can you tell me the case number that you are calling about?"

"Yes," said John, as he looked at his police papers and read off the number.

"Merci. Also, can you please give me your full name, date of birth, and your American passport number?" she said.

"Oui, of course." John located his passport to communicate the number on it, and gave her his full name and date of birth.

"Very good, merci. Keep in mind that we are continuing our investigation, because there are still some unanswered questions, but we can share with you a few updates today. Would that be helpful?"

"Yes, of course, merci!" John grabbed the hotel note pad and pen that was on the lamp table near his window seat.

"First, we did verify your identity, so that is the main reason that I can speak with you today. We have the case number for your American missing persons file, and the American Embassy has verified for us all records with your local sheriff's office and the State of California," she said.

"That's great," said John, listening intently.

"Oui," she continued. "We are building a large file for her, and the first detail that we can share with you is about her French identification papers. We have confirmed your wife's French passport, when it was renewed, and that it is up to date and current. She is a dual citizen of both France and America. Since she was born in France to a native French mother, but also has an American father that met the requirements of his American citizenship, this makes her a dual citizen after filing the necessary paperwork. Although she was born on an American military base, this is not the deciding factor because technically that was still French soil, but it is her mother's and father's citizenship that gives her a status in France as a dual citizen, as long as she stays current with all of her paperwork and obeys the laws of our country."

"Excellent news," John said, continuing to listen more than speak.

"The second item is that we have located some family members in the Bordeaux region of France with the name of Guerin. Your wife's grandparents are deceased, but she has some cousins and other relatives alive in this area of the country. We could not verify any Girard relatives that are currently living, but we are still searching to see if there are some relatives on this side of the family that might match up with her history," she noted.

"Do you have an address for any of the Guerin's?" asked John.

"Not yet, said the Officer, but we do have your wife's permanent address on file from her passport application, and I can give that to you before we finish our call."

"Excellent," said John. "That would be very helpful."

"One minute," she said, looking through her file papers. "Here it is."

John wrote down the permanent address that the police had on file for Mia from the passport application. It was a Saint-Émilion address.

Officer Moreau continued, "Unfortunately, we cannot find any evidence yet of what happened to her, or if a crime had been committed, so we are continuing our investigation on that part of the case."

"I see," said John.

Officer Moreau continued, "We also do not yet know the exact date that she reentered France, but we do have the date that she applied for her new passport and received a new copy of her birth certificate and some other national paperwork related to her employment. We are continuing that part of the investigation, and will be dispatching a team soon to help look for her. We may have more information for you again next week, if you would like to make an appointment to come into the department."

"That is extremely helpful," said John. "I am so appreciative that you were willing to take my call today and update me on the latest findings."

"De rien," said Officer Moreau. "We are happy to be of service, Mr. Marcomb. Please contact us again in one week and we may have more information for you."

"Oui. Merci beaucoup!" said John, as he ended the call.

John stood up from the chair and looked through the wide-open casement window and down toward the bustling street.

He paced around the room for a few minutes, and then landed across the comfortable hotel bed.

John looked up at the ceiling, and thanked the great Lord for the blessings that were coming his way.

CHAPTER 27

Saint-Émilion

John woke up in the same position that he had ended the afternoon. The sky had turned dark, and the window was still wide open. The excitement of the week, the news from Danielle that Mia was indeed alive, and the additional verification by the police, had all coalesced to knock him out for a long nap. He woke up late in the evening, and went down to the main lobby to see what he could locate in the way of food. He had missed dinner, and noticed that his smartphone had numerous messages from Jordan, Olivia, Anne and others.

He sat in the hotel lobby for nearly two hours, texting with Jordan, Olivia, Anne, and Charley. John really liked the *Grand Hôtel de lucarne.*

They were all very happy for him, and wished him well. Many reminisced about how far he had come, and were thrilled and amazed that he had verified her presence in France.

He missed his friend Charley, and provided some all-encompassing updates to him about how helpful he had been in their meeting at *BP's*, and what had transpired since their early discussion about Amelie at *Vintage Rags.*

Jordan was ecstatic about the news, and could hardly contain herself.

"I'm so excited, daddy!" said Jordan. "When are you leaving for Saint-Émilion????? I love the name of that town! Call me as soon as you arrive!" She added a long string of emoji characters.

John updated Olivia about the news from Officer Moreau. He thanked Olivia for setting up the call, and asked if she would send a note of thanks to Officer Philip.

"That's wonderful that they gave you her passport address!" said Olivia. "You will be able to start with that location and see who lives there!" Olivia could not have been more thrilled on behalf of John. What an incredible person, thought John, as he wondered what spiritual forces had been at work to place such an exceptional person in his path.

Olivia also confirmed that Andréa was planning to be in Saint-Émilion over the weekend, and passed along Andréa's phone number so that he could get in touch with her. Andréa would be arriving on Friday night, she said, but it would be fine if he gave her a call on Saturday morning.

Danielle and Anne had also talked, and Anne updated John about how much Danielle had liked him and wished him well in his search this weekend. Anne talked about how Danielle was still crying about his daughter Jordan. There were tears of sadness for the time that Mia had lost with Jordan, but also tears of joy that maybe they would be united again.

"She is normally not a highly emotional person," said Anne. "Your story made a sizeable impression on her life."

Danielle also told Anne that she had been unable to contact Mia the entire afternoon, but maybe she had just turned off her telephone due to the concern that Christine had placed in her mind early that morning. They assumed that she was safe, and possibly wanting to be alone for a while.

Laura had also heard the news from Anne, and sent along many kind thoughts and wishes.

"Mr. Johnhood!" she texted, "you *américain ace*! I am so happy for you!" Laura had been one of the staunchest believers that somehow John would find Mia. It was as if she had already visualized it, and spoken it into existence.

John returned to his hotel room, and packed a light bag for his trip the following morning. He would keep his hotel room for now, and could always cancel it if his trip extended longer than anticipated. He spent another hour texting with Jordan, and decided to rest up again for what was sure to be an eventful weekend ahead. The night had crossed midnight and turned toward Friday morning. He took his spot again on the bed for a second round of rest.

The morning came quickly, but John had doubled up on his rest and felt ready to go. His mind was less tired than the prior evening, and after a shower he was his usual self as he passed through the hotel lobby and made his greetings to Enzo and Zoé. He had packed a small bag for his trip, and told them he would return in a day or two.

Nicole at *le patisserie* was happy to see him. John spoke about his travels plans to Saint-Émilion, and she was thrilled for him. She spent some time talking about the latest frolics of her daughter, who was growing faster than she could believe.

John left the café and jumped into a taxi for the twenty-minute drive to the train station. He was heading to the Gare Montparnasse, and would take the high-speed train to Bordeaux.

John had never been to the Bordeaux region of France, or anywhere in the far southwestern direction of the country. He was excited about seeing a new area of the world, and particularly anxious to see some of the sights where Mia had been spending time over the past two years.

John looked at the map during the taxi ride to the station. The country of France was about the size of Texas, and the Bay of Biscay was a noticeable inlet near Bordeaux that was surrounded by the western coastal arc of France and the northern coastal frontage of Spain. The bay connected directly into the expansive Atlantic Ocean to the west. At a total of nearly 600 kilometers, he would be nearly halfway between Paris and Madrid by the time he arrived in Bordeaux.

John paid the taxi fare and entered the modern station. It had a wide ticket lobby space, large metal ceiling panels and skylight areas much like an airport terminal. There were electronic television screens throughout showing train times and track numbers. Retail shops lined the walls, for travelers to purchase drinks and other travel needs. John purchased his ticket on the TGV line, and headed toward the platform for his train to Bordeaux.

John had noticed a large black and white photograph from the prior century. A steam train had crashed through the old station in 1895, and went through the station concourse, crashed through the masonry back wall of the station, shot across a terrace, and went through the back wall of the station. It plummeted 30 feet below onto the terrace area below, and the photograph showed the train reaching its final resting point where it stood vertically on its nose, coming through the stone wall from above. John was happy to know that train brakes had improved since that period.

He entered the train platform, found his train and settled in for the 3-hour trip.

The French trains usually ran on time, and maintained a diligent schedule. His train to Bordeaux departed the station at the appointed time.

John sat near the window on the right side of the train. It departed the city, extended quickly through the Paris suburbs, and burst into the open landscape. The sun was to his right, and the land forms laid out ahead. He watched the liberating French landscapes begin to pass in front of his window. There was beautiful terrain unveiling itself, and his mind was set at ease as he watched the unfolding French countryside.

Flights and train travel had always been a good place for John to clear his mind and get some perspective on life. He began to think about all that had transpired over the past month, and especially since his arrival in Paris. He thought about the intertwining of characters that had helped him so much in France. It was an extraordinary thing to experience, as if it had been fully pre-ordained prior to his arrival.

Of all people, it was Janey who got everything started by booking him into his hotel, and reserving an evening at the *bienvenue diner*. From there, a parade of events had unfolded, starting at the dinner in the *lumiere room* with Anne, Laura and Arne, and continuing forward to encounters with Alaïa, Juliana and then Olivia. Enzo was a consistent helper, and the return call from Dr. Gregor had an impact on his mindset. There was the stately Louis who was his only ally at the school, Philip with his influence on Officer Moreau, and then Danielle with the breaking news about Mia. When you add Charley and Jordan to the mix, they had all played a pivotal role in helping him get to this point.

John was extremely appreciative to all of them, for their friendship, selflessness, and unconditional support. I am the luckiest man in the world, thought John, as he watched the beautiful French landscape unfold. It was a noteworthy insight, given that he had lost his wife and best friend for two full years. This was how far John had come in his spiritual development, which reflected the magnitude of his appreciation for all who had played a role. Now he hoped that maybe Andréa could assist him in Saint-Émilion, to close out this final step of the process. He couldn't wait to see who else might cross his path, as he tried to visualize how Mia might be found and reunited soon with him and his daughter.

John continued reading about the small town of Saint-Émilion, and the general Bordeaux region. As the hub of the famed wine-growing region, Bordeaux was world-famous for its red wine production. He was intrigued by the primary grape varieties used by the châteaux, particularly the Merlot and Cabernet Franc.

John read up on the history of the Cabernet Franc - Merlot Wine, as an established and important variation on the classic Bordeaux blend. The two varieties had complementary features, which were Merlot's dark, juicy fruit balanced by the herbal aromas and structure of Cabernet Franc. This blend was used in the prestigious Saint-Émilion designation, which made some key wines including the famous Château Cheval Blanc. He read about how Merlot was used in higher proportions in this blend, thanks to its broad appeal and higher profile than Cabernet Franc.

John remembered that these two varieties, the Cabernet Franc – Merlot wines, had seen experimentation from other corners of the winegrowing world, including some top wines in California. They had been made from Cabernet Franc and Merlot, often with the addition of Cabernet Sauvignon.

John was fascinated with the small-town character of Saint-Émilion, the Bordeaux region, and its history back to the Romans and early vineyards. He had always enjoyed visiting the vineyards in California, and this would be a very fascinating region to explore. John wondered if southwestern France would have a similar climate and terrain to the vineyards in California. He had always loved walking the vineyards, with the rows and rows of grapes growing in perfect unison on their stalks.

John looked out to the right as the train buffeted through the green hills and vegetation. It had sprinted past a mountain that was tightly carved out to the right, and exploded over a river with a series of Roman arches spanning the deep blue water below. It was a classically proportioned Roman arch bridge, and John wondered how far back the bridge structure might be dated. Strong and sound, the masonry structure easily carried the flying train over the curving blue river below. John was nearing his destination in this beautiful part of the world.

He arrived on the high-speed TGV line into Bordeaux, slightly more than 3 hours after his departure in Paris. He had taken a direct route which did not require any stops along the way. The train slowed during its final approach, and seamlessly guided itself to a resting spot in the Gare de Bordeaux St-Jean. It was located near the Garonne River, the Pont Saint-Jean, and in the central area of Bordeaux.

John grabbed his small set of belongings, and headed for the exit.

He rented a BMW nearby, and headed back across the river and east toward Saint-Émilion. It would be a short 40 minutes or so to the hamlet.

As he drove the ring rode around Bordeaux, he eventually saw his connection and headed due east toward his destination. The experience and scenery was more than he could have imagined. Much of his excitement had to do with the idea that he was finally nearing an opportunity meet up with his wife. He certainly had some trepidation about the event, but his courage and faith carried the day, as John raced directly east toward the ancient vineyard setting.

He could see the designs of Alaïa in the local terrain, which had been notably etched into her designs at the boutique of *la Capelle*. The mix of colors, forms and textures were written across the architecture, lines and landscapes of the Bordeaux region. It was also written into the delivery and mannerisms of Danielle, a quiet calmness, sustaining beauty, and a forerunner of the style and substance that her daughter had become.

John came around a hill area, and stopped the car. His breathing became noticeably present, as he looked across the rooftops and quaint commune setting. The vineyards were intermixed and tucked around the outer perimeter, and the ancient small town sat like a beacon of future hope within its distant past. The continuity of buildings, rooftops, winding streets and green terrain all formed into a small but powerful unity. The tall Romanesque cathedral sat in the middle left and pointed to the sky, reaching about three times the height of any other building in the area. The cumulous clouds floated above like they belonged to the community, approaching from beyond in a friendly manner. It was a panoramic view unlike any he had seen, reminiscent of other ancient villages in France and Italy, but uniquely its own. The cobblestone streets indicated its history, and the building facades appeared to contain many stories about all that had lived and happened there over the centuries. John was in love with the view, the surroundings, and the idea that Mia might be somewhere within the scope of his current view.

John got back into the car and descended into the winding streets. He roamed between the buildings, noting the white window shutters and the residents walking the streets. Many watched closely as he drove past, and some openly waived as they welcomed him as an obvious visitor. Most of the buildings were two or three story structures, many with shops below and residences on the upper floor or two. A few of the buildings had curved corners, like the apse areas at the end section of old Romanesque churches. There were many distinguishing Roman features, set into a distinctly French setting. Saint-Émilion had a slight mix of hills affecting the contour of the community, with trees intermixed along the way, but was not a mountainous area. The vineyard setting served as its platform for existence.

John thought about the thoughts that can go through a person's mind when friends are discussing a location that he had never seen, and then the new thoughts that arrive when a person finally sees the context and setting. Saint-Émilion was everything he had imagined in some ways, but much more in many other ways. It brought home the personalities of some of the people he had met, particularly Danielle, Alaïa, Juliana and Andrea. He could see why they had been so calm and unified, professing an extreme loyalty to each other and happy for their individual and mutual successes. This was a very small town, thought John, but with a very powerful history. Being from Saint-Émilion was not a common thing, and the small-town unity and identification point had become a powerful part of their identity.

He drove past what appeared to be some old cloisters, right in the heart of the old medieval town, and made a mental note of where they were located to return there later in the day.

John looked up the address that the police had given him, and headed toward that destination. It was leading him just outside the center of town, and into an area with some individual homes of about seven or eight acres each. He came upon the address, and saw a structure sitting back on the site. It had the same building façade colors and forms as in the central town area, but had a slightly more single family residential layout and what appeared to be a couple of additional small storage structures toward the rear of the property. John pulled up in front of the home, looked around, and proceeded toward the front door. There was no activity taking place, and he could see a couple of older vehicles sitting toward the back of the acreage. He knocked on the front door, but nobody answered. He walked around toward the back of the house, but nothing seemed to be stirring on this day. John looked around again at the overall acreage, and wandered back toward the storage structures. He was beginning to feel a bit conscious about entering that far into the property, but had two years of his life at stake and was not about to be denied now. He would claim either innocence or ignorance if needed, and hopefully come across someone that spoke a shred of

English if he were to surprise the owners. His French had improved dramatically, and he knew all the basic greetings, niceties, toasts and goodbyes, but many of the sentences still moved too quickly for his comprehension.

The back area of the site was completely silent. Nobody was home.

John got back into his car, and waited a few minutes. He looked at his maps again, to get a better idea of exactly where he was now and what else was in that area of town.

Finally, he exited the home site, and returned to the center of town.

CHAPTER 28

Nicolas Chante

John returned to the heart of Saint-Émilion. A restaurant came up in front of him near the base of the old monolithic church, as he tried to find a place to park. He didn't have a large vehicle, but the streets were very narrow in that area of town. The café looked somewhat crowded, but had a good vibe to him as he pulled to the edge of the street. It seemed to be somewhat of a tourist destination, but there must have been a number locals also that had simply walked to the café. John found a place to put his car in a city designated area further north, and walked back through the winding streets and hills to the café.

The restaurant sat at the base of a three-story building, with a flat façade and the typical white shutters on the windows above. It had a simple glass storefront, with the words Bar, Brasserie and Créperie separately spaced along the upper exterior cornice and glass areas. It was a breakfast and lunch location, bar and brewery.

Old round cobblestones in various sizes filled the street, with larger and more uniform stones in a rectangular pattern defining the sidewalk area. A large outdoor area with white umbrella tables could hold many customers in the outer street area, and an additional three or four tables lined the storefront area.

The café was still serving both breakfast and lunch. It had several adjoining rooms inside, which could not be seen from the exterior, so there was plenty of room for John to take a small table at the main front space.

John looked around inside the restaurant, as he moved toward a table at the end wall. It was cozy and casual, with some local art on the walls. It was a Crêperie, which was essentially a pancake house that served other types of breakfast and lunch plates. The bar and brewery menu started after lunchtime, and the wine menu was specific to the region but with a couple of additional options to choose from.

The waitress was a delight, and greeted him quickly at his table.

"Bonjour," she said, handing him a menu. "Can I get you a drink while you look at the menu?"

"Bonjour," responded John. "Café au lait would be wonderful, merci."

There was a small white name tag that was pinned to her shirt with the name *Sophie* printed on it, in small and understated black letters. She looked like a Sophie, thought John. He remembered Sophie from their *bienvenue diner* two weeks prior, and wondered how she was doing with her graphic design business.

John picked up the *Carte and Menus*, and looked inside. It was not until then that he noticed the restaurant name *Nicolas Chante*, listed prominently across the front of the menu. He seemed to have a thing about doing this, especially with clothing stores and restaurants. This was a new revelation about himself, and had happened at *Vintage Rags, la Capelle*, and now *Nicolas Chante*. I must be more interested in the vibe than the name, thought John.

He opened the menu, and considered the specialties that were available. A crêpe was a type of very thin pastry, usually made from flour and mixed with eggs, milk, butter and a pinch of salt, and he decided to go for one of those.

Sophie returned with his coffee and cream. "Have you looked at the menu?" she asked.

"Oui," said John. "I'd love to try a crêpe, which one would you recommend with fruit on top?"

"Well, maybe something simple like an open crêpe with whipped cream and strawberry sauce on it? C'est très bien," she continued, nodding up and down with her head.

"That sounds perfect, merci," said John.

"Do you like wheat flour or buckwheat flour?" she continued, speaking fluent English and clearly having mercy on him. He already liked her.

"Blé, s'il vous plait." he responded. John wasn't sure if he liked buckwheat flour, and didn't want to chance it since he didn't require a gluten free diet.

"Bien, farine de blé," she said with a smile, as she wrote out the ticket order.

Sophie went to place the order at the kitchen, as John continued to look at the menu. "Nicolas Sings," thought John, that is an interesting name for a restaurant. A bottle of Château St. Émilion Haut-Segottes from Saint-Émilion Grand Cru had been placed in a small photograph on the lower left corner of the menu. There were categories of food selections to choose from, organized by price range. John was happy with the specialty that had been recommended. Maybe he would return another day to sample some of the wine selections on the menu.

John sent a text message to Olivia, and told her that nobody had been home at the address provided by the police.

"Where are you now?" she replied.

"Nicolas Canta, a café in mid-St. Émilion," he said, "near the old cathedral."

She responded right away that she would check in with Andréa and get right back to him.

John pulled out his mystery novel and read part of a chapter.

Sophie delivered his crêpe with strawberries and whipped cream, served on a plain white plate.

"Merci!" said John. "It looks great."

John enjoyed the late breakfast, watching the people come and go from the restaurant. The Créperie had a very nice feel to it, was very homey, and all the staff seemed to get along well with each other.

Olivia finally responded with an update that Alec would stop over and meet up with him at the restaurant. Alec was Andréa's boyfriend, and had arrived in town last night.

"He's on his way now," said Olivia, "will be there shortly." Andréa had called Alec with the request, and then sent an update back to Olivia.

"Andrea won't arrive until Sat.," she continued, "but Alec can get you acquainted with St. E."

Olivia doesn't mess around, thought John, and Andréa was not far behind. They were both genuine and highly efficient, not letting anything get in the way when they set their mind to accomplishing a task.

"You're a blessing of major proportions," said John. "Merci, ma sœur."

Olivia returned some smiley face emoji's, and some additional best wishes.

It is a very small town, thought John, so arriving shortly by someone who lived there was probably very possible.

John finished his lunch, and ordered a coffee refill and some light desert.

A young man entered the restaurant, and scanned the room as if he were looking for someone. John stood up to see if this was Alec.

"Bonjour, Mr. Marcomb," said the nice young man, "my name is Alec." He reached out to shake John's hand, who had stood to greet him.

"My pleasure, Alec. Won't you please join me?" said John, pointing toward the extra chair in front of him.

"Andréa asked that I come and meet you here," said Alec, "did she tell you about it?"

"Yes," said John, "I received a message from Olivia that you were coming. She had spoken with Andréa. Thanks for coming over."

"No problem, Mr. Marcomb," said Alec. "Andréa doesn't arrive until tomorrow, and asked me to help out with anything you might need."

Sophie caught a glimpse of Alec sitting with John, and came toward the table, "Hi Alec, how have you been? Do you two know each other?" she asked, pointing toward John.

"We just met," he said, "but Andréa knows Mr. Marcomb, and asked me to come and meet up with him."

"Have you met Mr. Marcomb?" Alec asked to Sophie.

"Yes," said Sophie. "I have been his server today, but I didn't know his name."

"Please call me John," he said toward both.

"Yes, sir," responded Alec.

Looking toward Sophie, Alec continued, "John is a friend Andréa and Alaïa, and in town to follow-up with some family members."

"I see. Welcome to Saint-Émilion, John," said Sophie.

"John is a very nice man," said Sophie, looking toward Alec.

Another girl had joined them at the table that was on staff at the restaurant.

"Lauren, this is John," said Sophie, "he is a friend of Andréa and Alaïa!"

"Hello, John," said Lauren. "Two of my favorites in the whole world!" she said, speaking about Andréa and Alaïa.

"I heard that Andréa was coming into town this weekend," said Sophie. "How is Alaïa doing? I miss them both."

"Good," said Alec. "They keep in touch all the time, and Alaïa is busy with her boutique and new clothing line."

"Did he treat you well as a customer?" asked Lauren, all in good humor as she looked toward John.

"Why yes!" said Sophie, he has been very nice, and he even pronounced my name correctly. Americans usually accent my name on the wrong syllable, but he has been saying it correctly!"

Alec filled them in about John, who is looking for his wife. Alec had heard the romantic story from Andréa, and began to tell them about it. They both took a seat at the table and listened in. Since they both knew Alaïa and Andréa, they were curious about how it all connected to their town.

"You're kidding!" said Sophie. "That is the most romantic story that I have ever heard! Do you know for sure that she is here?" she asked John.

"I'm hoping so," said John, "that is what I am here to find out."

"And you know Alaïa and Andréa?" asked Lauren. "How did you meet them?"

"Mostly through Olivia Martin, who I met through Anne Avé. They have both become very good friends. I've been to Alaïa's boutique, and met Juliana and Andréa one night at a catered event. You all have some very nice friends."

"Oh, you know Juliana Dubois too?" said Sophie. "What a small world."

"Yes, Andréa Renaud just texted me," said Lauren, "and told me the story of the search for your wife. That is amazing that you have come all this way to find her. She asked me to look out for you in the restaurant."

"Is there anything that we can do to help you?" asked Sophie.

"Yes, there might be something," said John, "I went over to the house where the Guerin family was supposed to live, but nobody was home. Do you know any Guerin's in the area?"

"Yes, of course," said Lauren, "they might be out at Henri Lemaire's vineyard, they are often out there this time of year helping with the business. I think they live out there sometimes, because there is so much room and they do some operations work for Mr. Lemaire. Andréa's family owns a vineyard and is good friends with their family."

"Alec, do you know where that is?" asked Sophie.

"Yes, I do, why don't I drive you out there and we can check it out!" suggested Alec. "I have been there a couple of times."

"That would be outstanding," said John. "When could you go?"

"Right now, if you want," said Alec.

"OK, let's go have a look," said John.

"Sophie, you have been a delight during my time here this morning," said John. "Thanks to both of you for your insight into the Guerin family and vineyard contacts."

"You're welcome, John," said Sophie. "We hope to hear good news from Andréa about this."

"Good luck, said Laura. "Alec, be sure to let us know what you find out."

John and Alec departed the restaurant.

John had left Sophie a very large tip.

"Good luck!" yelled Sophie, as they made their way through the doorway and onto the sidewalk.

CHAPTER 29

Château de Mathieu

Alec and John loaded into Alec's small European car and headed out toward Henri Lemaire's vineyard. It was in the Saint-Émilion region, northwest of the main town, and out toward the direction of Pomerol.

"Thanks so much for driving me out here," said John. "You have been extremely helpful today."

"You're welcome, sir, I am happy to help," said Alec with a smile.

"You're a fine young man," said John. "Andréa is a lucky girl."

Alec appreciated the complement. "Any friend of Andréa and Alaïa is a friend of mine," said Alec.

John was texting with Jordan and Olivia as he was riding along with Alec.

Olivia updated John that she had spoken again with Danielle. Olivia gave her the police verification of John's identity, and the case that had been confirmed by the American Embassy. Officer Philip had been helpful in authenticating this trust. Olivia passed the information along to Danielle, so that she could share it with Mia or her extended family. The family had never met John, and might be more at ease if they had some police verification about the situation.

"Olivia is a phenomenal person," said John to Alec. "Have you ever met her?"

"Yes, a couple of times, and I have always heard great things about her from Andréa," said Alec. "I know Alaïa also thinks the world of her."

"I hope Olivia meets someone who is a match for her wide-ranging exceptionalism. She deserves the very best, someone who can match her kindness, spirituality, talent and convictions, and that truly cares for her."

"That's very nice of you to say," said Alec. "Andréa told me about your gathering at the small dome, and was very impressed with both Olivia and Laura for putting together the event. It sounds like Olivia has been a key person in bringing you together with Alaïa, Danielle, and the people here in Saint-Émilion."

"That is true, Alec," said John. "Anne and Laura have been phenomenal friends, but Olivia is the person that has really made it all happen. I could never thank her enough for all that she has done."

"Andréa tells me that Alaïa often calls Olivia when she really needs something important done in the fashion world," said Alec. "Olivia just seems to have a natural talent to know the right person and make the right call. Andréa says she is very personable, and exudes such kindness that people can't help but want to assist her, especially when she is doing it on behalf of one of her friends. I know that Andréa relies on her for many things as well."

"Alaïa's mother is also amazing," said John. "I just met her yesterday, and was very impressed. She is a longtime friend of

Mia's, way back to their college days, and I would not be here today without her help in revealing that Mia had traveled here."

"Yes, Danielle is unbelievable," agreed Alec. "She is highly respected in this area. She has been traveling down here more lately, now that her work at the school has transitioned to her successor. She worked so hard building that program, the same way that her mother had done, but she took it to a new level."

"Her mother ran the same program?" asked John.

"Yes, her mother was its founder, back before Danielle was a student at the school," said Alec.

"I had no idea," said John. "Her mother must have known Mia, back when she took her classwork in Paris," he continued, thinking on this for the first time.

"Probably yes," said Alec, "if she went to school at the same time as Danielle."

"And now Alaïa has followed in those same creative fashion footsteps," said John, "but in more of a hands-on approach with her own line of clothing and her own business."

"Yes, Alaïa is extremely talented, much like her mother," agreed Alec. "Danielle is very modest about her work, but could have easily had her own high-end fashion line. She chose more of an educator role, helping others reach their dreams, so it was her style to blend the two together. But she could have easily had her own fashion line, and the school focus is the only reason that she did not start her own business."

"Amazing," said John. "What a talented group of people you have from this area."

Alec looked at John and smiled.

"I know that Danielle also had a significant influence on Anne Avé," said Alec. "I've heard Anne mention it a few times during parties that I attended with Andréa. Anne would begin talking about fashion programs related to her charity work, and always mentions Danielle as her primary mentor as a fashion designer and her grace in handling the higher profile charity events."

"Those are a couple of wonderful stories to hear about. Thanks for sharing about Danielle and Anne," said John.

"You're welcome," said Alec.

After a slight pause, Alec continued, "The girls at the restaurant really liked you."

"How do you know that?" asked John.

"Because they like the locals that come in, but rarely enter any lengthy conversations with the other visitors," said Alec. "They are nice to them, but don't tend to spend a lot of time with small talk. With you, they sat down and listened to the entire story, and even helped with some solutions. They never do that. The other waitresses picked up the slack for them when they were sitting with us, because it was so unusual. They are a great bunch of people at that restaurant, and the staff always look out for each other when needed."

"That's very nice," said John. "I like both very much, and Sophie had a special spirit about her. She reminds me a little bit of my daughter. I hope she finds her role in life and finds something that she really enjoys."

"I think she will," said Alec. "She is very talented with her advertising and marketing work, and has been working many hours on the side to improve her branding and electronic skills. I think one day she will be able to step into it more fully, and be able to support

266

herself in that role. She already represents some of the vineyards on a freelance basis with her creative ideas and communication skills. Hopefully some day she can do that full time."

"That's outstanding," said John. "She is great with people. I could easily see her in a creative field related to communication and marketing or branding."

The two raced along the countryside, getting closer to their destination.

"I'm not sure how much English they will be able to speak, when we arrive" said Alec. "I can help as an interpreter, if you need any help."

"Yes, of course, merci," said John. "My French is improving, but I am a long way from being able to carry on a conversation of any depth. I could most certainly use your help. Besides, you are an incredibly well spoken young man."

"Thank you," said Alec.

Alec pulled to the curb at the right.

"We are here," said Alec. "This is the place that Lauren suggested. It is owned by Henri Lemaire, who is a very nice gentleman and has done very well for himself. We can start at the main building, and go from there."

"OK," said John. "I'm ready."

Alec turned right, and passed under the outer gate area that said *Château de Mathieu* at the top. There was a large metal arch that spanned both the entry and exit lanes, and the metal scripted letters sat within the full span of the arch.

"Who is Mathieu?" asked John.

"I believe he was Henri's father, who founded the vineyard," said Alec. "They use a different name for the bottling company, but he was the person that assembled the land, built the winery buildings, and turned it into a highly profitable business venture."

Alec continued down the long entry drive, bending right around a large fountain area and then curving back to the left under a covered entry.

The buildings and grounds were in excellent condition, and the landscaping had all been trimmed to perfection. The main front building was much more modern that John had expected, which large amounts of glass, metal awnings, and expensive stonework at the base, archways, and hardscape along the entry area.

Alec pulled to the curb at the right side near the entry, and turned off the engine.

Alec and John looked at each other, and exited out of the car.

They moved toward the tall double entry doors, and rang the doorbell. The door opened wide, and a gentleman said hello.

Alec spoke to the gentleman in French. "Hello, my name is Alec. This is Mr. John Marcomb, who is a friend of the Leroux, Renaud and Dubois families, and is visiting us from America. Is Mr. Lemaire at home today?"

"Oui, trés bien" said the gentleman, an assistant at the vineyard. "Entrez."

"Merci beaucoup," said Alec, and the two entered the modern castle.

"I am Denis," said the gentleman. "Please wait here. Mr. Lemaire is just now finishing his lunch on the outer terrace, and I will tell him that you are here."

Alec and John took a seat in the central entry hall.

In less than 5 minutes, Denis returned.

"Gentlemen, will you please come this way," said Denis.

"Oui," said Alec. "Merci."

John and Alec followed Denis through a series of rooms and out to the rear terrace area connected to the house. It had large awnings covering different table and seating sections. A large round table sat in the center. Several comfortable low backed lounge seats were arranged at the perimeter, with thick white cushions and stone capped corner end tables.

"Please come in gentlemen," said a voice as they entered the terrace area. "I am Henri Lemaire," as he reached out to shake their hands.

Alec greeted Mr. Lemaire in French, "I am Alec, a close friend of the Renaud's, and this is Mr. John Marcomb, who is a friend of the Leroux, Renaud and Dubois families, and is visiting us from America."

"A pleasure meeting you Alec, and welcome to our château, Mr. Marcomb," said Henri.

"Merci," said John. "Please call me John."

"Merci," said the stately gentleman. "Please call me Henri."

"Merci, monsieur," said Alec.

Henri asked about the Renaud's, specifically how Andréa's parents have been doing. Alec filled him in on the latest news, and how well Andrea was doing at her new job in Paris. Henri was pleased to hear the news.

Alec respectfully turned the conversation toward John. "Mr. Marcomb, or John," he said to Henri, "is good friends with Danielle Leroux and Anne Avé, as well as Alaïa and Andréa. I think you might know all of them."

"Yes, I do!' said Henri, "You run in good company, sir John."

Henri looked toward John, "How do you like our small village?" said Henri.

"It is magnificent," said John, "and everyone has made me feel right at home."

"That is excellent," said Henri, "we have some wonderful people in this community." Henri continued, "What can I do for you gentleman on this fine day?"

"We know you are a busy man," said Alec, "but we were hoping that you could assist us with some information."

"Certainly," said Henri, "I will help with what I can."

"Thank you, sir," said Alec. Alec converted back to French, and filled in Henri on the reason for John's visit to Saint-Émilion. Alec told him the story about John's reason to visit Paris, the acquaintances that he had met, and the story about him searching for his wife. He had gone to the school, but Mia was not there. He had met with Danielle, who filled him in that Mia may be here in Saint-Émilion. Danielle suggested that he come here and try to locate her. John is a very good man, he continued, and has been highly recommended by Andréa Renaud and Alaïa Capelle, two of his closest friends. He also thought that Henri might know Anne and her friend Louis, from some of the charity events at the school. He asked in respect for his help with any information that he might have. Alec also spoke about the police, the verification process, and the connection to the Guerin family, and how John had gone to the Guerin house but nobody was home.

Alec continued, switching back to English so that John could hear the final question, "Lauren at Nicolas Chante today thought you might know the Guerin family, so that is the main reason that we have come to see you today. Do you know of them? They are relatives of John's wife, Mia."

"You are an impressive young man," said Henri, in English with a heavy French accent, and looking directly toward Alec. "You have made your case very well, my dear sir."

"Thank you, sir," said Alec, smiling toward Mr. Lemaire.

Henri sat back in his chair and absorbed the information.

After a long pause, he looked up toward both.

"The Renaud's have been dear friends of mine for many years," Henri began. "When we went through some financial difficulties during one of the recessions, there were no greater supporters of this family than the Renaud's. Your friend Andréa comes from the finest of families, and it sounds like she is following in their footsteps. I also know Anne very well, and of course Danielle. There are no finer individuals in all of Paris than Anne and Danielle, and I have great admiration for their successes and kindness. You also have mentioned Louis Durand, who is a friend of Anne and a fine gentleman. He is an investor in our operation, and has been instrumental in helping up reach new distribution channels. And of course, I have heard about the fine work being done by Alaïa. She is a direct extension of the talented Danielle, and I am happy to hear how well she is doing with her new clothing lines. So, you are in very good company, my friends, and you are welcome here at our château."

"Thank you, Henri," said John. "I have also been very impressed today by this fine young man. He has been extremely helpful, and I believe will be a great success for many years to come."

"I agree," said Henri.

"What else can you tell me about your wife?" Henri continued.

"Of course," said John. "The search has led to Saint-Émilion because of some new information yesterday from Danielle."

John pulled out a picture of Mia, Jordan and John standing together at the beach. "This is my wife, Mia," said John. "Do you know her?"

Henri took the picture from John, and sat forward in his chair.

"Yes, John, I do," he said, looking over toward John. "I also received a call this morning from the police. We do employ some Guerin's here, and I shared that information with the police."

John looked at him and listened.

Henri was still sitting forward in his chair. "Your daughter is a mirror image of Mia," Henri continued, looking again at the photograph. "She is a beautiful girl, and must miss her mother terribly."

"Yes, beyond words," said John. "Anything that you could do to help me locate Mia would be greatly appreciated."

"Please wait here," said Henri. He left the terrace area, and went back inside the house. He was having a brief conversation with Denis, and returned to the terrace.

"Where is your daughter now?" asked Henri.

"She is in California," said John, "at our home."

"I see," said Henri, "and you have come all this way not knowing if you would ever find your wife."

"Yes," said John, "but I have received great help along the way, and Danielle was the one that told me she had come to Saint-Émilion. Danielle has known Mia since back in their college days at the Sorbonne."

"Yes," said Henri. "Danielle is a brilliant person. There is nobody finer."

"I agree," said John.

Henri continued to hold the picture of Jordan with Mia.

Denis came back on the terrace and said some words quietly in French to Henri. John did not understand the words.

"Please wait here," said Henri, as he left the room again.

John looked toward Alec. "He is going to speak with the Guerin's," said Alec.

"I see," said John. John sat back in his chair and looked out across the vineyard. It was a glorious day, and the sun had filtered beautifully across the shaded terrace area.

Henri had taken the picture with him to meet with the Guerin's.

Henri had asked Denis to check in on Alec and John, and bring them some drinks and hors d'oeuvres.

Alec and John sat on the terrace, and chatted about Paris and Alec's other friends. They sipped their drinks and had a light snack while they waited.

After about 15 minutes, Henri returned. The Guerin's had joined him.

"Hello, gentleman, thanks for waiting here," said Henri. "I hope that Denis was able to get you some refreshments while you waited."

"Oh, yes, thank you," said John.

"I would like you to meet Richard and Gabrielle Guerin," said Henri. "This is Mr. John Marcomb, the husband of Mia Michelle Girard."

Both smiled broadly, and took a step toward John. John stood from the chair and shook their hands.

"It is my sincere pleasure to meet you," said John, looking at them, and then looking toward Alec. Alec reiterated the same sentence in French, for them to hear the exact wording by John.

"Merci," said both, and both bowed their heads toward John.

"Please sit down," offered Henri to all of them.

Richard and Gabrielle Guerin were a similar age as John, and a very nice looking couple with obvious strong local roots. They did not speak any English, but had a look of warmth in their eyes that did not need words. They were cousins of Mia, which John was very interested in observing. He had seen very few pictures of her relatives on her mother's side, and not for many years since their early days of marriage.

"The Guerin's are dear friends of our family," said Henri. "They have been helping us during this season on the vineyard. I have told them about you, and showed them your picture. They are very honored to meet you. Both were saddened to hear about all that you have been through, and the effect that it may have had on your daughter. They tell me that they had also spoken with the police this morning, who verified your identity to them, and the case on file regarding your wife."

Henri said some sentences to the Guerin's in French, to fill them in on his overview to John and Alec. Alec nodded in agreement toward John, as Henri interpreted for the Guerin's. The Guerin's said a few things in French back to Henri, and both smiled in the direction of John.

Henri smiled and returned his attention back toward John. "As Mia's relatives, they are very happy to meet you in person, and see the photograph that you shared of you, Mia and Jordan. They see the strong resemblance of Jordan in Mia, and appreciate the way that you have searched for your wife in such loving terms. They knew the Girard's, but they have all since passed away except for some distant cousins. They tell me their grandmother knew Mia, and had remembered that she was married, but they had always been confused about that until today. They thought maybe she was just getting old and had been thinking about the wrong person. Since then she has passed, but now they see you sitting here and know that she had been referring to you, because their grandmother thought that Mia had married and might be living in California. They are also appreciative of the police verification, and are greatly saddened by what you must have endured over the past two years. They believe your story, and would like to help you with Mia."

John felt a tear roll down his left cheek area. He was not a highly emotional person, but this news had touched him to his core. He stood and embraced both in a full hug. They all broke down with some tears, as the three of them continued to embrace.

"Merci," said John. No words had been necessary, but he wanted to squeeze it out just the same.

"Come," said Gabrielle, as she grabbed John's hand.

"Come," she also said to Alec, gesturing in his direction.

Gabrielle led John through the terrace and down the steps to the lower level, with Richard just behind them and Alec next to Richard. The stone staircase curved down and to the right, and there was a stone terraced floor on the lower level under the area where they had been sitting.

She continued through the lower terrace, and cut across the stone pavers to a second building about thirty yards down from the main house. It was a two-story structure, with a balcony above and a modern arched entry below.

Gabrielle held his hand firmly as they passed under the archway and into the neighboring structure. This must have been their living quarters, as she walked with conviction and knew all the nuanced detail of the living quarters. There was an open main room below that served as a meeting and lounge area, with seating areas sectioned in three locations across the room. Large color photographs of grapes, vineyards, crates and wine bottles covered the four walls, aligned across the entirety of the room in a unified manner. They must have been photos of the Château de Mathieu and its vineyard operations.

They continued past the seating area, and toward a doorway at the right rear corner of the room. Richard and Alec were still following behind them.

Gabrielle made a slight knock on the door, and slowly entered the room.

She said some French words very swiftly and softly ahead of her steps, as she led John into the space.

Sitting to the left side of the room was Danielle, who rose to greet John with cheek kisses and a large embrace. Sitting back in the left corner of the room was Mia, with a smile on her face and tears running down her cheeks. She was holding the picture of her with Jordan and John at the beach.

Danielle stepped to the side, and motioned toward Mia.

John moved across the room slowly, as Mia began crying with full tears.

John held out both hands toward Mia, and let her find the energy to rise from the chair.

Mia rose and gave John a full embrace, crying excessively on his inside shoulder.

"I'm so sorry, I'm so sorry," Mia repeated in French, over and over, as she continued crying into John's upper chest and inside shoulder area.

"She is so beautiful," she said in English. "I had no idea. Please forgive me for what you have gone through."

"It's not your fault," said John. "It's not your fault. You didn't do anything wrong."

Mia slowly composed herself, and looked across the room. The entire contingent was wiping away their tears.

She couldn't help but have a brief laugh of embarrassment, as she looked across at her family and dear friend Danielle.

It was a laugh of joy, and her tears of sadness were converting to tears of joy. They had all stood in silent support as she regained her composure and took a seat near where she had been standing. John sat down next to her, and Danielle sat directly across. They let her wipe away the tears, and assemble her thoughts.

Danielle began to smile, as she saw this conversion taking place toward tears of joy.

Gabrielle also had a warm look on her face, as she watched Mia begin to compose herself.

"She is so beautiful," said Mia, as she wiped away the final tears on her cheeks.

After a long pause, she looked at John, and then toward Danielle, and then toward her family.

"I have seen her in my dreams," said Mia.

She wiped away the teardrops that had gathered on the photograph, which was still tightly gripped in her left hand.

CHAPTER 30

A New York Minute

Mia and John touched down at John F. Kennedy International Airport in New York at 1:11pm, on their Air France flight from Paris. They taxied across the runway, and the airplane settled into the gate at Terminal 4. They had departed Charles de Gaulle airport just two hours prior at 11:01am the same day, but had gained several hours in time flying to the west.

John and Mia picked up their luggage at the baggage claim area, and passed into the American customs process. After filing their entry paperwork at the electronic kiosk, they proceeded toward the final queuing line ending at the immigration podiums. The immigration agent at their stand asked to see their passports, and had a welcoming smile for the two of them.

"Where have you two been traveling?" asked the agent, a middle-aged gentleman with a strong New York accent. The name on his jacket said Dominic Aiello.

"We are returning from Paris," said John, "it was a wonderful trip."

"Oh, were you there for business or pleasure?" asked agent Aiello. "I see that Mrs. Marcomb has been over there for quite a while."

"Mostly pleasure," said John, "yes, we reconnected in Paris, and now my wife has completed her stay with friends and is able to join our family back in America."

The agent smiled and looked at Mia for a couple of moments. He looked again through her paperwork, visa and passport.

"Welcome back to America, Mrs. Marcomb, and enjoy your stay in New York," said Dominic.

"Thank you," said Mia, with a distinctive French accent, "it is great to be back home."

They both smiled, and headed toward the main lobby area. Mia felt honored by the kind and sensitive treatment by Mr. Aiello. John & Mia both knew that he could have asked several more questions, but he let it rest at that.

John had decided to bring Mia to New York on the way home, for her to connect with the place that they had originally met, and for her to begin the rebuilding process of her memories of America. It might serve as a transitional place, he thought, before they made the full trip back to California.

Taking the advice of Dr. Gregor, he wondered if there might be portions of her memory from a couple decades prior that could possibly be activated before the more recent periods of her life in California. John didn't know how much she might remember about this city, or how far back her memories had been compromised, but he felt that it was worth the try to familiarize her with this segment of time when they were newlyweds in the city, and maybe help her to rebuild her early history as an American before they continued back home to California.

John ordered up a private car service at the main terminal area, and they made the 15-mile trip toward the island of Manhattan. The driver said that the lower tunnels and bridges were full of traffic because of some recent accidents in that area, so they headed toward the Midtown Tunnel. They passed under the East River, and surfaced up on the island of Manhattan. They took a left on 2nd Avenue, and proceeded down toward lower Manhattan and into the SoHo District.

They arrived in SoHo about twenty minutes before 3:00pm, and proceeded toward the hotel for an early check-in. The hotel was the perfect transition back to America, an urban setting in an artistic neighborhood. It had a similar scale to the buildings that Mia was familiar with in Paris, but was distinctly American in culture, language and amenities. The hotel was very modern, with an impeccable style, clean, sophisticated, and consisting of luxurious material finishes throughout.

They took a room on the 5th floor, and the front desk attendant made them feel right at home. John and Mia stopped into the lobby gift shop before proceeding toward the elevators, making sure they had everything they might need before retreating to the hotel room. They looked through the small book collection, periodicals, and some clothing items on the racks. They purchased a couple of books, a few bathroom supplies, and some water, and the porter helped them with their luggage to their room.

After they had settled in, John and Mia ordered up an early dinner of room service, and spent the remainder of the late afternoon and evening hours relaxing in the hotel room. Both were exhausted but exceedingly happy, and decided to just hang out for the evening in the hotel room. They each took a long shower, read their books, talked and laughed, surfed the social media sites, enjoyed the activity below in the streets, and watched some comedy on American television during the evening. They had all the time in the world, and there was no rush to be anywhere or do anything now that they had arrived in New York. It was the first night back in America, and the idea of being back on the home soil was reason enough for them to celebrate in private.

They decided that time would be under their control for a couple days. They would schedule whatever came to mind, and then visit those areas of the city when it was time. John had planned to spend at least two or three days in Manhattan, at whatever pace was most relaxing for roaming the streets, dining at the restaurants, and enjoying whatever fun and enjoyable activities came to mind on that day. Being unscheduled was the perfect schedule for the remainder of the week.

The evening concluded with a bottle of Bordeaux brought to the room, along with some specialties from the hotel kitchen. John had placed a special scented candle for them on the sitting room table. They had reserved a large double hotel room with two adjoining sides. It had a bedroom and bath area on one side, and was separated by a door leading to the sitting room on the other side. The sitting room had a large couch, two cozy arm chairs, a coffee table, side tables, and a large built in video cabinet on the entire end wall area.

They watched a movie in the sitting area until late into the evening, with the lights set dimly in a movie theatre fashion. Eventually, they made their way under the luxurious cotton sheets in the lightly dimmed bedroom area. It was the middle of the night in Paris, and their body clocks had not changed over yet.

John woke up early, and took a seat by the window of their hotel room. He had missed too many days with Mia, and was still on Paris time when he awoke. He made some coffee at the hotel room bar area, and nestled into the chair.

The morning sun was lovely, just coming up over the eastern horizon and filtering between the buildings in lower Manhattan. It reminded him of his days living in New York, having the loft windows wide open and the sights and sounds of the city rushing in with the air. The windows in this hotel were mostly inoperable, but the views of the street and the sun cutting through the roof scape, buildings, canopies and awnings below reminded him of his many years of living in the city. Late spring and early summer were his favorite months of the year in this place, when he would walk the streets and more frequently incorporate the sights and sounds of the city into his daily routine. Greenwich Village, SoHo, Tribeca and Little Italy were among his favorite places for doing this, and he thought about where they might go for breakfast after Mia had awaken from her long sleep.

John had begun reading a new fictional novel about a romantic mystery set in Argentina, and periodically peered over toward Mia as she rested comfortably. He gave thanks for all that had transpired in his life over the past month, his faith, his friends, his courage, his patient resolve, and most of all to the almighty God that had brought Mia back to him.

A small teardrop ran down his left cheek as he thought about how much he had been blessed. He needed to do his part, accept the circumstances, trust the process, and follow the clues, but beyond that, it was completely out of his hands, and in the control of forces well beyond his comprehension. He was supremely appreciative that he had been able to receive the message of how to approach the situation, how to follow the inner voices, and how to remain in faith during the process until it could be fully realized. It was a miracle to behold, thought John, beyond what he could have ever imagined or hoped for.

"Thank you, Lord," he said, softly into the room.

Mia stirred toward her right side, and brought her lovely face onto the pillow and began facing toward the window. She inhaled a couple of large breaths, as her eyes fluttered above the cotton pillow cover. Her eyes opened slightly, and ran across the room toward the outside wall of the hotel. A smile came across her face as she saw John looking at her from the chair by the window.

John folded the book across his lap and smiled back. No words were needed by either of them, just the peace of being together again in the private and cozy hotel room. It was a pleasure like no other, thought John, and they had all the time in the world to enjoy it.

John and Mia showered and dressed for the day. They took the elevator down to the hotel lobby, and crossed through the lobby area. Holding hands, they crossed through the entry threshold and dropped onto the SoHo sidewalk.

The street and sidewalks were active, with people going to work and deliveries being made. The city was also their heart beat, and they turned left down the artistically manicured street with its cast iron storefronts and modern window displays.

They didn't bring much along with them for the day – Mia had her sunglasses and small shoulder bag, and John just had his wallet and smartphone.

They walked up two blocks to the north, and turned left on Prince Street. They crossed over one street to the west, and then headed up Wooster Street, crossing over the wider Houston Street and into Greenwich Village. The freshness of the morning air was spectacular, and had the faint smell of ocean breeze that had sometimes filtered through the morning streets in lower Manhattan.

John suggested to catch a light breakfast in Greenwich Village, where they had both lived when they first met, and Mia loved the idea. They turned west down Bleecker Street, which made John reminiscent about the cafés and clubs along the way, noticing what was the same and what had changed since the years that they had lived there.

"Do you remember any of this?" asked John.

"It does seem vaguely familiar," said Mia. "I do feel comfortable and at home walking through the streets in this area."

After a few more blocks to the west, they turned back toward the south on Macdougal Street, and grabbed a sidewalk table under an awning at an expresso and breakfast café. This was the type of café where you could take a seat and became part of the urban fabric of city life, much like the cafés in Paris and across other parts of Europe.

Mia smiled, as she sat in the metal backed chair. "I like this place," she said.

"Me too," said John.

The two ordered some light breakfast and café au lait, and watched the people walking past. It was one of those mornings that John had dearly loved about the neighborhood, especially when his work life had not gotten in the way. The freshness of the air, the sidewalks that had been washed off in the early morning with a water hose, and the early morning before the street activity became too hectic – all were meaningful signs to John that he was in his happy place.

For Mia, she was simply enjoying the new surroundings, the somewhat familiar neighborhoods, and her time getting to know John again. It had been a leap of faith for her to travel with him to New York, but she trusted her family and friends like no other, and they had been extremely adamant that she was doing the right thing. She also trusted John – there was something about him, a kindness, and a deep, unspoken level of trust that she could not discount. It was the final decisive reason that she had decided to listen to her family and friends and travel to New York with him. She knew that somewhere very deep inside of her that she inherently trusted him, that he was earnest and heartfelt, and that he would help her find her identity and regain the missing parts of her life without sacrificing her other new parts along the way.

The coffee arrived, and they put in their cream and stirred it perfectly into the cup.

John pulled out his picture of her and Jordan.

"She looks just like you, you know," said John, "and always has since she was a very small girl. More than that, she has your personality. Jordan is very kind, creative and intelligent."

Mia smiled and took the picture from John. She studied it for a while, as she sipped her hot coffee.

"What have I missed?" said Mia, mostly speaking to herself, in a quiet fashion under her breath.

John let her continue.

"She is a very beautiful girl," said Mia, handing the picture back to John. "I hope that someday I can remember more about our history together. I see the picture of the two of us, but I don't understand it. I hope that someday I can understand it. I feel her deep inside of me, and I would like to know her again."

"You will," said John. "In time, you will."

They finished their coffee and jumped into a taxi heading uptown. Mia watched as they passed through Midtown, the tall buildings, and continued north through the busy city.

When they reached Central Park South at the perimeter of the park, Mia jumped forward and looked out of the car window. Something had caught her attention, as she looked at the trees along the edge of the park, and watched the horse drawn carriages passing beneath them along the perimeter.

The two of them got out of the car at the corner near the Plaza Hotel, at the corner of Fifth Avenue and Central Park South. Mia looked around at the hotel, observing the buildings lining the streets along Central Park South, the large fashion outlet names along Fifth Avenue, and the corner of the park.

They crossed the street and walked toward the park, which was a world onto itself.

"What a beautiful park," said Mia, "right in the middle of this large city."

They continued past a pond, down into the heart of the park, and grabbed a seat on a bench.

There was a fence in the foreground to the left side, and a large open field extending outward into the far distance to the right, with several tall buildings as a backdrop to the large open area.

This was the place where they had taken their wedding photos, many years ago following their marriage ceremony in lower Manhattan. The photos were taken in the middle of the field, with the tall buildings in the distance, on a beautiful sunny afternoon in the middle of June. Mia and John were 100% in love.

Mia sat on the bench and stared into the open field, not saying a word for over ten minutes.

"Absolutely, beautiful," said Mia, as she continued her silence for another long period.

"Yes, it is," agreed John, remembering that beautiful sunny day in June many years ago.

The morning hours had continued to impress, with a light breeze and a nearly perfect temperature. The green surroundings were incredible, with many flowers in full bloom, and the walkers and runners graced the sidewalks.

They noticed two doves chatting on the fence about twenty feet in front of them and slightly to the left - talking and chatting, chatting and talking. One was a bit smaller, which must have been the female, but they were a dynamic duo and traveling companions to be sure.

John had become well acquainted with doves over the past two months.

The birds continued chatting and talking, "whoah, whoo, whoo, whoo."

"It is like they are hoping for us to overhear their conversation," said Mia.

"Yes, it is like they appear to be speaking with us," agreed John.

"Look at those two lovebirds," said Mia, as she tipped down her sunglasses to take a better look.

To John, Mia had the most beautiful eyes on earth. She was also very observant.

"Yes," agreed John, "they are quite remarkable. What do you think they are saying?" he asked, not really expecting an answer.

"Stay in faith," said Mia, without hesitation. "Stay in faith."

John sat back in awe at the entire conversation, both from the birds and from Mia. What had prompted her to that? Stay in faith. My goodness, thought John. Central Park in New York. Stay in faith. This has been a worldwide excursion, he thought, the doves were still following him across the globe.

They both watched with extreme interest, as the female dove became very active. They both had been calm but talkative to begin. Now, the female was fluttering to and from the lower planted areas just beyond the fence area.

"I had a dream about two months ago about a girl," said Mia, without any warning that they were heading into this type of a conversation.

"You did?" said John.

"Yes, it was very unusual, I didn't know what it meant for the longest time," she continued, in what had become her beautiful mix of American and French accents.

John had learned to listen. He no longer needed to be the focus of every conversation, or any conversation for that matter.

Mia tilted up again and looked at the inside of her sunglasses, as if seeing through them more clearly might be tied to her comprehension of life.

"I thought maybe it was one of those dreams that never makes sense, but now I think differently about it," she Mia, staring into the distant field.

The doves had completed their stay on the fence, and were off to other adventures.

"Do you know what it means now?" asked John.

Mia continued staring into the distant field, as if she were waiting for the answer to arrive soon.

"And then," she continued, "I had another dream about three weeks ago about a similar experience to that one."

Mia was starting to piece something together, but didn't know exactly what it was. She was such an incredibly intelligent person, thought John, but it was almost as if she had temporarily drifted off into a separate, parallel universe, trying to bring the answer forward through a level of sheer will power. Something in the distant field was trying to get her attention.

John listened with patience.

"It was so vivid and real, like I was awake," she said. "I felt like there was someone that was going to come and help me, but I didn't know who that would be," she continued, staring in the distance with a blank stare on her face, as her head swayed back and forth a couple of times from the left to the right.

"I am just realizing now that maybe the two dreams were a part of the same dream," she continued, "like two halves of a sporting event."

The birds had gone, but her thoughts were fully active.

After a long pause, she trimmed the harvest, "I could feel myself wanting to be saved."

Mia continued staring into the distance, in a slight trance of some sort, peering deep into the unknown but at the same time trying to pull it into her current conversation. She must have deeply trusted John, and somehow knew that she should be sharing this with him. Her sunglasses stayed firm, locked into the distant sky.

She repeated her prior thought, "Yes, I could feel myself wanting to be saved," she continued, "but at the time I didn't know why I would ever need to be saved."

John let her continue.

"It was very peculiar, but now I see that it makes sense," she continued.

Her look pressed forward, and her face swayed slightly from side to side as the answers came forth.

"There are some things that everybody knows about me, but that I don't seem to know about myself. Maybe that is why I needed to be saved," she said. "My spirit was telling me that I needed to be saved," as her head finally went up and down, in one single nod.

And then she was done.

The two sat there for the longest time, with no need to say any words. That was always the best thing about a great friendship, thought John, the ability to hang out for hours with someone and not need to say a single word. Social creature that he was, the words were usually flowing, but it was nice that they did not need to be flowing to be perfectly content in a relationship.

This was one of those times when no words were needed.

Jordan had told him a story at the pond about a very similar dream.

CHAPTER 31

Greenwich Village

Mia and John spent the next couple days roaming the city, walking the neighborhoods, enjoying the local shops and restaurants, and resting up at the hotel.

John had been taking Mia to familiar locations from her past, with Mia able to consider ahead of time if that sounded like a good idea. She seemed to have a general familiarity with many of them, and most importantly a comfort level with being around those locations which gave her a general feeling of being home. She continued to unfold her personality, becoming more and more like the Mia that he had lived with for many years, but it was clear that she would still need a considerable amount of time for everything to fully come together.

John had time. John would be there for as long as it took. Unconditional love was a beautiful thing in life, and John certainly had offered it out for Mia.

He would be patient, he would be proactive if wanted, and he would be silent when needed. Most of all, he wanted what was best for her.

It had been two years since she lived in America, and that alone would take some time to transition. On top of that, she had a husband and a family to get reacquainted with, and John was not sure if he would be able to handle it as well as Mia was achieving it. He admired her for the faith in him, the resolve to move forward, and the effort to keep an open mind and enjoy the process. This was typically Mia. She was indeed strong and resolute, always willing to listen and learn new things, and was making a great effort to try and recapture what she felt she was supposed to know. Her inner guidance was telling her that this was the right pathway to take, but she was also being patient enough with herself to let it unfold in the right place and at the right time. It was a beautiful thing to watch, as each did their own part to try and piece it all together and let it evolve as needed.

"I am blessed to spend another day with you," said John, as they dropped onto the street the following day.

Mia looked at him with that characteristic look and bourgeoning smile that he had seen throughout the years. It was a silent expression of love that he had always known her to have, when she would be unspoken, but appreciative and in agreement with his sentiments.

John did not need or expect and answer. Deep down, he knew how she felt. Mia grabbed his hand tighter as they weaved through the crowd and in front of the creative SoHo storefronts.

The following two days consisted of easy and natural trips to selected places across the city, and Mia was becoming more and more interested in putting some pieces together and beginning to remember their life together. She also loved this city, as did John, and made it very easy to both to pick most any adventure and let it unfold in whatever time frame was needed.

They made a trip to the place where they got married, as Mia looked on and tried to absorb all that she could imagine about it.

They did some shopping at the high-end fashion outlets that she knew from Avenue Montaigne, along Fifth Avenue and other parts of the city, as well as the boutiques that had set up shop in SoHo.

She had a keen interest in stopping in at St. Patrick's Cathedral, during their walk along Fifth Avenue in Midtown, and spent over twenty minutes sitting in the church, taking in the sites, and meditating in private.

One late afternoon on the second evening, they attended dinner at Tavern on the Green in Central Park, which was a location that they had often attended in their newlywed years. It had closed for a while, but had reopened again for some time now, and was a place that both John and Mia immensely enjoyed.

Mia was something of a city girl and all the trimmings that came with it, but she also loved her landscaped settings, fresh air, scent of flowers, manicured lawns, plants, and interesting tree canopies. She loved sitting by the pond in Central Park, and going down near the harbor area to watch the ships and flowing blue water crash against the ferry and outer shoreline.

This was the girl that John had always known, with her love of flowing water, greenspaces, fashion, city life and interesting dialogue.

They spent the afternoon of the third day hanging out at the hotel restaurant, talking over a bottle of wine and hors d'oeuvres, and listening to the piano players in the bar area. It was extremely relaxing, as if it were their own home. The hotel staff was highly accommodating, and the design quality of the hotel was worth observing and absorbing as they relaxed near a large interior water fall area. The sculpture in the lobby was modern and colorful, and the surrounding walls forming a partial atrium toward one side had

295

a few some interesting metal rail balconies, reminiscent of the interior courtyards in Paris that overlooked the water fall area.

John stared toward Mia for a time. She had lounged back into the chaise lounge chair, sipping wine and watching the water fall across the rocks in front of her.

"Your beauty has never wavered," he finally said, looking back toward the waterfall. "Both inside and out. You are the same wonderful person that you have always been," he said.

"You are much too kind, my wonderful man," said Mia. "Apparently, you have always been the great charmer throughout our many years together?" she asked with a dry smile, loving the complement but giving John a witty nudge of inquiry.

"It is not a matter of charm, my dear" he responded, smiling but also serious as he looked in her direction. "The truth is never a matter of charm, but only a matter of fact. You have always had great balance in your life, and been a solid and loyal friend to all who have known you."

Mia gazed at him with appreciation.

John continued, "and you still have those cute little cheeks, and a beautiful smile and spirit."

"Now that is definite charm, my dear man," said Mia, never to be duped for long.

John smiled in her direction.

They were beginning to know each other again, the weaving wit of their personalities, their mutual respect, and their deep care for each other that was a treasure below the surface, like diamonds ready to be discovered.

"How about some dinner tonight in Greenwich Village?" asked John. "I know a little place off the beaten track, where we can escape through the courtyard and have a nice little dinner with the locals."

"That sounds perfect," said Mia. "Let's take a short nap and a shower, and maybe head over there after that?"

"*Oui, ma magnifique femme*," said John.

"*Parfait, mon adorable homme*," said Mia.

On this third evening in New York, John and Mia departed the hotel to have dinner in Greenwich Village.

They took a taxi up toward Bleecker Street, and then cut across west toward 7th Avenue. They got out of the taxi, and John grabbed Mia's hand and crossed the street. They headed down a couple of winding streets into the adjoining neighborhood area, off the beaten path. John knew of a local side street hangout that was reserved mostly for locals. He knew the place since he had lived in the neighborhood, but most outsiders would never find it without a local resident to show them the way.

"Where are we going?" asked Mia. This was a residential building, and Mia did not see any signs of a restaurant nearby.

"Right through here," said John, as he grabbed her hand and they cut through the small residential courtyard.

John opened the door and they went inside.

"You would never know it was here!" she said, looking back toward the small interior courtyard as they entered through the back door of the restaurant.

The small bistro was bustling with people, waiters, and activity.

There was one small table toward the outer third of the room, with plenty of room for two people to sit. The tables were very old, and the butcher-block wood tops had been carved into the top layer, showing many years of wear.

They ordered up a glass of wine, some appetizers, and a small salad to begin.

Mia loved the small bistro, and toasted John with her glass of wine.

"This is my kind of a place!" said Mia.

John knew that. He had proposed to Mia in this restaurant.

The appetizers and salad arrived, and there was plenty of activity to watch in the restaurant. Many of the people knew each other, and many of the waiters and staff knew the patrons. It was a very comfortable setting, with continuous activity throughout the medium to small sized room.

"How do you find these places?" asked Mia.

"Well, we lived in this neighborhood for a while," said John, "when we were first married," smiling at Mia with a look of fond memories.

John did not have a need to recount their days of proposals and matrimony. It was simply enough that she was here with him today, and there would be plenty of time in the future to reminiscence about the full story behind this restaurant.

The appetizers arrived, along with the mixed green salads for each with numerous additions and a vinaigrette dressing.

"I loved the clothing boutiques that we visited today in SoHo," said Mia. "Thank you. They were beautifully displayed and had some marvelous designs and accessories."

"My pleasure," said John. "Greene Street has really added some great stores recently, all the high-end names, but I also thought that the small shop on Thompson Street had some great items that would look incredible on you."

"Yes, it was a small shop that was very creative!" said Mia, "I did not expect to see that type of a shop on that street when we first turned the corner and walked up the sidewalk. It was a hidden gem!" she continued.

John thought about the small shop on Thompson Street. They had lived directly across the street during their second year of marriage.

"Simply wonderful," continued Mia, enjoying the salad with fresh toppings and a savory dressing.

"That neighborhood really speaks to me, John, I had a very good time shopping over there today," Mia continued.

They enjoyed the wine and salad, and went for a second glass. The appetizers were exceptional, large enough to share as a full meal as they sat and chatted about fashion.

"Danielle and Christine have been such wonderful friends to me," said Mia. "I hope that we can continue to stay in touch and follow the lives and careers of their wonderful children," she continued.

"Yes, of course," said John. "Social media makes it easier than ever now to stay connected and share photographs, but we should plan to work in a regular vacation to Paris every year to visit your family and friends, and enjoy the city."

"I would like that very much!" said Mia, with a smile that lit up her face. "I would love to keep in touch with my family over there, plus Danielle, Christine, Alaïa, Juliana, Andréa, and all the great people at St. Catherine's."

"Of course," said John. "Maybe we can make some private contributions to the school to send our regards and help keep in touch?" he asked.

"Oh, yes," said Mia. "That would be wonderful, they would be so appreciate of our financial support and continued interest in their programs."

Mia was feeling like the world had settled perfectly into her lap.

"Merci, my dear friend," said Mia, looking up at him, and slightly tilting her glass in the air. "You are a magnificent human being, with a great kindness in your heart and great courage in your soul."

Those words could linger forever, thought John.

John checked his phone, as he looked across at Mia.

"Do you trust me, my love?" asked John, in a sincerely inquisitive way.

"Why, yes," she said. "What do you need to know?"

"I'm glad that you do," continued John. "It is so remarkably wonderful to be back together, but I would like you to meet someone," he said.

"Yes, of course," said Mia. "Who would you like me to meet?"

"Hi, mama," said Jordan. It was the same way that she had said it to Mia when she was a very young child.

"Oh, my dear girl," said Mia, as she grabbed Jordan in a full embrace.

They openly sobbed and cried in each other's arms for a period of ten minutes. Trying to hold back the tears was an impossible task. They were two grown women, and neither one could control themselves. It was a sight to be seen.

John sat in the chair and watched it unfold. He could not help but have tears of joy rolling down both of his cheeks as well, as he grabbed his napkin and continued wiping his wet face. The locals at the tables nearby watched as Mia and Jordan cried and sobbed in each other's arms. They also started to tear up a bit, as they watched the two girls next to them in their long embrace. One girl at the adjoining table had to get up and make her way to the bathroom to compose herself. She didn't know exactly what had transpired between Mia and Jordan, but she knew that they were exchanging tears of joy.

"I knew you were alive," said Jordan. "I just knew it," with her head buried into Mia's shoulder.

"Oh, my dear girl, you are lovelier than your picture, and I am so sorry that I have not been here to be in your life recently," said Mia.

They sobbed for another five minutes, trying to collect themselves all the while.

Jordan had finally found a seat next to Mia, and John had gone to the server for a fresh large batch of napkins and tissues.

The group at the table next to them had also settled down a bit, but the girl was still tearing up as she watched Mia and Jordan unite, and had to leave the restaurant.

"How did you get here, my dear girl?" asked Mia.

"Daddy flew me in yesterday, and I have been staying with some friends in Tribeca," said Jordan.

"I couldn't wait to see you, but I didn't know if you would remember me," Jordan continued. "I have been a nervous wreck for two days!"

"Oh, my dear girl, I do know you," said Mia. "I have seen you in my dreams."

They hugged and sobbed for another three minutes.

John was completely silent, as he watched the two interact.

It was a milestone event. Mia did remember Jordan, and this interaction had completely confirmed it.

Jordan was the girl in Mia's dream.

"I have so much to talk to you about," said Jordan. "I don't even know where to begin!"

"Yes, I know," said Mia, in her calm and understanding style as a great mother.

Mia continued, wiping away Jordan's tears, "We will have plenty of time to talk, my dear Jordan. We will have plenty of time, *Ma chère fille.*"

CHAPTER 32

The Silver Bow

Mia sat in the beautiful chaise lounge chair on the veranda of her home in Southern California, entranced and amazed by the gorgeous view. She had on her white spring linen shirt, and a hat tilted across her brow. The air was warm, crisp and clean, and the plants and flowers were soaking up the sun and light breeze in a familiar way as she had remembered on many days prior to her disappearance.

Mia gazed into the distant mountains and watched the line of mountains move up and down in the distance. It was a simple line that reminded her of many childhood drawings she had made. The early drawings always had white horse fences, beautiful vistas, vibrant plants and palm trees.

She breathed deeply toward the beautiful and calming view, with fresh green stretching across the distant inclines. It occurred to her that she had seen this time and this place in her mind's eye, many years ago as a child, and it left a calming peace on her heart and soul.

"What more could a person really want in life?" she whispered to herself.

The flow of water was captivating to in so many ways. There was the sound of the water hitting the pool below, and the smell of the fresh mist coming from the face of the water fall. Heightened visual experiences had always seemed to put Mia in a bit of a trance, and captured her interest in a way that the other senses could not do. Curiosity would meet creativity during this state, and send her into an elevated trance of combining life with art.

Mia was incredibly artistic, and viewed everything from a lens of form and beauty. Mia's eyes would focus on the natural flow of each individual white curve and splash as it propelled down the gravity slope and off the face to the pool below, while at the same time she would drift into her deep internal and soulful abyss.

Mia viewed her waterfall as part of a larger emotional cycle, with water and emotions passing by her very own happy place enclave, as it landed at the base of her waterfall and mysteriously departed to an unknown place somewhere down the road. The flowing water helped Mia feel connected to the origin of life itself, and the natural rhythm and balance of the balance of the earth and nearby ocean. The mystics had always equated water with emotions, and Mia on a simple level could begin to understand this mystical connection whenever she placed herself in front of the falling water.

Her eye caught the main trunk of the tall palm tree at the corner of the yard. It was extremely long, and had already stretched beyond it wildest dreams. As it slightly bent toward the west, the branches at the top caught a reflective glow from the setting sun. While the tree was incredibly tall, and still had a great deal of growing to take place, it didn't appear to know just how tall it had planned to grow.

John brought out a cold glass of lemonade. The small square ice cubes were lightly banging against the side of the glass as he handed it to Mia.

She noticed that his other hand was holding a small package that he had tucked up under his left arm. The package was wrapped in beautiful silver wrapping paper, with a slight hint of white stardust embedded into the tint.

John sat down in the second chaise lounge chair next to Mia, which had been abandoned for two full years.

The package became a curiosity to Mia, but she was in no hurry to ask about it. It was simply something that had instantly become part of the visual beauty of the day.

They both enjoyed the sounds of the birds and wildlife, along with the sights and sounds of the waterfall.

John thought about the horizon line deep into the ocean, as viewed from the flats in Santa Monica. The horizon line did exist, thought John, but it was always deep in the distance. The water always looked darker and appeared tighter as it extended out, eventually kissing the sky with a thin white line before the light haze touched above it in a wide expanse.

Finding his horizon had been the equivalent of him balancing the important areas of his life, the balance between logic, emotions, and spirituality. It was clearly part of the process that he needed to go through to reach his next level of spiritual development, but in retrospect it had also been part of the process of finding the courage that he needed to go look for Mia.

John looked in the direction of Mia and marveled at the way she had nestled into the chaise lounge chair, as if she had been sitting there her entire life. Her magnificent *Céline* sunglasses floated across her eyes, and her brown hair lightly raised up on her forehead as it met the breeze under her stylish hat.

"I got this for you a few months ago," said John, as he handed the silver package across the chair to Mia.

The bow was a lighter shade of silver, and perfectly matched the wrapping paper.

"Merci," responded Mia, always loving surprises and feeling grateful that the package was for her.

Mia lightly pulled on the ribbon.

The ribbon fell off the top of the package with ease, and fell across her lap. It fell as if it needed to reduce itself to slow motion, so that it could more clearly watch the beauty of landing across the leg of Mia.

Mia opened the box beneath the wrapping.

Sitting inside the package was a thick stock of paper, that was gilded with white and gold print on it that held the words *"Gift Certificate"*.

It was from *Vintage Rags*, for her to use at any time near or far, and in any way that she pleased.

THE END

ABOUT THE AUTHOR

Tony DeAngelo is an author, architect and real estate developer. His fictional writings focus on the convergence of mind and emotions in the development of his characters and stories. In addition to receiving a Bachelor of Architecture, Tony attended New York University's Graduate Program in Real Estate & Investment Analysis, and also studied law in Los Angeles. He currently lives in Southern California with his wife and four children.

8 PALMS

PUBLISHING